HOW TO BE A BADASS VIGILANTE

HOW TO BE A BADASS VIGILANTE

HOW TO BE A BADASS VIGILANTE™ BOOK TWO

MICHAEL ANDERLE

DISRUPTIVE IMAGINATION

Copyright © 2021 LMBPN Publishing
Cover copyright © LMBPN Publishing
A Michael Anderle Production

LMBPN Publishing
PMB 196, 2540 South Maryland Pkwy
Las Vegas, NV 89109

First US edition, March 2021
Version 1.01, March 2021
ebook ISBN: 978-1-64971-606-4
Print ISBN: 978-1-64971-607-1

THE HOW TO BE A BADASS VIGILANTE
BOOK TWO TEAM

Thanks to our Beta Team

Rachel Beckford, Kelly O'Donnell

Thanks to our JIT Readers

Dave Hicks
Daryl McDaniel
Deb Mader
Dorothy Lloyd
Diane L. Smith
Wendy L Bonell
Veronica Stephan-Miller
Paul Westman

If We've missed anyone, please let us know!

Editor
The Skyhunter Editing Team

To Family, Friends and
Those Who Love
To Read.
May We All Enjoy Grace
To Live The Life We Are
Called.

CHAPTER ONE

A glossy black Volkswagen Phideon pulled up out front. It moved slowly and carefully, but the driver was not making any effort to conceal himself or his passenger.

He was always professional, eyes scanning the surroundings for anything unexpected, but so far, everything was going to plan. Their route to the shipping facility had been scouted in advance, and their point of arrival was carefully watched. Four guards armed with compact shotguns, submachine guns, and short-barreled rifles stood out front. Other men with concealed pistols had been arranged along the streets on the way there, providing real-time updates on sudden changes in the security situation. And, in the abandoned watchtower nearby, a sniper with a high-powered .308 rifle and a state-of-the-art scope watched and waited.

It was a warm, partly cloudy day in early summer, and aside from the armed guards, everything looked typical at the compound. The place had a long history of carrying out its business both inside and outside the law, generally without much oversight.

Recently, ownership had changed hands. The staff was skittish.

The Phideon finally parked about twelve feet from the front doors, at which point the two closest guards came out to pin the vehicle in and perform a quick inspection, ensuring that all was in order. They nodded, then stepped back.

The man who climbed out of the back seat was well-dressed and well-groomed but otherwise unremarkable. About five foot eleven, medium build. Age, somewhere between mid-thirties and early forties. Clear olive-hued skin. Clean-shaven. Nothing about his face was distinctive or memorable; he was neither ugly nor handsome.

His black hair was perhaps his most striking feature. It was parted on the side and relatively short but appeared to have been cut with the utmost care and precision, then combed lovingly into place with the aid of product, giving him an air of fastidious perfection.

It was his immaculate hair that had lent him the nickname by which he was known in Los Angeles: *El Peluquero*, the Barber.

As the man stood beside the car, smoothing his plain charcoal-colored dress shirt and black slacks, the front doors of the facility's main building opened, and out stepped Neron, his second in command.

"*Hola, jefe*," Neron opened, grinning. "You're just in time, my friend." Out of habit, he glanced around to ensure that nothing was amiss and noted the comforting presence of his SIG Sauer P320 Compact in its holster at the small of his back.

Neron was a clear contrast from his superior. Though he was slightly taller and more muscular, he often stooped or slouched when standing or walking, and he shaved his head. He also wore gold jewelry and alternated between casual dress and fancy suits, depending on the occasion. Today, he wore his best suit. Just to be safe.

El Peluquero's shirt and pants were of fine quality, but they were not flashy or obviously made by the types of premium brands that some people might want to show off. He wore no jewelry, not even a watch. His sole concession to extravagance was a tattoo of an ornate Catholic cross on his neck, shoulder, and upper chest. The top portion of it could be seen on the right side of his throat, emerging from under his collar.

El Peluquero nodded in greeting and wasted no time on pleasantries. "Please give me a full tour of the facility, and tell me what we are dealing with right now. Also about any shipments that are arriving soon." He paused and adjusted the cuffs of his shirt. "And any problems we have encountered."

Neron nodded. "Sure thing, sir. Just step right this way..." He turned and pulled open the front doors.

As they strode in, Neron reflected that, despite having worked for El Peluquero for over three years, he still did not know the man's real name or where the hell he was from. Some people called him "Pelu" behind his back, but to his face, he was only ever referred to by his full nickname, or, of course, as "sir."

As for his origins, it was generally accepted that he wasn't from the US, though beyond that, opinions differed. His accent was odd; nobody could place it with any degree of certainty. Most people assumed he was from an obscure region of Mexico or from somewhere farther south, maybe Nicaragua or Colombia. One guy had suggested he was from Southern Europe.

Neron had his own theory. El Peluquero spoke both Spanish and English with the careful, measured formality of one who was fluent but not a native speaker. Perhaps that was just how he chose to speak when discussing business, but Neron wondered if perhaps the man was from Brazil, in which case he would have grown up speaking Portuguese.

The main building at the compound was dedicated to packing, unpacking, and otherwise processing shipments before staging them for their next destination. They did some exports to foreign lands, but mostly they imported products to be distributed to America's streets.

"Okay," Neron announced, flourishing his hand across the broad floor. "As you can see, everyone is keeping nice and busy. We got a big shipment there in the middle of the floor, came in this morning. Want to have a look?"

El Peluquero started toward the four pallets of shrink-wrapped packages. "Yes. Show me."

With the aid of the foreman and three of the workers, they went through each individual parcel, comparing the contents to the invoices and ensuring that all was well.

Neron checked things off. "Right, two thousand bottles of prescription opioids. The brand name is clearly visible, too."

El Peluquero asked, "Is it in the quantities we requested? The correct number of milligrams per tablet?"

The men checked the labels, then allowed their boss to pick one bottle at random and open it. Examining the pills, he found them satisfactory and nodded, and the process continued.

They went through everything: pound upon pound of cocaine, including cheap crack, more bottles of prescription painkillers, ecstasy, acid, and various other party drugs, amphetamines of various sorts, esoteric drugs from Russia, China, and South America, and of course, heroin. Of particular interest was the black variety, which was especially popular in Southern California this year.

El Peluquero summoned the two men who had brought in the black heroin by retrieving it from a coyote at the border. Both were young, shifty-looking types—street thugs who clearly thought they could make it big by working for a major outfit and then expanding at the first opportunity.

He snapped his fingers before their faces. "You. This is genuine? And of the required potency? Please demonstrate."

"Yeah," said the first one. "Sure it is, absolutely. Here, look." He pulled out a box cutter and slit open the topmost pack on the load, lifting it for his employer to examine. When he did, another packet showed beneath, and its color was slightly off. Both El Peluquero and Neron noticed.

Neither said anything.

El Peluquero smoothed the hair behind his left ear. "Yes, this packet is good."

Having concluded the inspection, El Peluquero nodded curtly to the workers and overseers and turned on his heel to stride off, his pace brisk but unhurried. Neron followed him.

Once they were far enough away that the ambient noise of the building would cover their voices, El Peluquero turned to his right-hand man and told him in a low voice, "Those two who told us the heroin black was fine were lying to us, of course. They acquired only enough quality product for the top layer and filled out the rest of the pallet with poor imitation-grade stuff. They must be killed. Do it today so there is no doubt in the minds of the others as to why it has happened."

Neron was not shocked by the order. He, too, had noticed that the men had been bullshitting them and were stupid enough to think they could get away with it.

"Should I make an example of them, sir? Making it nice and messy would make a big impression on the others." He had a knife as well as his gun, and if either of them tried to fight back, the guards would see to it that they failed.

With a slow, deliberate motion, El Peluquero shook his head. "No, beyond doing it where they can see. I need your focus to be on the jobs to come. Ensure that our workers understand how stupid it is to try to lie to us, but make it quick. Death is enough, in this case."

Neron was disappointed, but he did not complain. El Peluquero could be ruthless when he felt it was necessary. He had ordered the prolonged and hideous torture of two men within the last year, but only for the purpose of extracting information. Once he got what he needed, he had them put out of their misery.

The boss did not seem to take any sadistic pleasure in such things. He was cool-headed, a real professional.

"Yes, sir," Neron responded. "Now?"

El Peluquero raised a hand. "In another minute or two. I am going up to the balcony. Do it after I am out of sight. I want them to understand that it was my order, but not to see me when it happens. That will help train them to think of what I want—and what I will not tolerate—even when I am not present. Good workers should always fear that I am watching over their shoulders."

It made sense, and Neron agreed.

The two men walked to the doorway leading to an elevator that would take El Peluquero to the third floor. When the door gave its pleasant electronic ding and opened, the boss stepped in, and Neron walked back the way he had come, his fingers itching for his knife and pistol.

In the elevator, El Peluquero did not trouble himself with wondering how things would go. Neron was competent, and his other men would step in if something went wrong. Nor did he waste thought or mental energy on being angry at the fools who had tried to deceive him. Such people always cropped up, and he had always been able to cut them back down.

The elevator ascended, depositing him in a short hallway which, to the left, led to an interior walkway that encircled the main work floor, and in the other direction, led out to the balcony. El Peluquero went to the right.

The view was spectacular. The balcony was basic, as befit an industrial building like this; the place wasn't a luxury hotel, after all. El Peluquero didn't mind. It calmed him to watch the city from above, glimpsing the Pacific in the distance and smelling its salt, along with the smoggy smell that he had come to associate with his new base of operations.

Behind and below him, a gunshot rang out and one man screamed in pain, while others shouted and cursed in terror. Feet stamped rapidly away, but the second man's attempt at flight was cut short by a thunderous burst of submachine gun fire, along with the boom of a compact tactical shotgun.

El Peluquero supposed the second man had been blasted to pieces, more or less. The first, having been shot once by Neron, was likely now having his throat cut to finish him off. The spectacle would make a big impression on the workers, no doubt. For every man stupid enough to cheat him, five more were considering it. Displays like these ensured they never took action.

He pulled out his phone as a sea breeze rose and threatened to put his hair out of order. He brought up a couple of invoices, as well as an app that allowed him to keep an eye on the shipping manifests. According to the most up-to-date report, another load of black heroin would be arriving tomorrow, so the bogus batch the two recently-deceased con men had tried to fob off on him would not cause any serious problems with the flow of product.

The communications used vagaries and code, of course; it was a standard precaution. Still, he knew their correspondence was safe. All the programs his business used were encrypted. Location tracking of the highly illegal but difficult-to-detect variety provided further cover. Finally, his phone had an advanced wipe option that would fry its insides if he were ever in danger of being captured.

Footsteps approached, and the elevator dinged open on the ground floor. Neron was coming up to confirm the obvious.

El Peluquero reflected on how quickly his men had resolved the situation. They were well-armed and well-trained, and *that*, more than anything else, was how he had risen to the upper echelons of drug importers.

He had started out as an arms dealer. The money was good, and it allowed him to gradually accumulate extra weaponry. At the same time, he mainly hired professional mercenaries with backgrounds in the military or elite police units. By the time he branched out into the drug trade, he was stronger than much of the competition.

Los Angeles would be his. Soon.

Behind him, the door opened and Neron walked up, cleaning his hands with a couple of sanitary wipes. "Done. I think the second guy knew what was coming before I shot the first one, or he wouldn't have bolted. We got him, though."

"Yes, I knew you would." El Peluquero finished examining the manifests and put his phone away.

Neron snapped his fingers and blinked. "Oh, something else I just remembered—Motorcycle Man. You heard of him? That fuckin' wannabe superhero was all over the news, and a lot of the lower-level gangs, especially downtown, were scared shitless of him. Or her; some were saying it might be a woman. Whatever. Been quiet lately, but whoever that asshole is, he took out some decent-sized outfits. So, I mean, might be worth taking seriously as a threat. These days, you can't talk about LA without mentioning Motorcycle Man."

El Peluquero furrowed his brow. "Yes, I had heard the rumors. I doubt this person will be of great concern. I have seen nothing to suggest that he, or she, can challenge us, and if he is stupid enough to try, he will discover that we are not a mere 'gang.' He is new to the underworld and has only faced weak opposition. If he attacks us, we will quickly discover his weaknesses and remove *him*."

Neron shrugged. "If you say so. A lot of the stuff I heard was superstition. Ghost stories, the kind that dumb street-level fucks tell when they don't know what's going on. Exaggerated."

"Yes, probably." El Peluquero reached into his other pocket. "Here are the plans for the next two days. The night after tomorrow, we will be moving against one of our new rivals. No one very important or intimidating, but I want a smooth, professional operation."

He handed a folded slip of paper to his right-hand man. Neron opened it and read.

El Peluquero continued, "Keep it long enough to memorize it and pass it on to your top lieutenants, then burn it. Inform me of any developments. I will be focused on coordinating our shipments so we can flood the streets as soon as the competition is thinner."

"Sure." Neron pocketed the slip. He stretched and stared out over the balcony at the vast urban expanse. Below them, the cleanup men were taking away the bagged-up remains of the two smartass liars. "Nice view from up here, isn't it?"

"Yes," his boss agreed.

CHAPTER TWO

Kera stared at the potato, which she had levitated about four feet into the air in the center of her garage area, making sure any flammable materials were far away. Plus, a fire extinguisher rested by her feet, just to be safe.

The converted warehouse that served as her apartment was an unusually good locale for what they were doing, but not an *ideal* one. She didn't like the idea of accidentally burning down her own home.

"Okay," she began, her focus as intense as if she were the one preparing to cast the spell, "you need to start by understanding that heat, like moisture, is something that's present in the air all around us. All you have to do is ask the spirits to gather it up and push it to do its usual thing in one particular place. That's it. It's simpler than you would think."

Standing four feet to her right and slightly in front of her— and closer to the potato—Stephanie audibly drew in a deep, sharp breath and raised her hands.

Kera watched as her friend performed the required gestures with her fingers and listened carefully as she spoke the incantation that would bring the spell into existence. All of that stuff was fine; she was doing it right and without any problems.

The difficult part was what was taking place in Stephanie's mind. And despite her own status as an increasingly advanced witch, or thaumaturge, or whatever term one chose to use in reference to those who could perform magic, Kera couldn't read anyone else's thoughts yet.

She could feel their moods, though, and Stephanie was nervous. Excessively so.

"Remember," Kera added, "that nothing near the potato will really be damaged by flames, and we can put it out easily if we have to."

As Steph refocused, Kera saw the air around the vegetable begin to waver and shimmer; the warmth was gathering. The idea was to create a kind of portable magical oven, a consistent concentration of heat that could sustain itself over an extended period of time.

The left half of the potato exploded in a shower of burning sparks, while the right half drooped in midair, slowly beginning to steam as if microwaved.

"Okay, cut," Kera said. Stephanie fell into a relaxed posture, closing her eyes, exhaling, and shaking her head.

The potato, or what was left of it, dropped to the floor with a moist thud and rolled a foot or two aside. The air around it smelled as though someone had cut open a raw spud and dumped a trayful of burnt tater tots next to it.

Twisting a braid around her finger, Stephanie muttered, "Sorry. I thought I had it for a minute there finally."

Kera rubbed her temples. "I did, too. And, um, you sort of did. Like, say, if we had combined the two halves of what you did and spread it equally across the *entire* potato, it would have been roasted quite nicely."

"Ha, ha," Step returned, her eyes rolling back in her head. "I don't know. Something about it doesn't make sense to me. I get to a certain point, then I panic. Like the way you drop something hot suddenly when it's about to burn you, even though you knew it was hot to begin with."

"Understandable," Kera assured her. "Everyone has different strengths and weaknesses, stuff they're better or worse at. I suppose you're not destined to be a great, uh, pyromancer or whatever, even if you seem unusually talented at other things. Still, let's try two more potatoes. After that, regardless of how well it goes, I think we both need a break. And food."

Stephanie didn't hesitate to agree. Performing magic took a lot of energy. Both of them, since they had begun casting, had their appetites and metabolisms increase three or fourfold, and they ate vastly more while slowly *losing* weight.

They fished two more spuds out of the bag, and once again, Kera levitated one in the center of the floor while Steph attempted to roast it to perfection.

Again, it seemed like she was about to succeed, only for a sudden rush of flame to engulf the potato, juggling it in the air, while pulses of heat flared up and down and up and down...

Kera allowed the ravaged vegetable to fall, then let out a long, rattling sigh. Until now, she had been trying to deal with her friend's difficulties with a mixture of warmth and snark, attempting to be funny to keep her spirits up and pass the repeated failures off as no big deal.

But at this point, she was burnt out. There was nothing much left for her to say. Stephanie simply couldn't do fire spells. They required a point of view that was too much at odds with her temperament and overall skills, which tended toward water.

Stephanie looked equally tired, not to mention sheepish. "Sorry," she apologized. "I can't seem to get the hang of it. Other things haven't given me this much trouble. Don't know why."

Wouldn't it make sense, though, Kera pondered, *if a person who could understand one element well could also understand its diametric opposite? Like they're complementary in a way. Yin and Yang, something like that.*

Which gave her an idea.

"Okay, one last try. And I promised that we'd take a break afterward, so let that inspire you or something. Think of it this way. You're good with water, right? Water and fire are opposites, but in a way, they're very similar. They both go wherever they can, even if fire goes up and water usually goes down. But both are relentless, flowing forces. Think of the heat as being like a body of water, shifting around something, gradually wearing it away from the outside."

Stephanie blinked, and her eyes went distant as she considered it. "I hadn't thought of it that way. It's worth a try. Here goes, then..."

Both watched as the air around the final potato began to shimmer. To Kera's mild surprise and growing excitement, catastrophe didn't strike. Instead, the spud began to smoke and smolder in a measured, consistent fashion.

She glanced at Stephanie. The other woman was clearly putting a great deal of effort into the spell and would not be able to sustain it for long. Also, she was over-roasting it somewhat. But she was doing leagues better than she had mere minutes ago.

"I can't..." Stephanie grunted. "That's as much as I can...do."

The heat vanished, and the potato hung smoking in air that rapidly returned to room temperature.

Kera floated it over to the counter. "Well, I'm impressed. That was a hell of an improvement, Steph. This one might be edible, even. If it is, I'll split it with you for lunch."

Her friend burst out laughing. "I have no idea how I did it. Well, your little metaphor helped, honestly. But it was like, I just had a breakthrough. I think I get it now. More or less."

When Kera cut the potato in half lengthwise, she found it to be crusty and overcooked on the outside and still hard and raw on the inside, but it was in good enough shape that she simply carved off the outer layer and tossed the rest into the microwave.

"Don't worry," she pointed out, "I'm making a lot more food than that, but I figure it will be the dish of honor in addition to the other stuff."

They ended up having an entire pot of fettuccine with alfredo sauce and leftover chicken, four burritos, a chef's salad with plenty of dressing, a couple of donuts, and of course, a small helping each of potato with butter and parmesan.

While devouring their massive lunch, it occurred to Kera that she was not as hungry as she had been lately. Performing spells, particularly basic ones like minor object levitation, did not tax her as much as it used to.

She knew the reason why, of course—Pavla's lessons.

She winced. Thinking of Pavla still hurt in ways she didn't entirely understand. In the realm of what she *did* understand, she knew it was iffy at best to take any magical advice from someone who'd been out to hurt her.

It was just that Pavla had been an extremely good teacher, as well as—in some ways—a good friend.

As if on cue, Stephanie asked, "Where did you get the idea for that? The thing about comparing fire to water so it would make more sense to me."

Kera frowned and hung her head. "Pavla," she stated, speaking the name quickly and returning to her food without further comment.

"Oh, right." Stephanie knew her friend well enough not to press her on the subject. The memory was still raw for both of them. Pavla, who had seemed like such a nice person, had tried to capture or kill them. It was miraculous that they had survived.

Then again, the official definition of thaumaturgy was "the working of miracles."

They reached the end of their meal, with Kera not quite able to finish her half of the repast. She let Steph have it instead; she had been working harder, anyway.

"So," Stephanie proposed as she took their dishes to the sink, "want to train some more? Honestly, it's pretty fun. Whether I screw up or not, I get a rush out of it."

Kera had secretly been hoping they were done for the day. Still, she tried to supervise while her friend went through the motions of several other enchantments—cloaking, telekinesis, throwing her voice around corners, all of which she found somewhat easier than fire spells. That was good; it meant that Kera didn't have to be as involved and could drift off into the gloomy clouds within her own head.

Soon enough, Stephanie noticed.

"Kera, I can tell you're getting tired. Or something's on your mind. Are you okay, girl?"

Kera wasn't sure how to respond. There was a whole bevy of potential answers to the question, some more truthful than others.

After an awkward pause of twenty or thirty seconds, she gave up trying to overthink it. "I don't know. I suppose I'm not entirely okay. Could be worse, but still. I can't stop thinking about Pavla and everything that happened with her."

Stephanie crossed her arms over her chest and gave the other woman a concerned look. "You want to talk about it? You could say we both have reasons to get all that off our chest."

It was true. In the duel that had erupted in the desolate alley, Kera probably would have succumbed without Stephanie's help.

"No." She sighed. "I'm sorry. It's stupid to bring it up and then say I'd rather not discuss it, but my feelings are still too mixed up. Like it's a big jumbled mess in my brain. How much I wanted Pavla to be who she said she was, a true friend and a good teacher. She betrayed me, but then she let us go. It's so confusing."

Stephanie walked over and hugged her, and they spent a moment leaning against each other.

"I know," said Steph. "Believe me. I still don't know what to make of it all."

"Yeah," Kera agreed. "And we got out of it alive, but not because I'm awesome. It wasn't a real victory; it was a freebie. Sorry. You helped a lot, and I'm not trying to disparage your, uh, contribution. You know what I mean. We barely squeaked by, and Pavla could have finished us off if she wanted to. What happens next time? If she and I meet again, I have to be ready for her."

They separated, both with somber, serious faces and reserved demeanors. In one another's presence, they were comfortable, but the dark cloud of external events hung heavily overhead.

Stephanie replied, "I understand. But you might never see her again. Still, it's good to be prepared. I gotta head home."

"Right," Kera murmured. "I need a shower, and I have to do the dishes. I'll see you later tonight at work though, right?"

"Yup, I'm on 'til closing time." She was a waitress at the cocktail bar and grill in Little Tokyo known as the Mermaid. Kera was a bartender.

Kera walked her friend to the door. "Take care. Oh, how's your sister doing? With, um, you know."

"Oh." Steph laughed, "Regina's still dating that Ted guy as far as I know. She said he's funny, which is," she coughed, "accurate. As long as she's happy, I'm happy."

Kera chuckled. "Yeah, I get it. Bye."

Her friend walked out, and she closed the door behind her. Slumping against the wall, she remembered something else.

Chris. Ted was his best friend. And right now, Kera had enough on her plate that, as much as she liked Chris, she wasn't sure she could deal with anything extra.

James Lovecraft shared the rearmost seat of the limousine with Ezeudo, their guest. James' partner, Mother LeBlanc, sat on the seat across from them. None of them had spoken for perhaps half an hour. All was well enough between them, but they were tired from the long journey.

The flight to New York City from Geneva had taken long enough. Since the layover to fly to Albany would have been about the same amount of time, they had instead opted to drive to James' mansion upstate.

Ezeudo looked out the window. "Beautiful country," he remarked in his Nigerian accent. "Nearly as striking as Switzerland, in some ways. The mountains are not as high, but the terrain is interesting, and you have lovely forests. Also, I should like to see more of New York sometime. It is one of the major cities I have never visited before."

James smiled. "Thanks. Regarding NYC, though, I would have thought you had seen plenty of it, given how long it takes to drive through all that congestion. Good Lord, I had forgotten what a chore it was. That's part of why I live upstate. The other part, of course, is for privacy regarding the whole 'magic' thing."

"That is sensible," Ezeudo agreed. "And I should think the city would be a better place to walk through than to drive."

Mother LeBlanc chimed in. "It is, but then again, most traditionally-designed large cities are. It is less the case with the more modern American cities, which consist mostly of commercialized suburban sprawl and were designed to be driven through. Los Angeles is perhaps the worst offender."

Not long ago, she and James had been there, so they knew what they were talking about.

"I see." Ezeudo looked back inward. "I have heard similar things, and when I was in Australia, I found that much of Sydney and Melbourne could be described that way, too."

James shrugged. "Never been there myself. Oh, that reminds

me. I hope you don't find it too cold here. I mean, yeah, it's summer, but it will be autumn before long, and winter closes in fast up in the Adirondack region. People from warmer climes are sometimes shocked by the difference."

LeBlanc, who was from New Orleans, nodded in empathy.

Ezeudo tilted his head back and laughed. "Hah! You say that because I am from Nigeria. Remember, my friend, I have lived in Switzerland for some time now, and I have worked for nonprofits all over the globe. I can pretty much deal with any type of weather."

James leaned back and folded his hands behind his neck. "Good point. Well, that's for the best. If it should come to pass that we need to go elsewhere within the US, there's no telling what sort of conditions you might be in for. That's one of the interesting things about America. We have virtually every biome on the planet somewhere within our territory."

Smiling, Ezeudo quipped, "I doubt that is *exactly* true, but perhaps close enough."

The limo continued to wend its way up the road through the forested hills, coming at last to the expansive property on which the Lovecraft estate stood. Though James was not the leader of the council, which technically had no head member, the largest number of America's thaumaturges resided in the Northeast and Mid-Atlantic regions, so his house had been chosen as the closest thing they had to a general headquarters.

LeBlanc watched Ezeudo's face. "Are you concerned about Guillaume?"

The man turned to look at her. "Yes, I am. I am certain that you are, too, though perhaps your focus is different from mine."

James acknowledged the little exchange between the two of them without offering any commentary of his own. Things had improved, but there was still a lingering tension among them.

He and LeBlanc had gallivanted off to Geneva after noting the presence of magic users there, whose activities had hitherto been unknown to and therefore unsanctioned by the council. There was a man called Dartmoor with very weak powers, but far more important and interesting were Ezeudo and the young boy Guillaume.

Knowing they couldn't control people living so far away and fearful of the consequences if Guillaume accidentally harmed other kids or otherwise drew large amounts of negative attention to himself, James and LeBlanc had reluctantly cut the boy off from the divine power of the universe, leaving him bereft of his inborn talents.

Then, for the first time in either of their lives, they had reversed their decision.

Ezeudo had convinced them to restore the child's powers in exchange for his submission to their training and an agreement to act as their agent in Europe once the regimen was complete. At first, they had intended to train him on the spot in Geneva.

But there had been...developments.

For one thing, it had become clear that Ezeudo's latent potential was greater than James or LeBlanc had suspected, and furthermore that the habits and self-taught lessons he had picked up would require more "correction" via their standardized methods than they'd previously thought.

Second, the rest of the council, spearheaded by Lady Mitchell, had found them, contacted them, and demanded their immediate return to the States, asking that the ongoing farce of their adventures come to an end so normalcy could be restored. In James' opinion, it meant that Mitchell and her supporters within the group didn't want to be bothered with any new information.

Nonetheless, there was a risk of the council fragmenting into two or more parallel and independent bodies, which might well be a disaster for the American magical scene.

So, after much cajoling, James and LeBlanc had booked a

flight back across the Atlantic, bringing Ezeudo with them on the condition that it would not take more than a year. And, of course, that he speak to Guillaume and the boy's mother beforehand, reminding them not to do anything foolish or drastic while he was away.

And now, here they were.

"Home sweet home," James announced as the limo slowed and then stopped out front. "Frankly, we have been away too long. The place looks strange to me."

LeBlanc shrugged. "Such is the way of things. I probably would not recognize New Orleans at this point. I had but a single brief visit there six years ago, and that was the first time in a decade."

Ezeudo seemed faintly amused by their feelings. "I myself have not been 'home' in many years," he pointed out.

As they got out of the car and unloaded their minimal luggage, James had to appreciate the man's situation. Ezeudo had been chased out of his home village by locals who were uncertain about his power and was now a modern-day nomad.

The double door out front opened as they approached. Behind it was standing Mrs. Ryker, one of James' two housekeepers. "Hello," she announced. "Welcome back, sirs and madam. Everything should be ready for you."

James thanked her and led the way into the foyer, where they paused to set down their luggage. James and LeBlanc took in the sight of the old place for the first time in months, while Ezeudo appreciated it for the first time.

"If it's all right," LeBlanc quipped. "I'll see myself to my usual place on the second floor." She started for the stairs.

James followed her, with Ezeudo at his side. "Yes, we're right behind you. I figure we ought to lodge our guest before anything else." He wanted to head to the study where they did the bulk of their work and where the council usually met, but it could wait.

Once upstairs, James, stepping ahead of the others with the assured gait of one who knew the house better than any other person on the planet, made a beeline for a particular door—the third down the hall on the left. He opened it, turned on the light, and flourished his hand as Ezeudo came up behind him. LeBlanc moved past them out of sight.

"Your quarters for the duration of your stay," he announced. "It is neither the best- nor the worst-quality room in the house. Somewhere around the middle. It is also the one best situated, relative to the construction of the place and the utility lines, to remain cool in the summer and heated in the winter for the lowest possible cost. Much of the time, these rooms sit empty, so there's no point in running conditioned air into all of them, is there? Anyway, make yourself comfortable."

Ignoring James' spiel about utility bills, the tall Nigerian stepped, looked around, and set his suitcase down near the foot of the bed. "It is very nice, to be truthful," he opined. "I am now curious to see the *best* room in the house. Hah! You live in a luxury hotel."

His quarters were spacious and equipped with old yet high-quality and well-maintained furniture and decorations, including an original oil painting depicting the wooded mountains beyond the tall, curtained window.

"I suppose," James conceded. "If this were Europe rather than America, my family would probably qualify as aristocracy. As it is, we're just rich. But my funds aren't *unlimited*, hence the utilities issue. But enough about that. Let's review the gist of your training regimen."

Ezeudo turned to face his host, his expression neutral but guarded. "You told me a year or less."

"Right." James folded his hand behind his back. "Normally, getting someone properly trained in all the basic spells and fundamentals of thought, philosophy, ethics, conduct, and so forth is a project requiring a minimum of, say, sixteen months, and often more like two years. Completing the entire course within one year is not unheard of, but," he sighed, "it will require a fairly grueling schedule, and it won't be easy unless you turn out to be one of the finest students in our history."

The other man grimaced. It was the look of one who grasped what was to come without shying away from it, but without pretending to like it, either. "I will do as well as I am able," he stated.

"I don't doubt it." James walked in and went to an ornate mahogany desk, flipping open a ledger that lay there. "I had this brought in before we arrived. It's the record of a previous student who was able to complete the course in thirteen months. Not a perfect analog, but close. Look it over. I will be making some improvisations, of course."

Ezeudo began skimming the pages. "What kind of improvisations, if I may ask?"

"Well," James explained, "I've formed a hypothesis, based on what I know of your skills and background as well as other students who were your age or had your approximate level of talent. It's that if we teach you all the basics at once, you will be able to quickly ascertain where your strengths and weaknesses lie, then you can reinforce the weak areas by practicing the skills that come more naturally."

Ezeudo made a low sound in his throat. "That makes sense. We shall see when we begin."

LeBlanc wandered into the room, sidling up to the desk and looking over the ledger alongside Ezeudo. He seemed mildly annoyed by her intrusion.

"Matthias?" she mused. "James, you mean to train Ezeudo the way we trained him? Are you certain that's wise? I am *not* certain, or I wouldn't ask such a question."

Ezeudo continued to read, pretending not to notice LeBlanc's ominous insinuation.

Stony-faced, James shot back, "Not *exactly* the same way." He repeated the plan he'd described to their new student.

LeBlanc frowned. "We are in your home, but you agreed some time ago that your home would no longer be entirely *yours*. It belongs, to some extent, to the council. They will be along shortly, you know. Some of them, anyway. They might stop by at any time. And the mere fact of us being back in the US means their authority is no longer ambiguous. We will be under close scrutiny."

"Yes, yes," James grumbled. "Don't remind me."

Her eyes hardened. "I'm afraid I *must* remind you. After all that's happened these last months, any crazy plans of yours will bring the rest of the council down on your head with greatly increased force. We had a good reason for doing what we did, James, but they still do not see it. I have tried to support you even when we have had our disagreements, but I cannot protect you forever should they continue to fail to see the value in your actions. Or to put it another way, if you should continue to fail to convince them."

James put a hand over his eyes. "Is it really necessary for our new friend to hear all this? Ezeudo, please continue looking over the book and ring if you need anything. The bathroom is down the hall and to the right. LeBlanc and I are going to take a walk."

"Of course," Ezeudo replied mildly.

Returning to the ground floor, they surrounded themselves with a magical sound shield and strolled out onto the grounds before resuming their conversation.

"Tomorrow," LeBlanc began, "I must leave for New Orleans. Ironic, I suppose, that I mentioned how long it's been since I visited the place on the ride here. A contact of mine has agreed to meet me to discuss some things. No one you know. I will inform you of anything that affects you. Primarily, though, you will be affected by my absence. You will have to train Ezeudo alone."

James looked at the sky. "You could have mentioned that

earlier, but it shouldn't be a problem. And regarding what you said about the council, I ran the whole thing by Lauren Jones. She approved of it and volunteered to evaluate Ezeudo's training at regular intervals."

"Good." LeBlanc reached into the folds of her brightly-hued dress and pulled out half of a Cuban sandwich, taking a small bite before speaking again. "I have told you my concerns. What are *yours?*"

James tried to conceal his annoyance but probably failed. LeBlanc knew him too well. He wanted to project an image of total confidence in his new pupil and what was to come.

"I am most worried about one of Ezeudo's strengths rather than any of his weaknesses," he confessed. Lying to LeBlanc would be pointless. "He worked for nonprofit groups and other such large bureaucratic organizations, so it should be quite easy for him to get used to working with the council. *Which means...*" his tone sharpened "that he may find it too goddamn easy to deceive us and skirt around regulations and such, which could compromise his training and get us in trouble. He's a willful man and a pretty smart one."

LeBlanc raised a finger. "Everything you just said applies in turn to when we—well, mostly you, though I contributed—convinced the council to let us publish that book, then set off across the country hunting for newly arisen magic-users, then disregarded the council's request to come home in favor of our recent Swiss adventure. Does it not?"

"Oh." James groaned. "It does indeed. Thanks."

His friend continued. "Ezeudo has some training of his people's traditional sort, as well as many years of minimal self-training behind him. It demonstrates that he is not a complete fool, but he also needs to understand why we do things our way. Make it clear to him what the stakes are. *Show* him the history of magic. Show him what has gone wrong in the past when people act without a guiding framework. Then, we must trust that he'll do what is necessary."

She had placed a hand on his arm, and he put his opposite hand over it. "That's *roughly* the plan," he pointed out, "but a good reminder, anyway. Enjoy your trip to NOLA, though I imagine it's going to be muggy as hell this time of year."

LeBlanc smiled. "I shall try."

CHAPTER THREE

Lia had finally prevailed upon Johnny to visit her house again. Despite their mutual concern for Sven, a friend and former coworker of them both, Johnny had been skittish and distant lately.

She couldn't blame him, given all that had happened. But now more than ever, the three of them needed to pull together.

Lia had pulled her vehicle out to park it temporarily at the curb so Johnny could pull his distinctive Mustang into the garage. She had told him again and again that he ought to get rid of the damn thing since it was easy to spot and easy to track, but he had refused. It was his pride and joy.

The distinctive car cruised down her street in the residential part of eastern Long Beach, turned smoothly into her driveway, and then vanished into the garage. Lia went out to meet him as he emerged and closed the big door manually.

"Hello," she said. "Let me move my car, then we'll head in."

He nodded, his eyes shifting around to spot anyone following or watching him. Lia was frankly amazed that their various enemies hadn't traced them here yet. She was considering moving again, perhaps to somewhere outside the LA metropolitan area.

Once her car was back in the driveway, she let Johnny in, and they both went straight to the living room. Sven still lay on the couch, recovering from his bizarre injuries.

He was a ways away from making a full recovery, but he was better than he'd been when Johnny had first found him, stumbling and bloodied and delirious, on the side of the road in Manhattan Beach.

And he was awake.

"Mr. Torres." He groaned, his voice weak and pained, as he turned to look at his friend. "So nice of you to join us. Ha, ha. Fuck. I can't remember how long I've been here."

Lia put a gentle but firm hand on his shoulder, pressing down to urge him to lie back. "It's been close to three weeks," she reminded him. "I thought you were improving, but it's clear that you need more time. I think you pushed yourself too hard last time you tried to get up for a while, and now you're having a relapse."

Johnny grimaced, but his face was soft around the edges, with traces of warmth and sympathy. "Better do what she says, Sven. Lia's smart, eh? And we both want you to get better. Sit back and relax. At least you're not working some shit job or on the run still."

Or, Johnny thought, *back in the clutches of whoever those* pendejos *were who captured him.*

He had been trying not to think very hard about it. There were too many elements to the whole affair that scared the shit out of him, especially if what had happened to Sven could be connected to what had happened to all of them on the terrible night when Motorcycle Woman had stormed their headquarters and killed Pauline.

He had a nasty feeling that there *was* a connection.

While Sven settled back into a more comfortable position, Lia turned to Johnny. "I had a gunshot doctor take a look at him. He basically said there was no way he could treat him properly without access to a fully stocked hospital but that he was pretty sure Sven would be okay with enough rest. I'm not so certain anymore. I've been wanting to face the music and take him to the emergency room, but..."

Her voice trailed off, and Sven laughed. "Yeah, sure, that would be a great way to fuck us all. Hospitals ask questions, and cops ask hospitals questions about the questions. You know how it works. Not to mention, do you know why it's taking me so long to get better? They did something to me internally with *magic*. I bet it's still rolling around in there, the curse or the demon imp or whatever it is, tearing shit open right when we think it's going to get better. How would a surgeon react to that? They'd misdiagnose it, and if I told them the truth, they'd pack me off to the goddamn psych ward."

Johnny tensed, and the fluid in his spinal column suddenly felt half-frozen. The last thing he wanted to hear was the notion that Sven, or any of them, was under a curse.

Lia waved a hand at Sven, then spoke to the other man. "Johnny, once Sven started talking more, he began saying that the people who captured him were...witches, cultists—magicians of some sort. It sounds crazy, but we were all there at Pauline's place. I think we need to accept the prospect that something very, very abnormal is going on here."

Johnny turned away from her, staring blankly at the dim evening light that barely penetrated the curtain over her front window. "Yeah. I've been trying *not* to accept it. After that fuckery, I wanted to go clean. I got a regular job and everything, finally. The people I'm staying with are getting antsy for me to leave, but they're okay for now. I might be looking at a normal, peaceful life soon. You think I want to start digging all this shit back up?"

Narrowing her eyes in irritation, Lia snapped, "None of us do.

We all agreed to go straight, to go our separate ways and pretend nothing ever happened. But it's impossible. Whatever is going on in the city lately, we are inextricably linked to it until it's over. We don't have to like it, but refusing to acknowledge reality is the same sort of thinking that led Pauline to end up where she did."

Lia shuddered at the memory. Not only of how Motorcycle Woman had stomped through their defenses, beaten Pauline in combat, and finally cracked her head open. But also, before that, of how Pauline's sanity had frayed beyond all hope of recovery.

Their former boss had been both ambitious and visionary. Lia had agreed with her and supported her at first, even believed in her. But in the end, she had gone mad. Though it hurt to admit it, it was perhaps for the best for everyone else that Pauline was dead.

Johnny turned back to face her. "All right," he growled, "what do you think we should do, then? Hire a fuckin' merc company to go kill the assholes who did this to Sven? Go enlist at Hogwarts so we can fight magic with magic? What?"

Lia took a deep breath and ran her fingers through her long black hair. "I have been thinking it over, and there is no reason to assume that the people who captured Sven and tortured him are affiliated with Motorcycle Woman. Why would she let us go, telling us to go away and keep quiet, only for her friends or allies to scoop Sven back up like this? He said they kept asking him about MW and about the LA Witches. He also mentioned that he hadn't been doing anything illegal, which MW warned us not to do. I have to conclude that these people are her enemies, or her former partners or employers looking to hunt her down."

"Yeah." Johnny shrugged. "When you put it that way, it makes sense. It's what I suspected too, except I didn't want to fuckin' dwell on it because Motorcycle Woman *didn't kill us*. These people are probably a lot worse than she is."

Lia steeled herself for Johnny's inevitable reaction to what she was about to say. "Right. So, I propose that you find Motorcycle Woman and tell her what's happened."

He was stone-silent for a few seconds, staring at her with mouth agape and eyes bulging, before he sputtered, "What? What the *fuck?* Are you *loco en la cabeza?* Jesus Christ, Lia, that's about the last thing I would ever want to do for the next two hundred years. Fuck!"

She exhaled slowly. "Oh, I know. I didn't expect you to be happy about the idea, but like you said, she only fought us as far as was necessary to stop Pauline from having us blow up that stupid bar. I think Pauline might have died accidentally during the fight, anyway. It wasn't as though she executed her with a nine-millimeter double-tap to the head or something. I suspect she wants to do good, so if there are very bad people after us and after her, we have something in common with her, don't we?"

Johnny continued to balk, and while Sven lapsed in and out of consciousness beside them, paying partial attention, they argued on and on.

"No," Torres insisted. "As far as I'm concerned, our business with Biker Witch-Lady is over. She made her point, and if she's on some kind of crusade against crime, best of luck to her because I'm not into that life anymore. If you want to do good deeds, start a charity with your embezzled money, or go work at a soup kitchen."

He started for the door, but Lia dashed ahead of him and blocked his passage with her arm, her hand laying on the knob. She was smaller than he, but she had the martial arts training to counterbalance his street-fighting experience. She would not be physically intimidated by him, and he was smart enough to know better than to try to shove her away.

"No, Johnny," she insisted. "Sven suffered and came close to dying because of this. You saved him, yes, and that's great, but it's not over yet. We are going to see this through and salvage something from the wreckage Pauline left us. If you're too frightened to go after Motorcycle Woman, then so be it; I'll track her down myself. But in that case, you're going to take over the duty of watching over Sven. There are sayings in multiple cultures that if you save a man's life, he becomes your responsibility."

He roiled with unspoken rants and profanities, finally saying, "My whole life will go to shit if I can't hold down a job. I can't stay here all the time."

"You don't have to," she pointed out. "Move out of your friends' house and stay here instead. Go to work when you have to. I know it's a longer drive, and I'm sorry, but you owe us that much. Sven doesn't need to be watched constantly, but he needs someone to check up on him and help him out at least twice a day."

Johnny threw up his hands and gazed at the ceiling. "Fine. Give me another day or two, and I'll move in with you. Will you even be around? And why the hell are you doing this? Do you think that we *owe* MW something?"

She took her hand off the doorknob and relaxed her posture. "Thank you, Johnny. And no, it's not that. It goes back to when Pauline and I first met, and I signed on to her whole crazy scheme to make this city a better place to live. I believed in that. Unfortunately, I also bought in to the premise that the only way to improve things was through control of everyone's behavior. In retrospect, maybe I should have seen how flawed that was."

Johnny, who, along with Sven, had worked for Pauline because it was a secure and well-paying job with the possibility of advancement, stared at her.

Lia went on. "You remember some of the nonsense she convinced herself of. It sounds crazier in hindsight. Drugs prey on people's crude, stupid desires, so getting them all hooked makes it easier to lead them around by the noses. She wanted to be 'the best' at everything too, which was why she went off the deep end when Motorcycle Woman proved to be a little bit better. Maybe there was a real reason behind all this. I'm going to find out."

Judging by Johnny's slack-jawed expression, he wasn't as sure. "You're nuts," he stated. "By saying all that, you're kinda sounding like Pauline yourself now. If you go after MW, you're going to get yourself killed. Me, I'm not sticking my neck out for another crazy bitch with delusions of grandeur."

Lia bit down on the desire to ask him to clarify who he meant by that.

"But," he added, running a hand through his short black hair, "if you're that dedicated to getting it over with and moving on to the afterlife, I saw a bike that looked an awful lot like Motorcycle Chick's at Kim's Convenience around the southern part of Little Tokyo once or twice. Might be a coincidence, but it wouldn't be a bad place to start your search."

Lia managed a weak smile. "Well, thank you. I'll try not to end up in the afterlife any sooner than necessary, though. I'd rather give Pauline more time to calm down first."

Again, Johnny stared at her in befuddlement. Then he threw his head back and cracked up. "Yeah, you'd end up having to spend eternity listening to her rant about profit margins or something. Fuck that."

After putting on her leathers and helmet and climbing astride Zee, her Kawasaki Z900, Kera had cast a low-level glamour spell on herself to make both the bike and the helmet look bright red instead of black. She wasn't going out in the persona of "Motorcycle Man;" she was visiting friends.

The drive to the little convenience store was short. She could have walked it if she'd had more time, but she had to work this evening and preferred to devote her available hours to face time with the Kims.

Once there, Kera secured Zee to a post outside. She took her helmet off as she pushed through the door. The bell rang, and Sam Kim looked up at her from the register.

"Oh, hi, Kera," he greeted her. "Are you here to buy stuff, or did you just want to talk to my parents?"

She waved. "Hi, Sam. Parents, but I might need to stock up on some groceries on the way out."

"Okay." He stepped out from behind the counter. "They thought you might drop by and told me to close up the store for an hour if you did." He walked past her and flipped the Yes, We're Open! sign out front to Sorry, We're Closed.

Kera cocked an eyebrow. "Oh, really? I didn't think they could still, um, sense the future. Then again, it's been a week or so since last time I was over, so I suppose I'm due."

Sam winced, and Kera regretted her choice of words. His parents had lost their powers because of her. She was far from proud of that.

He led her behind the counter and into the short hallway beyond, which opened into a landing for a staircase that led up to the family's living quarters on the second floor of the building. Their home was hidden from the street, and here in the middle of the city, it always impressed her as an oasis of peace amidst the noise and lights and gas fumes outside.

Mr. Kim appeared on the second-floor landing. His appearance always reassured her; a trim, aging Korean man, weathered by time but full of good humor. "Kera! Hello, finally. Where have you been all this time? Anyway, you are welcome, as usual. In fact, we have a surprise for you, ha. Although it is an unintentional one since we had no way of being certain you would show up today."

Kera started up the steps, with Sam following her. "Now I'm curious. Before we get to that, though, how have you been? How's Mrs. Kim?"

"We are fine," the man answered her, "for the most part. Ye-Jin is still sick, but she is stable for now. It won't be long until she can get in at the hospital and get professional treatment."

Kera smiled in relief. She had been using her talents to combat Mrs. Kim's cancer, staving it off until the poor woman got past the waiting list. She might be dead by now otherwise.

Beyond the landing lay the living room and the dining room. There was a person in each room, indicating that the "surprise" was a guest. The individual in the dining room was Mrs. Kim, and she was setting plates out for a meal. Kera couldn't see who was in the living room. The wall blocked her view, and she saw only a pair of legs and feet wearing khaki slacks and black shoes and socks.

Mrs. Kim turned to face her. "Hi, Kera." Her face was lined with pain and fatigue. When she was at all able, she insisted on fixing dinner, though her husband and Kera had often advised her to do otherwise.

"Hi." Kera ambled over and took the last two plates. "Here, I'll help." She evenly spaced them on the table. Enough for five people.

"Thank you," the woman said, "but I could do it. I am okay. Better soon." Her English was not as fluent as her husband's, though Kera sometimes suspected she was even more intelligent than he was.

Before Kera could ask who the mysterious guest was, Mr. Kim took her by the shoulder and showed her into the living room. "Look who it is! Ha, ha."

It was Chris.

Kera blushed, annoyed that she hadn't taken any special measures to make herself look nice. "Oh. Um, hi, Chris. Sorry it's been a couple days since we talked. I've been busy with work and helping Stephanie."

He knew everything. She had finally spilled the beans to him not long ago, and it was no longer necessary to hide what she was or the strange lifestyle she lived. Still, opening up to anyone was difficult for her.

Christian smiled. "Nice to see you, and don't worry about it. We both have lives. You hungry? They've been forcing me to sit here inhaling mouth-watering cooking fumes for the last half-hour. Not sure how much more I can take."

Kera laughed and approached him. He stood and hugged her. "I'm *always* hungry. Not as much lately, but still."

Behind them, Mr. Kim pointed out, "Don't worry. There will be *plenty*."

There was: heaps upon heaps of *jjimdak* chicken, a huge bowl of *tangpyeongchae* vegetables, lovely greasy noodles, dumplings, and an incongruous but welcome apple pie, along with strong green tea.

Mr. Kim strategically placed Kera and Chris next to each other at the table.

I never updated them that we're pretty much officially dating now, she realized. *They might think we're still in romantic limbo and are trying to make sure we get together. Well, it's nice of them, and we can always pretend that they helped make it happen. They deserve that much.*

As they ate, the sporadic conversation was casual and cheerful, but Kera couldn't help noticing that Sam was glum. He had an obvious crush on Kera, though he had never been anything but a younger brother figure to her. She wondered if he was jealous of her and Chris.

She suspected there was more to it than that. She thought back to what she'd stupidly blurted when he had first let her into the store.

"Are you guys getting on okay?" she asked the family. "I mean, now that things are...different."

Mr. Kim waved a hand in dismissal. "Why do you keep asking that? I have told you that we're fine. It is a relief to not have to worry about that garbage all the time. Magic is more trouble than it's worth. I don't envy you still having it. Hah!"

Sam, however, asked, "How come that weird couple didn't take anything away from me? I guess I don't have the gift after all."

Kera nodded. *Ahhh, that's it. Poor kid. He probably has a trace, but I guess thaumaturgic talent can skip generations.*

"It's more of a curse than a gift, really," she commented. "Not as much fun as it looks." It sounded more awkward than she had intended, probably because it was obvious that she was trying to cheer him up.

He sulked. "Yeah, sure."

Chris chimed in. "No, seriously, Kera complains about her powers constantly. Like having three times the homework, or something. Any time she's around, I never hear the end of it."

That raised a chuckle from the boy, though Kera turned to Chris with a glare and flicked his earlobe.

"Ow," he whined.

Kera was surprised by how little she ate. Only about two, maybe two and a half times the food a normal human being would consume, as opposed to her usual triple or quadruple helpings. Her body, mind, and will were growing more efficient at processing energy. She hoped it meant she'd stop losing weight too since she was getting downright scrawny.

The Kims noticed her diminished appetite.

"You eat less," Mrs. Kim observed. "I hope this means you are working less, too. Do not do too much at once. You must have breaks to recover and be your best when you need to."

Mr. Kim's mouth was full, but he nodded and pointed at his wife to emphasize his agreement.

Kera breathed out. "Yes, I'm trying not to overburden myself. Every time I get a handle on one thing, though, some new crap comes up that I have to deal with."

After swallowing, Mr. Kim said, "Such is life. One thing at a time."

They lingered and talked over tea after the food was gone, though not for long; Kera had to be at work soon, and Chris had to get home and go to bed for work tomorrow. Kera had occasionally wondered if their relationship might be doomed simply based on him working a nine-to-five shift and her working late at night.

The couple said their goodbyes to the family, thanking them for dinner and promising to call again soon, and found their way out as Sam resumed his place behind the register and reopened the store.

Outside, Kera and Chris walked arm in arm the short distance to her bike.

She asked, "Do you have a ride home?"

"Eh," he responded, "I took an Uber out here. Not a big deal. I can walk or get another one. Mr. Kim offered to drive me, but he's got other things to do."

Kera put her hands on her hips. "Bullshit. I'll take you *halfway* home, which will only be, like, a mile out of my way. I could use the company on the drive to work anyway."

He laughed. "I guess I can't refuse, then."

As they climbed onto Zee and buzzed off into the evening, neither noticed the petite young Asian woman standing across the street at the other end of the block, pretending to be absorbed in looking at her phone. She glanced up and watched the bike speed away.

"Coincidences happen," Lia muttered under her breath, "but there can't be *that* many women with bikes like that. Even in LA."

CHAPTER FOUR

Pavla had already been reprimanded for her first failure in all her numerous years with the powerful coven known as the Orthodoxy. She did not understand why it was necessary to go through it all a second time. It seemed less like discipline than vengeance.

She was a slim, unremarkable-looking woman with wavy brown hair, and she appeared to be in her early thirties, though in fact, she was closer to sixty. She had spent the bulk of her life in the Orthodoxy's service, ever since they had recruited her as a university student in Prague.

For decades she had carried out the organization's will, dispassionately tracking down and recruiting potentially promising witches—and if necessary, kidnapping or eliminating them. Never had she encountered a serious problem or made a major mistake until she had at last come to Los Angeles and met Kera MacDonagh.

The building the Orthodoxy had chosen as their new regional headquarters in North America was an old abandoned Orthodox church. Anezka, the grandmistress, found it amusing to select such buildings in mockery of the mainstream Orthodox Christian faith that prevailed in the coven's Eastern European home territory. The church lay in a derelict neighborhood where they were unlikely to be bothered.

Pavla stood in the nave, which was hung with draperies and occult symbols and lit by green-burning braziers. She faced the altar. Behind it, an ornate chair with bronze trim and deep green cushions had been set up. No one sat in it yet.

From the side, Belen approached. Belen was the caretaker of the church and an American affiliate of the Orthodoxy, an unpleasant little old woman who clearly had no love for Pavla and thought herself worthy to be made a full member of the coven soon. Pavla doubted it.

"Hello, dear!" Belen chirped with syrupy falseness. "Anezka will be along shortly, then they'll begin the conference. Just stand right where you are, and everything will be taken care of."

Pavla, not bothering to look at her, replied, "Oh. Thank you."

Belen yanked a cord, and the sable draperies at the sides of the empty chair fell to the ground. Behind them were black-rimmed mirrors, four each to the left and the right. Their surfaces were dull and indistinct.

A moment later, Anezka appeared, striding seemingly out of thin air to Pavla's left. She was wearing a long jet-colored dress, which, with her black hair, made a striking contrast with her milk-white skin. She did not look at Pavla or speak to her until she had ascended behind the altar and seated herself on the throne.

Belen scurried off since she had not been invited to observe. Pavla breathed in through her nostrils and waited for whatever was to come.

At a snap of Anezka's fingers, the eight mirrors burst into lime-hued flames, and their surfaces grew brighter before disclosing the visages of the nine senior witches and warlocks of the Orthodoxy's top advisory echelon. Most of them remained behind in Russia, and one or two were on assignment in other countries. Their dark faces loomed and stared.

At last, Anezka looked at the woman standing in front of her. "Pavla. You were called here tonight for a disciplinary hearing before the High Council so that we may discuss what is to be done with you in light of your recent and unprecedented failure." She spoke Russian, the Orthodoxy's standard internal language, with a slight Ukrainian accent.

Pavla bowed her head. "I understand, Grandmistress."

I understand, she lamented, masking the emotions from her face, *that this is a time-wasting formality since I have been chastised, and I'm well aware that I mustn't fail again. Why the charade?*

The nine senior witches weighed in with brief, redundant comments that sounded appropriately grave and nebulously menacing. Pavla stood and waited them out until Anezka resumed speaking to her.

"Most of our advisory board," the grandmistress explained, "voted to have you expelled from the organization. Do you comprehend the significance of this?"

Despite her best efforts, Pavla could not suppress a brief tremble. "Yes, Anezka."

The Orthodoxy refused to allow loose ends; it insisted on tying them up. If she were kicked out of the coven, then there were only two possible fates in store for her. One, execution, which tended to be a gruesome and drawn-out process since it was a ritualistic affair based on the methods used to destroy Slavic witches many centuries ago.

Two, she might retain her life, but not her powers or her memory. Removing them both would also have meant an agonizing and terrifying process that would leave her helpless, confused, dumb, and traumatized, then turned out into the uncaring world. It was difficult to decide which would be the worse option.

Suffering one of the two or perhaps both was beginning to look highly probable.

Anezka's full lips turned upward at the corners. "However, at my insistence, you are to be given a second chance. You do, after all, have a long record of exemplary service, and all the information we have suggests that the girl Kera is an extraordinary specimen. Perhaps you grew overconfident in your abilities after so many years of unbroken success and neglected to consider your own reports that Kera's power was far beyond what we usually encounter."

"Yes, Grandmistress," Pavla agreed. The worst of the tightness and coldness within her abated. "I underestimated how difficult it would be to bring her in."

The other eight elder witches buzzed and grumbled within their mirrors, but Anezka lifted a slim white hand, silencing them.

"You may retain your position, your abilities, and your life, Pavla, provided you complete the task to which you were first assigned. Kera has proven that she has no interest in joining us. Therefore, she must be destroyed."

Pavla's gut clenched, but she nodded.

Anezka continued. "You will be assigned a partner to ensure that we can devote sufficient force to the job at hand. It is conceivable, albeit unlikely, that a witch of your standing could be overwhelmed by an especially powerful novice. For Kera to defeat two of our talented trackers, though, will be impossible. Thus, we are pairing you with Olina."

Bile rose at the back of Pavla's throat. She had no fondness for Olina. The woman was well-known as a snitch who constantly tried to undermine whoever occupied the same rung in the hierarchy as herself, pushing them down far enough for her to clamber atop their shoulders and pull herself upward to the next rank.

Pavla was almost certain Olina hated her personally for being Anezka's favorite and most trusted tracker.

This is a sham, she concluded. *They're assigning Olina to me as a way of keeping tabs on me and determining if I need to be replaced rather than because they think I need the extra firepower to take Kera down.*

Pavla asked, "If I may, when will Olina be arriving?"

"Tonight," Anezka stated. "She is on her way as we speak and ought to be here within the next half-hour."

Pavla's spirits sank further if such a thing was possible. She would not even have time to try to change Anezka's mind or formulate a plan to work around Olina's subversion.

The grandmistress glanced to her right and left. "Do the other members of the High Council have any other questions or concerns for the subject?"

Two did, but they were simple requests that Pavla restate her account of the battle with Kera. Probably, they wanted to ensure there were no discrepancies that might indicate Pavla was lying.

In point of fact, she *had* lied. She had claimed that Kera and her friend overpowered her and escaped. In truth, she had subdued them...then turned around and stormed away, leaving them there.

She still didn't know why. Her feelings on the subject were a mystery to her.

At last, Anezka ended the conference, clapping her hands to extinguish the magical flames that flowed along the edges of the mirrors and rising from her chair to descend past the altar.

Now that the formal ceremony was over, Pavla could speak on a personal basis. She pressed as close to Anezka as she dared.

"With all due respect, this decision will hamper my ability to accomplish the mission," she told Anezka. "Olina dislikes me and covets my position. Everyone knows as much. No job I do will be good enough for her. She will constantly watch for me to make a misstep and will pounce if I put so much as a single foot wrong. Wrong according to *her*, that is. And if I do everything perfectly, she will make something up. She is a talented witch, but she cannot work with others. She cares only about her own advancement."

Anezka gave a slow nod. Her cold, imperious manner had given way, but she was still not in a yielding frame of mind.

"Oh," she began, "the High Council knows what sort of person she is, and we will take her character into consideration when reading her reports. But we *must* be hard on you. It is the only way to restore the integrity of your image within the coven. Were I to be excessively lenient—and please recall that I argued against your expulsion—I would fail in my duties as grandmistress."

Pavla simmered within, but she could not argue further. Voicing her misgivings openly had been a major risk at this point. Anything more would be outright disobedience.

Sucking in a long, shaky breath, Pavla said, "I understand, madam. With your leave, I would like a breath of fresh air."

"You are dismissed." Anezka seemed distracted by other concerns. "I will be returning to Russia in the morning. Our small operation here is well established. Good luck, and do not squander this opportunity."

She turned and swept away, her long black dress trailing along the floor behind her.

Once she was gone, Pavla trotted toward the front doors, pushing them open with more force than was necessary and barging out into the mild air of night, the faint starshine, and the closer lights of the city, though the neighborhood surrounding the church was dark.

Off in a far corner, hidden within shadows and behind a cloaking spell, Belen watched. Beside her, so did Olina, who had been present since Anezka had made her entrance.

"My, my." Belen clicked her tongue. "This ought to supply some high drama, don't you think?"

Olina, a small blonde woman with hands that always seemed to be moving, smiled. "Yes. And since I am here, I might as well get started."

She walked toward the door, following Pavla's path and watching her from behind.

Over the past two days since her now-infamous potato roast with Stephanie, Kera's thoughts had drifted back to the unpleasant subject of Pavla. It was taking on the allure of the forbidden. She knew it was bad for her mood and focus to think about it, which made her keep doing so as a masochistic act of defiance.

So, late that afternoon, before she made herself dinner, she was pretty well overwhelmed by the need to beat the living crap out of her punching bag. Given that she and Steph were going out tonight, it would be good to have a warm-up session anyway.

She changed into her gym shorts and a t-shirt and added ankle and wrist wraps, though she did not wear shoes or gloves. After five minutes of intensive stretching, she emptied her mind of everything except her long years of martial arts training— Shotokan karate back when she was a teenager, and a mixture of Judo, Hapkido, and Taekwondo with Mrs. Kim more recently. Though still not a master, she was progressing toward a high level of competence in her own blended style.

That alone remained in her head. That and the seething undercurrent of rage and frustration.

She let out a loud *kiai* and charged the heavy bag, faking out as if to punch it but then pivoting and striking it in the center of its mass with a powerful side kick. It flew back, swinging upward until it was nearly parallel with the floor before falling back toward her.

Her increasing education in the "soft" techniques of Judo and Hapkido, which emphasized redirection or manipulation of hostile force, flashed in her mind, but for the moment, she discarded them and went back to the "hard" philosophy of Shotokan. Force was to be opposed with force; attacks were blocked, then the attacker was crushed with superior violence.

Kera fell into a stable blocking stance and took the onrushing bag against her arm and shoulder. The impact barely moved her, and she felt it as a stinging slap but nothing serious. The bag rebounded and she pounced on it, hitting it at maximum speed with a flurry of punches, palm strikes, and knife-hand chops from every angle available to her.

As she assaulted the sack, her mind kept putting faces on it, but they varied, shifted, melded into one another. Half the time, it was Pavla's face.

The other half of the time, it was an array of imaginary, fictitious faces, Kera's unconscious way of filling in the blanks representing the people Pavla worked for. Those who had put her up to it. Those who were truly responsible for the nice Czech lady's betrayal.

After taking the edge off her aggression, she settled into a groove and started incorporating evasive maneuvers and redirection techniques into her routine. She imagined attacks coming her way, making them up on the spot so she had no time to "expect" them and had to react instantly based on instinct, reflex, and intuition.

Goddammit, she thought as the bag continued to miss her and be pummeled for its insolence. *Why did she have to spare us like that? Well, I'm glad she didn't kill Stephanie no matter what. But if Pavla had finished me off, at least I could have gone to the grave feeling justified in hating her forever.*

Instead, she muddled things. Now I don't know what the fuck to feel. Yes, she was working for some coven or secret society or whatever, trying to recruit me. Maybe to kidnap me if that didn't work. Maybe even to assassinate me if I wouldn't play along.

But was some part of our friendship genuine after all? Is that possible? Do I want it to be possible at this point?

The bag provided no answers, but it gave her an outlet for the outpouring of chaotic and primal emotions that surged out of the core of her being. It was a solid target. Nothing about it was confusing or ambiguous.

Kera moved on to launch a sequence of Taekwondo maneuvers: high kicks, flying kicks, hook kicks, and axe kicks. Risky moves, but when they connected, they tended to end a fight quickly. They also made her more tired than she'd anticipated.

When she glanced at the clock, it was a good seven or eight minutes later than the time she'd planned to finish by. Stephanie would be leaving for the meeting place soon. Since tonight would be her first time out on a nocturnal vigilance run, she might lose her nerve if Kera didn't show up on time.

Worse, fatigue was setting in. Kera was in good enough shape that she had energy to spare, but she had overdone it in terms of taking out her anger and anxiety on the poor bag. She could not afford to be drained tonight. If they got into anything serious— like an epic brawl, which Kera had had to deal with on several occasions—she might not have enough strength to make it out in one piece.

Before jumping into the shower, Kera made a small pot of strong coffee and prepared a cup with extra cream and sugar. It was a crude way of reenergizing herself, but it was better than nothing.

After the shower, she drank the coffee while gathering her things—various tools and weapons, as well as emergency snacks in case the need to use magic depleted her strength further— which she stashed in her pack. Her leathers and helmet, of course. Her phone, which she had managed to rig with a combination of an audio amplification spell and a scanning app to pick up police radio signals and relay them into her helmet.

Finally, it was time to go. Though she'd had to rush, she would be on time.

"All right, Kera," she told herself, "you've done this many times before, and you and Stephanie got through that fight with Pavla together. The two of us can handle foiling a car theft or breaking up a gang fight. Everything will be fine."

Inexplicably, she was seized by the desire to tell someone

what she was doing and why, and where she would be in case something happened.

Chris was the most likely candidate. She wanted to call him and see what he was doing and hear any reassuring stuff he might have to say.

"No," she murmured, opening the warehouse's front door and wheeling Zee out to the curb as cars zipped by on the lighted streets. "That would be pointless. He'd probably say not to do it, and I'd be reduced to asking how his day at the office went or some shit. He would think I was being...ugh, needy."

Then again, couples did that all the time, didn't they? It was *normal*.

It still felt uncomfortable. She mounted the bike, started the engine, and roared off into the street, wondering vaguely what "normal" was.

CHAPTER FIVE

For their meeting place, the two young women had chosen a relatively quiet (by Los Angeles standards) street corner in the northern Fashion District. It wasn't far from where either of them lived.

Kera remained nervous that she would be late, but she arrived at the spot one minute early. Stephanie wasn't there yet.

There were, however, two thirty-something couples in swanky club clothes staggering down the street. They looked drunk, though there weren't any nice bars or clubs nearby that Kera was aware of. They saw her sitting astride her black bike and pointed.

"Hey," one of the men called, "look! Is that who I think it is?"

The presumed girlfriend of the other guy added, "Yeah, it has to be. Shit! Hey, you! Are you—"

Kera turned toward them and took off her helmet, rapidly casting a minor glamour spell to make herself look darker and chubbier. "Motorcycle Man?" she finished for the woman. "Pfffft, hahahahaha, no. I ain't no superhero, honey. In fact, I can barely ride this thing. Always moving up in the world, though, and who knows, maybe the real deal will take me as his apprentice or something."

Laughing but seeming a tad disappointed, the inebriated quartet stumbled past her, waving goodbye and telling her to say hi to MM if she saw him.

Kera exhaled, put her helmet back on, and canceled the spell.

Just then, Stephanie appeared on foot. She must have parked her car down the street.

"Hey there," she announced, waving and jogging toward Kera and Zee. "You are who I think you are, right?"

In a low, faux-impressive voice, Kera said, "Motorcycle Man? Or Woman, technically. Yes, ma'am, that is correct."

Stephanie grinned. She looked exuberant, but there was a sheepish, nervous quality to her, too. "Damn. I can't believe we're doing this. Anyway, you're the veteran here, so tell me what we do to start out."

Before they worried about choosing a place to begin the prowl, though, or discussing potential strategies and tactics for dealing with crime, Kera examined her friend's choice of outfit. Stephanie had selected what had to be the most nondescript clothes in her wardrobe.

Kera marveled, "So, what? Motorcycle Man's sidekick is going to be spoken of in hushed whispers by the media as Yoga Pants Girl? That'll be something."

Stephanie laughed. "You bet your ass. They won't never see it coming. I'll show up and ruin the bad guys' day by asking to speak to their manager."

Shaking her head, Kera quipped, "Shit, that might be worse than anything *I've* ever done to them. You're mean. Anyway, climb aboard. There's plenty of room; Chris fits behind me, and he's bigger than you are."

"I should hope," Stephanie remarked and swung a leg over the back of the seat, then wrapped her arms around Kera's waist. "Lead the way."

Kera recalled her earlier thought about tactics.

"Yeah, yeah. First, a quick rundown. The way this works is, I keep an eye and ear out for anything suspicious, and you help me. If we notice something, we keep driving past it, then we sneak back. When I'm in vigilante mode, I have enough of a reputation by now that we might be able to scare criminals off simply by showing up. But if not, then think back to our fight with Pavla in that alley and how we managed to work together despite not having time to plan anything out, only with more people and less magic. If in doubt, leave the heavy hitting to me. I can fight without casting spells, which helps a lot."

Stephanie blinked, turned her head to crack her neck, and breathed deep. "Okay, got it. Let's go."

They cruised into the city, alert and ready.

Twice, the de facto magical receiver in Kera's helmet crackled, and she heard the cops reporting on minor disturbances, only to dismiss one of them as nothing after all—a mistake. As for the other, a domestic, two cars arrived on the scene, and an officer reported it as under control by the time Kera had driven a block in that direction.

"Well," Kera snarked, "the LAPD have to earn their paychecks, so we can't do all the work ourselves."

Driving around at random, they also saw a few groups of people who looked sketchy. However, after doing a second pass by them while cloaked, the individuals were not doing anything overtly wrong, so Kera left them be.

Then they passed a house where a guy, grimacing and mumbling to himself, was attempting to pry open the window.

"Aha," Kera said. "Now that's interesting."

Stephanie chimed in. "Hold on, I think he locked himself out of his own house. He's standing right in the streetlight and didn't try to take cover when we passed. He's wearing a bright red shirt, and he's barefoot. Doesn't look like any burglar I've heard of."

Kera had to admit she had a point. "Okay then, but if that

house shows up on the news tomorrow, it's on you. Still, I think you're right."

Despite the mixed messages from the police band radio and the minor instances of potential crimes they had seen so far, Kera sensed something else—a nameless, dreadful impulse, a bad vibe emanating from a point somewhere to the west of their location, toward Mid City or maybe Crenshaw.

Since Kera had started practicing magic, her senses had sharpened and opened up to the point that she effectively had developed a sixth sense. She now had the ability to sense things happening, feel people's emotions and attitudes from a distance, and be aware of what *Star Wars* geeks would call "disturbances in the Force."

She wondered if Stephanie was developing the same ability.

"Hey, Steph?" she asked. "Do you feel that? A nasty premonition somewhere west or southwest."

Her friend spent a couple seconds in silence, then answered, "I don't think so, but I trust your judgment. You want to head that way, then?"

"Yeah." She took a right turn, bearing westward. "It's more than just a hunch, I swear. Could be something bad. Get ready."

Stephanie's arms tightened around her waist.

Kera's instincts led her onward, and the sensation of foreboding grew stronger as they continued. After a couple more miles, she was close to positive that the problem, whatever it might be, was happening in Crenshaw or one of the adjacent neighborhoods.

Soon the evil vibe was screaming within Kera's mind. Stephanie piped up,

"Hey. I think I feel it. I don't know, might be all in my head because you said it was there, but I definitely have a bad, *bad* feeling."

Kera perked up. On the one hand, she was overjoyed at the prospect that Stephanie's gifts might develop along much the same course as her own had. It meant her friend could be equally talented and powerful and Kera wouldn't be alone. She would have someone else to talk to about such things.

On the other hand, it meant they *both* could be about to walk into a world of shit.

They came to a neighborhood where the overall character didn't suggest a nice part of town, but where the houses were larger and more widely spaced than was usual for the area. And then they saw the parked cars, the flashing lights, and the orange barricades blocking off part of a street up ahead by a big, older, two-story house surrounded by a high hedge and eight or ten palm trees.

What was odd, Kera realized, was that there was an LAPD cruiser present, yet she hadn't heard anything reported on the police scanner. She wasn't intimately familiar with law enforcement procedures, though. Maybe the cops hadn't had time to report the incident yet.

As she buzzed up, a man wearing a suit jacket, whom Kera somehow suspected was carrying a concealed weapon, strode to the edge of the barricade. "You can't come through here," he announced. "Go around. Keep clear."

"Okay, sorry," Kera said and drove onward, peering past the man at the various figures standing or milling around.

Once they were a block away, Stephanie asked, "Did you see all those guys with guns? What the hell was that?"

"I'm not sure." Kera had her suspicions, though.

They stopped and secured Zee near a small neighborhood park, then crept on foot back toward the house that seemed to be the epicenter of the night's shenanigans. They cast spells to cloak themselves from sight and muffle any sounds they might make.

The pair cut through the gap between two properties, ducked under a strip of yellow streamer-tape that had been strung across the sidewalk, and circled around the hedge to examine the spectacle on the front lawn.

As Stephanie had pointed out, there were at least a dozen armed men surrounding the house, with nine of them near the front door or on the nearby street. Perhaps half of them were carrying pistols; the other had rifles and shotguns, and one or two had submachine guns. High-end private security, Kera guessed.

Next to the police cruiser, a cop was speaking to the apparent leader of the men.

"...can delay the report by maybe another hour, but you guys have *got* to get your story straight ASAP, okay?" the officer insisted. He was squinting and looked tired and irritable. "I need to get going, or they're gonna suspect some shit is going down. I already had IA breathing down my fuckin' neck two months ago."

"Yeah," the other man rasped, his tone cold and bitter. "Real shame, that. But we appreciate your cooperation regardless, Officer."

Bingo, Kera's mind declared. *Organized crime. That guy's a dirty cop who's running interference for them. But what the hell happened here? Did someone get murdered? Was there a major theft of a million in drugs or something like that?*

She whispered her suspicions into Stephanie's ear as the officer climbed into his car and drove off. Steph nodded and shuddered. She didn't complain or ask to leave, though. Her courage was nothing to scoff at.

Some of the armed guards were talking to each other in low voices, and they sounded depressed and frightened. Kera, focusing on various conversations, heard snippets that disturbed her immensely.

"...son *and* the daughter, for fuck's sake. Yeah, they're grown up, and they half-ran the operation alongside the old man, but shit. They wiped out a whole family. Who the fuck is gonna pay us now?"

"...told him, you can't put a price on security, especially these days, with all these goddamn foreigners trying to move in. He thought I was being greedy. Yeah, I like having work, but that's my legitimate professional opinion. In fact..."

"Hold on," another man said, louder and more sharply than the others. "Someone just called me on the boss' phone. No idea who it is. Encrypted caller."

A hush fell over the crowd. The man who had answered the phone covered his mouth and turned away, discussing something with the mysterious caller. Kera could not hear anything he said unless she got closer and used fairly powerful magic, which might drain her beyond what she could deal with if violence broke out.

Stephanie asked, "Are we gonna take these guys out? They ain't law-abiding citizens, that's for sure, but they seem sad. I think someone killed their boss and his kids, or something like that."

Kera examined the group and contemplated the issue. She and Stephanie, with the element of surprise and enough magic, probably could defeat the whole group. By doing so, they would break up a crime outfit and put mobsters, illegal mercenaries, or drug-dealing thugs behind bars. But it would be extremely risky.

And she wasn't sure it was *right*. Something about the situation did not feel like it required her to intervene and hurt people more than they'd already been hurt.

Her instinct was that she and Stephanie were, at least on this specific night, looking not at perpetrators but at victims. Who, she wondered, had ordered the hit? Who had carried it out?

As if answering her mental question, the guy with the phone turned to the others and announced. "El Peluquero. He said he's on his way. To *talk*."

The man's voice was twisted with anger and sarcasm, and after finishing his curt report, he cocked his pump shotgun. Clearly, talking was not what he had in mind.

"Hold on," someone else shouted. "We open fire as soon as someone pulls up, and maybe the whole city blows up. Not to mention people will say we're loose cannons, and we won't get comfy security jobs no more. Have to go down to fuckin' Mexico and behead police informants for a living. I ain't doing that shit."

A third man shouted, "Fuck it, my old boss would take me back. And this piece of shit can't get away with stuff like this." He clicked off the safety on his rifle.

Stephanie inhaled. "Oh, crap. Should we get out of here?"

Kera's mind raced. "Steph, I'm sorry we walked into something like this your first night out. If you want to go back to the bike, I won't say a word. But I can't just let this happen. I have to do something."

Her friend hesitated. "Fine. If you're sticking around, so am I."

Kera smiled and immediately prepared a big, powerful shield spell. If these guys started shooting, at least she could block off the worst of the carnage to come in time for the legitimate police to intervene.

A black car, possibly a Volkswagen, rounded a corner beyond the barrier and approached the house. As the dozen guards fell into positions to begin their attack—or defend—if necessary, lights suddenly shone on them from the second- and third-story windows of the surrounding houses.

A voice, amplified by a megaphone, barked, "Move and you're dead. Stay right where you are. And lower your weapons."

Kera's jaw dropped. "*Now* what the hell is going on?"

The men cursed and obeyed, realizing their enemy had planned everything two steps ahead by commandeering the neighbors' houses to act as sniper spots.

The black car continued its leisurely approach and stopped before the orange barricade. The doors opened, and three men stepped out.

Kera squinted and cast a minor spell to see farther and clearer, as though she were zooming in with binoculars. The details burned themselves into her mind.

Two of the men were huge, imposing-looking brutes in full

black paramilitary gear: helmets, goggles, plate-carrier tactical vests, harnesses. They carried expensive assault rifles, probably made by European manufacturers, and wore pistols at their hips.

The third man was completely different. He was on the taller side of average and dressed in snappy-casual business attire. Nothing about his appearance stood out, save his salon-perfect black hair. He didn't appear to be armed.

He stared at the dozen guards, not flinching from their desperate or hateful gazes, for perhaps a full minute before he spoke.

"Hello, my friends," he began, in a clear, almost mechanical voice with a slight accent Kera didn't recognize. "I am El Peluquero, and I have come to claim responsibility for the elimination of your late employer and his son and daughter. Trying to avenge them would be very foolish. All of you would die in the time it took you to squeeze off a single shot."

Kera's blood ran cold. She had come into contact with some unpleasant people in recent times, but never anyone who was so calm, frank, and casual about murder.

"Furthermore," the well-groomed man went on, "I know all of your names and your records. Tracking you down later would be very easy. So, I have come to discuss an easier way for all of us to benefit. What happened tonight was not personal. Your employer was simply an obstacle, which I have removed. And since I benefit from having quality people in my organization, I would like to offer all of you a job. I would guess that you have all been thinking about who will pay your salaries now that he is gone."

There was a moment of total silence as the dozen guards thought it over. It looked to Kera like a couple of them were still furious enough to try something stupid, but the rest seemed to be giving the proposal serious thought. They had to make a living, and excessive sentimentality was not wise in their line of work.

El Peluquero gave them a calculatedly gentle smile. "I will give you time to think it over. Two days. Please remain in Los Angeles during that time, or I will have to find you."

Then, with a curt nod, he climbed back into his car. His decked-out bodyguards lingered a half-minute longer before joining him, and the vehicle drove away in the opposite direction from which it had come. The spotlights from the neighboring houses were not shut off until the black vehicle had been out of sight for a full minute.

Once relative darkness returned, the men huddled and began discussing things among themselves. Based on the chatter she could hear, Kera suspected most of them would end up agreeing to transfer their loyalty.

"Steph," she commented, "let's get out of here. We could beat these guys up, but *that* man might think another rival gang did it, and he might have even more people killed. I don't want to do anything hasty till we have a better idea of what's going on."

Stephanie shuddered again. "Yeah, agreed. What the hell did we get ourselves into?"

They snuck back toward Zee, thankful their cloaking spells had worked. As they remounted the bike, Steph asked, "Who *was* that guy? You've been fighting crime for a while. Anyone you've heard of? And what does '*el peluquero*' mean? I had some Spanish, but it's not ringing a bell."

"No," replied Kera. "I never heard of him."

As for his appellation, her mind was blank, too...and then, recalling his appearance, her memory flared up. "It means 'the hairdresser' or 'the barber.' He did have a nice head of hair, but you'd think a guy like that would go around calling himself 'the butcher' or something. Ugh."

"Charming." Stephanie held on tight, and they drove off in numb silence.

It amused Pavla to think there had been so many layers of observation going on, a veritable hierarchy of people spying on each other and having the drop on one another. With her at the top of the pyramid.

Along with Olina.

"Well, that was an interesting display of indecision," the other witch observed. "I have a theory about why you did not destroy her just now, Pavla. She and her friend are distracted. Watching those criminals threaten and posture must have upset them. They would be easy prey."

The two had noticed the developing situation in Crenshaw over an hour ago, and, suspecting that Kera might show up, they had camped out on a roof. They'd watched the covert operatives working for that Peluquero gentleman quietly subdue and evacuate the neighbors before setting up with rifles in the highest available windows. They had watched the other drug dealer's hired muscle debate with each other and with the corrupt police officer, and they had watched Kera and Stephanie sneak up.

No one had watched *them*.

Pavla turned to her shorter, unwanted partner. "Allow me to guess," she began. "Your theory is calibrated to make me look as bad as possible to our superiors."

Rather than respond directly to Pavla's accusation, Olina launched straight into her own. "You did not, in fact, *lose* the fight when you confronted her previously," she gloated. "She lacks discipline and finesse. And even if the black girl, who barely qualifies as a witch in terms of her aura's strength, managed to help, there was no good reason why one of your vaunted status could not have overcome them."

Pavla's insides roiled. Below them on the street, Kera and Stephanie had crept away from the big house with the hedge and were almost to the bike.

Olina finished with, "You *let* her get away, didn't you? And you have done so again."

Under no circumstances was Pavla going to curl up and die because Olina was more intelligent than she looked.

"*Or* rather," Pavla shot back, "having more than a single functional brain cell in addition to all the dead weight devoted to petty grudges and self-promotion, I know more about her than you do and am capable of making informed decisions based on that knowledge. I worked with her. This potential confrontation would not have gone well. And that is *before* you count the horde of people with guns down there who might easily have taken us out with a stray bullet and that sociopath trying to take over the LA underworld. We were not ordered to interfere with *that* business alongside dealing with Kera."

Olina smirked as though she knew something Pavla did not, which was doubtful. "The more you say, the more you convince me that I am right."

Pavla laughed. "Fine. Do you want to take a shot of your own, then? They are only now getting back on the motorcycle. Go ahead, Olina; be my guest. I will back you up in front of Anezka, even, and follow your lead. *If* you think highly enough of our odds to insert yourself directly into the middle of this clusterfuck."

They had been speaking Russian, but Pavla said "clusterfuck" in English. It was the perfect term to describe what would happen the instant the men below thought anyone was shooting at them, and sadly it had no direct equivalent in most other languages.

Olina stood poised at the edge of the roof. Though she was a small woman, there was a quality to the crude animal cunning that emanated from her when she saw something she wanted that frightened ordinary people.

But she did nothing. Slowly, her impish smirk drooped into a frown. A moment later, she turned and asked, "Was that a *genuine* offer, Pavla?"

Pavla smiled. "You tell me."

CHAPTER SIX

James Lovecraft reclined in a chair in the study of his mansion. The central portion of the floor, where the tables were generally set out for meetings of the council, had been cleared aside or moved to other rooms, providing a nice open space for training and practice.

Of course, the weather was nice out, and it would have been easier to train outside, and James did not like the idea of their new student fucking up his paneling or annihilating his carpet. But a good thaumaturge needed to be able to cast as well indoors as out.

Ezeudo stood in the middle of the room, eyes closed and arms outstretched. "I...think I see what you mean. Yes." He didn't sound sure.

Lauren Jones, fellow council member, let out an "Ahem" and scolded him, albeit gently. "Now, now. If you *think*, then you do not *know*. Thinking you see means the images are still forming and have not yet coalesced. Relax, and we will start over. This time it will be easier. Have no fear."

She and Ezeudo were working through a standardized set of techniques for visualizing the nature of a spell as well as the desired effect, then projecting one's will through the image to bring it to bear upon reality. The tall Nigerian had taught himself to use magic on a more intuitive and less intellectual basis. That was impressive in its own way, but it meant he had a lot of entrenched habits to overcome to learn to do things *their* way.

James sipped his rum and Coke through a biodegradable straw. He had been quite sincere, at first, when he'd told LeBlanc that he would be training Ezeudo, and Lauren would simply be checking in occasionally.

He should have known better. Already it was shaping up to be the other way around. Lauren was the best teacher among them. She enjoyed it, excelled at it, and lived for it. James' own experience as an instructor, by comparison, was both limited and lukewarm.

He contemplated selecting a book from one of the shelves to flip through and wondered what to have for dinner when the voices of both the teacher and the student rose in volume.

James looked up. They had repeated the visualization exercise, but Ezeudo appeared to have failed again.

The man's face was drawn, and the vibe emanating from him was full of restless frustration and self-doubt.

"Miss Jones," he said, "I am not certain I can do this in the way you describe."

She raised a hand, palm outward. "Please, it's Lauren, not Miss Jones. Or 'Hey, lady,' as some foolish boy called me once. And yes, you can. You simply require more practice, and if that doesn't do the trick, we will approach it from a different angle. Every spell, every exercise, is a puzzle that *can* be solved."

"But," Ezeudo countered, "are not most of your students young people? I am forty years old. There are reasons our species teaches its most important lessons to children and adolescents, rather than waiting until they are adults of my age. My background, and the worldview, which shaped how I use my power, may be too different to reconcile with your Western method."

Lauren stood, holding his gaze and listening intently, allowing him to speak. She had the odd quality of being simultaneously stern and friendly. With her, students rarely felt diminished or condescended to, yet they also had the sense that they would not be permitted to slack off.

And she was patient. When a student went into a self-critical rant, her usual method was to allow them to talk until they stumbled onto the cause of their problem or accidentally arrived at a solution. Watching her, James decided, was like watching a master painter bring a landscape to life with what *looked like* careless ease.

"But," Ezeudo continued, and he sighed in a way that turned into puffing himself back up, "my power has always been stable. I have good control, and I suppose that age brings wisdom. I have better knowledge about how to use magic judiciously rather than in the rash and stupid manner of youth."

Lauren nodded. "Indeed. Which is why I have no doubt you will succeed. Perhaps it would be best if you...how should I put this...translate my instructions into a mental or visual language that makes more sense to you. Find the best analog within your tradition while hewing as close to what I say as possible."

Ezeudo rubbed his broad chin. "Yes, that could work. May I take a break to walk and breathe fresh air? You began by telling me that such breaks were beneficial."

"Of course," said Lauren. "But only for twenty minutes. Then we resume the lesson."

With some reluctance, the man agreed and walked past James into the foyer, where he let himself out the front to amble about the grounds.

James turned to Miss Jones. "Lauren, you're doing a great job as usual, I'd say. If by some slim chance you actually need me to do anything, chances are I'll be enjoying myself doing something else or possibly asleep. If not, I'll be happy to help."

She adjusted the hem of her dress. "Highly amusing, James,

but you should be paying attention since I can't stay here indefinitely, and you will have to pick up with him wherever I have left off."

"Oh, I know," he conceded. "It's just so much fun watching you do all the work without being asked."

Lauren shrugged. With the lesson interrupted, she had nothing to do and was growing bored. "It's odd, though. He mentioned that he is forty, yet he has an impatience that reminds me of a boy half his age. What was it again that he was doing when you and LeBlanc pulled him out of Switzerland?"

"Oh, I don't know," James drawled. "Some nonprofit stuff, saving the whales or whatnot. And keeping an eye on the little French boy, of course. He might be worried about him."

Ezeudo, meanwhile, had rarely been so grateful to have open air around him and the open sky above. The Lovecraft estate was beautiful and comfortable, but it was increasingly reminding him of a prison. Or one of those oppressive boarding schools from older English literature that differed only marginally from a prison.

He ambled to the left, toward an area where trees and bushes were spaced widely enough to walk around and between them comfortably but dense enough to provide some seclusion. He would not be visible to James or Lauren through the windows.

Unless they were using magic to observe him at all times. He doubted it.

Nonetheless, there were *so* many rules here. Rules dictated by the council at large, dictating the behavior of thaumaturges, which he would have to follow for the rest of his life. Rules regarding his personal behavior as a guest in someone else's house. Rules pertaining to his status as a student; he was a schoolboy again at four times the usual age.

Rules intended to keep him here and away from his usual affairs.

He had spent twelve years in various locales across the globe. He had worked for the United Nations for a time. Though he often found them inefficient and overly hamstrung by regulations, they were in some cases a good springboard for doing good in the world once one learned to navigate the system.

He had also served in various nonprofits. Usually he sought places that were experiencing the worst strife and tried to find positions that would allow him to help. Ways he could employ his rare gifts to influence the course of events and make sure humanitarian aid flowed to the people who really needed it, rather than being tied up in red tape on the giving end or being stolen by greedy officials or warlords on the receiving end.

It had always been difficult, of course, to use magic without getting caught or raising too many questions, but it was worth it. He had saved entire villages on at least three occasions.

More recently, however, he had been waylaid in Geneva. It had become the closest thing he had to a permanent home, insofar as it remained a safe haven, a nest to which he had flown many times after weathering a storm somewhere else. He had friends there, other expatriates from Nigeria or elsewhere in Africa, as well as native Europeans he had become acquainted with. It was a beautiful city.

But he was not so much homesick for Switzerland as he was frustrated. His progress on this American council's strange program for magical education was going too slowly. James' promise that he would be done in a year at most now rang false.

All the while, the world continued to churn and boil without him. He had always stayed abreast of the various crises going on across the globe. Despite the best efforts of well-intentioned people, there were always terrible problems occurring. Problems he could be helping to resolve.

Ezeudo strolled past the stand of trees and down a slight

slope that led deeper into the low, forested hills surrounding the estate. He wanted to keep walking into the woods, but he could not.

He ought to simply talk to his hosts about his concerns, but he was afraid.

If he was honest with them, they might take it as a sign that he was preparing to go rogue. That he would be dangerous and disobedient, and then the combined might of the council would descend upon him. He might be mind-wiped and have his power cut off forever, as they had done to Guillaume before he had prevailed upon them to reverse their decision.

Then he would be dumped back in Geneva with nothing. He had neglected to renew his previous job contract to come to the United States for training, so he would be unemployed. He would have no magic, none of the abilities that had subtly and without him always realizing it helped him so much on his previous assignments. And he would have no memory of how things had reached such a sordid and difficult state.

"No," he insisted, clenching his hands into fists. "These people are controlling, and they did not tell me as much as they should have. But I cannot let them do *that*. I will play by their stupid rules for now and get back to training. When it is done, I will be in a far better place than I have ever been my whole life."

Breathing deeply in and out, he walked back to the mansion.

Christian piloted his Jeep down the streets to the northeast, with Kera in the passenger seat and Stephanie in the back. The three had reached the conclusion that they could use a short day trip to unwind and learn to defend themselves better if it came to that.

"To be honest," Chris admitted, "I wasn't even sure there *were* shooting ranges in California. Well, maybe out in the desert and mountains, and I suppose there are some people who carry concealed in the city, even though prosecutors in this area would try to convict them of terrorism if they so much as shot a chainsaw murderer in the leg."

Kera laughed. "As far as I know, the only place in America that is entirely gun-free—*officially*, anyway—is New York City. My parents owned a townhouse there, and once I started getting interested in firearms, I was always looking for excuses to stay the hell out of New York so I could go shooting more easily."

She thought back to those days when her dad, to his eternal credit, had indulged her sudden desire to learn a traditional if slightly dangerous skill. At home in Connecticut, the laws were almost as bad as New York, though. The best places to go were all the way out in Pennsylvania or up in Vermont and New Hampshire since if she remembered right, they didn't have bullshit restrictions on what types of guns you could have or how big a magazine you could use.

She said as much to her friends.

"Oh, yeah," Chris commented, snapping his fingers. "Aren't we still limited to ten-round magazines here, even though a federal judge ruled that was unconstitutional a couple years ago?"

Kera couldn't recall and made a mental note to ask someone once they arrived at the range.

Stephanie chimed in. "Well, as long we can get something that goes boom a few times, enough to scare off people like that Barber guy, that's a hell of a lot better than nothing."

"Yeah," Kera muttered. Dealing with him and his men, they ideally would need a turret-mounted .50-caliber anti-aircraft machine gun. Even in the US, that might be difficult to get away with.

They arrived at the place, which, situated in a less populated area out toward the mountains, had an indoor handgun range and an outdoor rifle range and a variety of weapons available to rent. There were other locations closer to downtown, but Kera felt this one sounded the most promising.

Chris parked, and Kera noticed how much more adept he'd become at handling the vehicle. It was the first manual one he had ever owned despite being well into his twenties, and his driving had been a touch awkward at first.

There was a main building out front. Presumably, the handgun range was in the basement, and it appeared that the outdoor portion was well behind the structure and fenced off for safety. Sporadic loud cracks like thunder or fireworks emanated from said area.

Stephanie commented, "Louder than I thought. They make you wear ear protection though, don't they?"

"Yep," said Kera. "And safety goggles. That stuff should all be rentable."

Kera took the lead as they entered and explained to the guy behind the front desk they wanted to rent an assortment of rifles and pistols and try them at both ranges. Looking at them gravely but not unkindly, the man asked, "So, do any of you have any prior firearms training or experience?"

"I do," Kera declared, "but they don't. And in my case, it's been about four years. I remember most of it, though. I've fired rifles a couple times, but mostly handguns."

Nodding, the man went over the basic safety rules and procedures with them. For Kera it was largely a review, but she welcomed it. Once it was all firm in her mind again, she could keep the other two in line.

Pointing a loaded gun at someone was a death threat, and a gun should always be treated as loaded unless one was a hundred and ten percent certain it wasn't. Fingers stayed off the trigger until one was prepared to shoot. Never cross the line at an outdoor range to check your target unless you've confirmed that no one else will be shooting until you're back. The breathing techniques and basics of stance and grip that allowed for accurate firing.

It all came back to her pretty quickly.

Kera, for obvious reasons, had become the day's unofficial master of ceremonies, and Steph and Chris waited for her to instruct them and lead the way. She gave it a moment's thought and then spoke.

"Okay. I think we'll start with rifles since despite being bigger, they're actually easier to shoot in a lot of ways. The size and weight absorb more of the recoil, and they're inherently more accurate. We'll see how we do with a couple different rifle types and then move on to semi-automatic pistols and revolvers."

When making their selections, Chris looked disappointed to discover that AR-15s were banned in California. Nonetheless, they found a decent semi-automatic rifle equipped with a ten-round magazine and a higher-powered bolt-action hunting rifle with a capacity of five.

"Five isn't very many," Kera pointed out, "but this is designed to be a weapon where you only need one shot. Maybe two at most."

Outside, there were only two men in lanes near one side of the range. The trio took a lane on the other side, and Kera went over the manual of arms for their rifles while the other shooters finished. Once it was clear, she set up a target at fifty yards, intending to move it back to one hundred once they had all attained halfway decent proficiency at the closer distance.

Chris was loading the ten-shot rifle. "Man, this is a pain in the ass. I guess the springs have to be strong to push the bullets up into the gun, but pressing down on a rounded object with another object against that much resistance isn't a lot of fun."

"Yeah, I know." Kera had embarrassing memories of barely being able to do it as a teenage girl. "They make loading devices that are a lot easier, but I forgot to buy one or ask if they had them for rent at the counter."

Finally, they began shooting. Kera went first so she'd be in a better position to advise the others. Firing the first rifle, the semi-auto .223 Remington, went pretty well, though she was rusty enough that it wasn't until the last two out of ten shots that she felt like she was on the ball. From what she could see, her shot placement reflected as much. One of her early rounds grazed the target's edge, and only the final two were close to the bullseye.

As for the second, the .308, it had more recoil than she remembered, but not vastly more than the other gun, so she managed to get about a two-inch group.

Chris went next. With both rifles, he started off decently, putting all rounds within the target circle though generally not hitting the bullseye, and his performance remained consistent through two mags of each. Kera suspected he was the kind of shooter who might never be a master marksman but would be acceptably competent at getting the lead where it needed to go at close to medium range.

Stephanie was another matter entirely. At first she could not hit the target, seemingly intimidated by the kick and noise of the weapons, but after the initial shock and a bit of coaxing from her friends, she improved rapidly.

"There," Kera soothed. "Remember that you're in control. It's like driving a car in that regard. A big noisy piece of metal that can be dangerous, but only if you're careless with it. Otherwise, if you pay attention and do what you're supposed to, everything will be fine."

Stephanie looked more comfortable with herself after the second round with the bolt-action .308. "Mkay, I think I'm starting to get it, at least on a basic level. Like, it's a matter of lining up the sights and timing it just right for when your lungs are empty, and that's also when you squeeze the trigger. You sort of have to make everything perfect, but you also have to not force it too much and let the moment be right."

She frowned and added, "But waiting wouldn't work in a real firefight, would it? We're not going to have much time if someone else is trying to shoot us."

"True," Kera acceded. "Otherwise, though, what you said is a good way of summing it up. And your accuracy toward the end was impressive for a new shooter. I guess if the three of us end up functioning as a fire team, you'll be our sniper. Back away from the fast-paced front-line shit and take potshots from a nice elevated position. Ideally."

Stephanie allowed herself to smirk. "That sounds cool when you put it that way."

Kera put up a new target and moved it back to one hundred yards, and they all fired a couple more mags. Obviously, it was more difficult at twice the range, but everyone managed to perform with a baseline level of competence. Especially Stephanie.

They headed back indoors for the second phase of the excursion. For the handguns, they chose a 9mm Glock, which Kera had a fair amount of experience with and was one of the world's most popular pistols, as well as a Ruger .357 Magnum revolver.

"And .38 Special," Kera quipped. "They're the same size diameter-wise. It's just the difference in powder charge, so this gun can fire either."

"What?" Chris marveled. "How are '357' and '38' the same number?"

Kera sighed. "I could explain it, but it would take too long. Bullets like to switch back and forth between imperial and metric measurements even more often than beverages do, and I say that as a bartender."

They started with the revolver due to its relative simplicity and used .38-cal ammo for its lower recoil. Everyone fired three cylinders and did fairly well.

Next they switched to Magnum rounds. To Kera's annoyance, she had some difficulty with them, given what a powerful cartridge it was to be blasting out of a handgun. Stephanie did too. Chris, however, burst out laughing the first time he fired Ruger, and his accuracy didn't suffer.

Men! Kera thought. It must be nice to have more upper body strength, thicker wrists, and bigger hand bones.

The Glock was last. It and pistols like it had always been Kera's favorite weapons platform, and she was pleasantly surprised by her ability to put most of the rounds through the bullseye, even at twenty-five yards. Her speed wasn't as good as she remembered, but her rate of fire had picked up by the third magazine.

Stephanie and Chris fared less well, though by the end, Kera had them doing okay. Chris seemed to have trouble with the sights on the pistol, and Stephanie found it tough to rack the slide. Still, they had a basic grounding in the weapon's use and function.

Two hours had passed. They turned in their weapons and headed toward the Jeep, discussing what they'd learned.

Kera summed things up. "Successful test run. We all know how to use four different guns at a minimum level of competence, and everyone found one they're particularly good with. A striker-fired semi-auto for me, a big-boy revolver for Chris, and a nice hunting rifle for Steph."

Stephanie again smiled in an off-kilter way. "Never would have seen myself as a hunter, let alone a sniper, but I'm not complaining."

Her coworker chuckled. "Keep at it, and that's a real possibility. Rifles are an elite weapon, in a way. They're what humanity invented to replace the bow and arrow, and someone who's good with one can kill anything that moves."

"Damn," Chris lamented. "Of course, it's my luck that I'd turn out to be best with the weapon that's slow and out of date. Though it's also badass as fuck, if I may say so. The boom of those Magnum rounds... I might have to shoot more of them purely for fun. I'm just not sure how useful a revolver would be in a modern combat scenario."

Kera shrugged. "Wheelguns are old-fashioned but not obsolete. They're simple and reliable, and they'll get the job done. Not the best choice in a lengthy firefight due to the lower capacity and slower reload time, but in a short altercation, they can actually be better in some regards. No need to rack the slide, so everything can be done with one hand. Feed jams don't happen, so if you get a bad round, you can just pull the trigger again and rotate the cylinder to the next one. And the frame being all one piece of material, as opposed to semi-autos being mainly two pieces between the lower frame and the slide, makes them stronger. Which is why the really big, scary cartridges like .44 Magnum and up are mainly revolver rounds."

Chris asked, "Uh, so should I upgrade to a big, scary cartridge? I think I could handle shooting it. My biggest fear would be that people would start sarcastically asking me if I think I'm Clint-fucking-Eastwood now."

"Nah," Kera told him. "Stuff at .44 Mag and above is mostly for dealing with grizzly bears if you live in Alaska, or I guess rhinoceroses if you live in Kenya. And for *fun*, of course. For stopping mere humans, .357 Magnum is about as much power as you'll need. .38 Special isn't bad either, plus it's nice to be able to shoot two different calibers out of the same gun."

Chris waved a hand. "I've known people who reminded me a lot of grizzlies or rhinos, but fair enough."

She patted his shoulder and bumped her hip against his. "And I've heard people say that the best gun is the one you can shoot well. So stick with what you're good at, and we'll put it to use. Next step is buying guns for ourselves. And ammo, worse yet. I should be able to pony up most of the money for all three of us, but I'll have to look into it."

Frowning, Steph remarked, "That's the hard part, ain't it? I don't imagine anything worthwhile is cheap."

Chris started the engine and suggested they go out for lunch next. The two hungry magic-users instantly agreed.

Kera sighed, satisfied with a day well spent. "We should all get together and do this again and soon."

Chris and Stephanie agreed with the caveat that it might depend on their schedules and budgets, though Kera said that she could spot them a bit of money from her savings if need be for training as well as buying their weapons. It was worth it to her.

"Also," Chris added, "if you want to go shooting by yourself, Kera, I won't be offended if you go without me."

She winced. "Ehh. I'd rather have your Jeep on hand."

"Why?" Stephanie asked.

"Yeah, why?"" Chris echoed.

Kera considered the answer obvious, but she humored them all the same. "Because I don't want my bike sitting at a place where everyone is armed. Sure, I could cloak it or put an illusion spell on it to make it look like it's a different color, but that stuff doesn't always work, and there's already enough speculation about the so-called Motorcycle Man as is. It would be a good way to set myself up to 'accidentally' get shot."

She grimaced, remembering what had happened in the back lot of the Mermaid after the dude in the Mustang had tried to shake Cevin down. "Or, worse yet, Zee might get shot again."

CHAPTER SEVEN

After a long, hard day of discharging firearms and driving through half of Greater Los Angeles, everyone agreed that what they really needed was a gargantuan amount of fattening Mexican food. They found a drive-through known for its quality and large portions and ordered food enough for six people.

Chris was perplexed. "Wait a minute. Neither of you has been doing magic, so why do you need to recharge to that extent?"

Kera and Stephanie exchanged glances.

"Good question," Kera admitted, raising a finger, "but we *were* using a little bit to stabilize ourselves and get a clearer bead on the target. Plus, I was thinking that on the rest of the drive home, Stephanie and I would practice recalling everything we did and coding it into our personal physical augmentation spells and luck charms. What do you say, Steph?"

Her friend pursed her lips. "Sure, why not? If magic can help speed up the training, it will save us a *lot* of money. More to spend on burritos."

When Chris pulled up at Kera's warehouse, they evenly divided the duty of carrying all the food in between them, though

Chris would be eating a mere one-sixth of the total, leaving the other two and a half meals' worth each to the ladies.

They piled in, took their shoes off, and tore into the masses of tortillas, beef, rice, cheese, and refried beans with abandon, liberally dressing it all with salsas both red and green, as well as guacamole and sour cream.

First, Kera switched on the television set. She was used to having the news on while she ate. She used it largely as background noise, not to mention it allowed her to keep an ear out for criminal activity that might be of interest to Motorcycle Woman.

After the initial pleasantries were out of the way, the biggest story was one involving the worst form of criminal activity of them all.

"Two people were murdered in their own home," the newscaster summarized, her voice and face grave with concern and subdued disgust. "LAPD responded to a call on a normally peaceful street in a western LA neighborhood where two friends who shared a house were found slain execution-style following a break-in. Nothing was stolen from the house, leading some officers and citizens to suspect it was a targeted hit."

Kera's head snapped toward the screen, and she listened intently as the broadcast cut to brief interviews of eyewitnesses and cops who had been on the scene. Beside her, Chris and Steph watched with equal focus.

Stephanie queried, "Is that what I think it is? Wait, no, it's something else. Oh, Lord…"

"Yes," Kera muttered. "I'm afraid it very much is, but probably part of the same problem."

Chris glanced at both girls. "Do you two know something I don't? If so, I'm not sure I *want* to know."

"I don't blame you," Kera admitted. "But you might as well since it's something I'll be dealing with, possibly for a long while yet. Now, hush for a minute. We need to hear this."

The report returned to the newscaster, who summed up the incident in the context of recent public safety concerns throughout the city. "This comes only a day after another triple homicide in Crenshaw of a father and his two adult children. All appeared to be gangland slayings, leading some to worry about a generalized uptick in violence that may yet spill out of the criminal underworld and begin affecting ordinary citizens. Back to you, Rita."

Kera lunged for her laptop. "Time to hear the other half of the story." She grunted. "The news is a decent place to start, but you need to read what random people are saying on the Internet to get a fully-rounded idea of what the hell is going on."

"No shit," Chris agreed. "Steph, while she does that, do you want to tell me about your personal involvement?"

Stephanie squirmed in place. "I'd rather not, but Kera's right; you need to know. We were looking for trouble the other night and hoping we could help. We found it, but we were too late. Big house in Crenshaw, belonged to a drug dealer or a mob guy, something like that. This new rival dealer who calls himself 'the Barber' killed the man and his kids. His bodyguards were all freaking out, then the man himself showed up and basically said, 'Work for me, or I'll kill you.'"

Chris' expression darkened. "Hoo boy. That sounds phenomenally awesome, doesn't it?"

From her position on the bed, Kera replied, "In a manner of speaking, yes."

She pulled up a few alternative news sites that had run with the story and skimmed them for extra details, as well as proceeding to the comments section. In some cases, all one could expect to hear was various individuals' opinions, but as time went on, she more and more often found that the electronic equivalent of street-level gossip was a good way to pick up on important info.

"Oh, man," she groaned. "Those two guys were killed over in

Dockweiler, and they had their throats cut with what they're pretty sure was a straight razor."

She recalled out of nowhere that straight razors used to be a common tool used by barbers, and an involuntary shudder rippled through her.

Chris blinked. "Jesus. That's even worse than I would have guessed."

Stephanie seemed to be on the same page as Kera. "Do they know who did it? Or is anyone saying they got any idea who's responsible? Like if it's 'friend of a friend' shit, that's still better than nothing."

Grimacing and reading on through the user commentary, Kera eventually stumbled onto a morsel that made her eyes go wide.

"Holy crap. Here's a guy saying that he's pretty sure that these two were killed because…wait for it, they refused to join El Peluquero. His comment has received seven upvotes in the last hour, so clearly there are other people who have heard of our friend the Hairdresser."

Chris snorted. "The *Hairdresser?* What, did he rise to the top of the underworld via the superior floral arrangements in his salon or something?"

Stephanie pointed out, "You wouldn't laugh if you had been there and seen what happened."

He relented. "Yeah, I suppose not. Seems like a weird nickname for a scary criminal mastermind, though." Scowling, he added, "But it does seem like he's no one to fuck around with. Were you guys spotted? Were they aware that you saw the whole thing?"

"No," Kera said at once. "We were cloaked. They couldn't see or hear us, and we chose not to intervene, though it was a tough decision."

Stephanie crumpled a burrito wrapper and tossed it in the trash. "We could have intervened. Maybe we should have, though it would have been dangerous as hell. Ugh. I haven't been able to stop thinking about that. Did we make the right choice?"

Chris asked, "Well, you said it was already too late by the time you arrived. Why did you choose not to do anything? I'm not saying I disagree at all. I'm glad you're both still here, on Planet Earth, for example. But I'm curious."

Kera finished scanning the comments, and she closed the article as well as the laptop. Sitting up, she looked at her near-boyfriend.

"Good question, and it's one we've been asking ourselves, too. I'm confident we did the smart thing. First of all, we would have been surrounded by people with guns, including automatic weapons. El Peluquero had snipers posted on the neighbors' houses above us and all around the house, plus the bodyguards were pretty heavily armed. If we had done anything, both sides probably would have assumed the other was making a move, and we would have been caught in a crossfire. We might have died, and so might everyone else."

Chris nodded. He looked relieved, so perhaps his respect for Kera's prudence and judgment had increased.

"And," she went on, "it's worth pointing out that all of these people were drug dealers. It wasn't as though one side was innocent, so taking a side didn't make much sense. Still, El Peluquero is showing that he has no compunctions about killing lots of people as the cost of doing business, so we're leaning toward him being the biggest threat right now. If we're lucky, he won't move on to killing innocents. Aside from indirectly via drugs, I guess. But we're probably going to have to deal with the bastard one way or another, no matter what."

Chris and Stephanie stared at her, taken aback. Reflecting on what she had just said, it occurred to Kera that it sounded more ruthless than she had intended.

Is fighting crime getting to me? Am I starting to turn into the same species of monster I've been trying to stop? God, I hope not. That's some-

thing to be careful about. But what I said isn't factually wrong. The most important thing is defending regular law-abiding citizens.

Steph peered at her, her eyes pained with concern. "Kera, you need to be careful. This man knows what he's doing as far as dealing with people who could threaten him. And you can bet he's heard about *you*. Your alter ego. Nobody in LA hasn't."

"Yeah, well," Kera retorted, waving a hand, "the good news about dealing with professionals is that they like to avoid too much collateral damage that attracts scrutiny from the police. It's not like random violence against passersby."

She glanced at Chris, who was not saying anything. Judging by the way his brow had wrinkled in thought, he was every bit as worried as Steph was.

If not more.

The television screen was incongruous, perhaps even anachronistic, set amidst the medieval church interior. Stone columns and draperies and green-burning candles could be glimpsed to the sides of it.

Anezka had changed her mind and canceled her trip, remaining in the States for the time being. She sat in her plush chair, her black-nailed hands curled over the armrests, and next to her stood Belen, who smiled and clucked at random intervals. She made no effort to disguise how honored she was to be so near the Grandmistress of the Orthodoxy and to serve as her personal handmaid.

The newscaster's face was drawn with concern.

"...a normally peaceful street in a western LA neighborhood, where two friends who shared a house were found slain execution-style following a break-in..."

Anezka shook her head, and her lips twisted in a sardonic smile. "It is truly amazing," she declared in heavily accented

English for Belen's benefit, "what normal humans can do to each other *without* the use of magic. It makes me think we have grown too reliant on our inborn powers. True, we are mighty and have had few problems with ordinary people, but their cruelty and ingenuity are most impressive. It would be disturbing if they were to turn their attentions to us. But that will never happen."

Belen chortled. "Of course not, Grandmistress. They're too credulous, too stupid. Their memories are fragile and can be wiped away in an instant, and as for the few who see things without being mindwiped, no one seriously believes them, anyway."

Someone breached the invisible tripwire-like forcefield surrounding the church and it registered instantly in Anezka's mind, but she recognized the auras as well as the cadence of the footsteps. It was Pavla and Olina, returned from their mission to offer their reports.

She hoped they had been successful.

At a snap of the grandmistress' fingers, two of the eight mirrors lit up and burst into emerald flames. The pair of senior council members who were available would thus be summoned to observe within the next minute or less.

"Pavla, Olina," she announced, tilting her head upward to throw her voice via the splendid acoustics of the church and switching back to Russian. "Welcome back. As you can see, I am still here. Another elder member became available to see to the matter I was going to supervise, so I chose to stay here and oversee this affair. Please tell me all that has occurred."

She kept her tone neutral. She did not want either of them to think she was assuming anything of favoring one witch over the other. It would be better to simply wait and hear what they said. All would be revealed quickly enough.

Pavla spoke the instant Anezka's voice faded. She came within a fraction of a second of talking over her mistress, in fact. She was no fool. She knew that being the first to make her report would give her the benefit of a first impression, in contradistinction to whatever Olina planned to say.

"Grandmistress, we have made excellent progress," Pavla stated. "We have discovered the perfect means of luring Kera into a position where she will be vulnerable and can be dealt with safely."

Olina began trying to insert her own commentary, but to head her off and further test Pavla's response, Anezka replied first.

"Oh? While that is *perhaps* encouraging, it was my hope that Kera would already have been destroyed so that I might rest easy, knowing the threat was past."

Two witches were behind Anezka's chair. The grandmistress had not turned to look at them, but she could *feel* the sour expression on Pavla's face—the barely perceptible wince, the frustration.

Anezka turned and saw the grim expressions of the two senior witches who had appeared in their respective mirrors and were now attentive to all that transpired.

"Kera has grown more cautious," said Pavla. "She is alert to the possibility that I will return for her, so a direct confrontation would be unwise. Our plan is to use a certain man as bait to distract her via an altercation with him and his followers, then move in to sweep up the detritus ourselves."

Olina made a sharp little "hmph!" sound in her throat and quipped, "Oh, the way you failed to do when you could have?"

Pavla pretended she had not heard. "If you will approve this plan, I believe it will bear fruit within a matter of days."

Anezka raised a hand and made a slow twisting motion. Her chair pivoted one hundred and eighty degrees to face the two lesser witches. "And who is this man, if I may ask?"

"They call him 'El Peluquero,' the Barber," Pavla answered her. "He is a new drug kingpin who apparently has arrived from somewhere farther south in the hemisphere and is making a play to take over criminal activity in the city via threats of violence. We observed one such incident in which he had the heads of a small crime family assassinated, then delivered an ultimatum to the old man's soldiers to join him."

"Oh?" Anezka raised a single black eyebrow. "What makes you believe Kera cares about this man at all? If she styles herself a fighter of crime, would she be disturbed in the slightest by mobsters fighting among each other?"

Pavla stiffened more from resolve than from reproach. Her determination had long been admirably consistent.

"Yes, Grandmistress. She and her friend witnessed the entire incident. Their fear and indignation were obvious. They did nothing, but I strongly believe Kera will not allow El Peluquero to dominate the Los Angeles underworld. He is too vicious and unfettered, and she seems to feel pity even for criminals when tensions go beyond mere fighting and into the realm of murder and death."

"So," Anezka shot back, "Kera witnessed the incident. You witnessed the incident. Does this mean Kera was in your sights the whole time?"

At this, Olina's lips drew back from her teeth. She looked like a cat about to pounce upon a hapless injured bird. Anezka had thought it odd that she hadn't tried to insert her commentary into the discussion yet, but the reason was clear at last. Olina had been waiting for the right moment to spring her trap.

"Correct!" Olina pronounced. "We had the opportunity to strike them down, but Pavla chose not to take it. She was afraid the gangsters would return fire, you see. As though there weren't spells to deal with such hassles and contingencies. I was most perplexed by her decision..."

Belen smirked, and she and Olina exchanged glances of mutual pleasure.

Anezka found their pomposity mildly annoying, so she observed, "And yet, Olina, you did not act either. How odd."

The small blonde woman's smile evaporated.

Though Pavla was obviously roiling with anger inside, she maintained her composure, having expected Olina to snitch on her.

"The gangsters," Pavla explained in a firm voice, "had people in hidden positions. We were aware of most of them, but it was possible that they brought other auxiliaries once El Peluquero arrived in his car. Accounting for every last one of them would have been exceedingly risky. Destroying Kera would have had to be done in a rushed and sloppy fashion that would have been obvious to others. One or two of the criminals might have escaped and spread the word before we could hunt them down."

Anezka shook her head. Before she could speak, the warlock in the mirror to her left snapped, "This is nonsense, Pavla, and we expect better of you. Your mission's order of priorities was clearly laid out. Kill Kera MacDonagh first. All else comes second."

The witch in the mirror to the right added, "Indeed, you should have known as much. We prefer expediency over artistry. Did you think you would reinstall yourself in our good graces by delaying the objective so you could kill the girl more *impressively?* Or *honorably?* Hah! Besides, dealing with these American thugs would be easier than allowing Kera to go free again, based on *your own reports* of her strength and cunning."

Anezka stared at Pavla. "I have nothing to add. Pavla, we must consider this another short-term failure, although your plan to lure her out via this Barber person may succeed. But do not delay it any further. We expect the girl dead and soon. Now, go. Complete your mission."

She waved a hand, dismissing the pair, and rotated her chair back toward the TV, where the news had moved on to a dull human interest story about a boy who had taught his dog to paint crude pictures with its paws. The mirrors winked out, leaving Pavla looking at the back of the grandmistress' throne.

"Yes, Anezka," Pavla said, with a curt bow of her head, then she turned and walked to the door, with Olina following close behind.

Outside it was growing dark. A lone man, shabby and dark-eyed, probably a homeless addict, stared dumbly at the two women emerging from the supposedly-disused church. Pavla flicked a hand at him, striking him with a light memory-wipe combined with temporary confusion so that when he recovered in twenty or thirty minutes, he would not recall having seen them.

As the man reeled and sat down hard against a wall, Olina hurried up to Pavla's side. They were near the alley where the fight with Kera and Stephanie had occurred.

"So," Olina began, her tone full of patronizing mockery, "it sounds like you should have heeded my advice. Next time, you will know better than to—"

Olina flew off her feet as though a truck had hit her, sailing through the air and slowing only enough so that when she collided with a brick wall, the impact was jarring and painful but not enough to break her spine. She writhed in place and tried to raise her hands to counterattack.

Pavla stood before her, one hand held at chest height, maintaining her control of the spell, her face expressionless and her eyes cold. Olina managed to squeeze off a quick but powerful Firefly spell, but Pavla saw it coming and neutralized it with a sphere of freezing water. Steam wafted about her shoulders.

As Olina struggled, she was aware of something else. Strong yet invisible hands were clamped around her throat, gradually compressing her windpipe and cutting off the flow of blood that ran from neck to brain and back. She saw spots and tried to think of a counterspell that could save her.

There was only one opening: a tiny gap in Pavla's unseen shield that would have allowed Olina to send a lightning bolt or a shard of debris straight through one of her eyes and into her brain.

But the penalties for killing another member without the grandmistress' approval were...severe.

Pavla lowered her hand. The choking relented, and Olina slid down the wall to crash hard on her rump on the ground.

"Yes," said Pavla, "we will both know better than to try anything foolish." She spun on a heel and walked away, leaving the other witch in a pile in the alley.

Olina coughed and massaged her throat as her vision and breathing started to return to normal. Hatred and disbelief swelled within her, but she attempted to suppress her emotions and to think about the significance of what had just happened.

She would not, in all likelihood, be able to defeat Pavla in an open fight, which in turn meant that Kera might pose more of a threat than she had guessed. That possibility only strengthened her resolve.

Anezka had been right, Olina concluded. One of them should have taken the cheap shot when the opportunity arose and damn the consequences. By hesitating and allowing herself to believe Pavla's nonsensical assertions, she had miscalculated.

Next time, *someone* would have to cast the sneaky spell that put an end to the MacDonagh girl once and for all.

CHAPTER EIGHT

With the day's lessons concluded, Ezeudo thanked Lauren Jones for her help and efforts, then trudged up to his room to retire. They had taken a break for supper, but the schedule James had set was so dense and hectic that there was one final session each evening after they ate.

Lauren called, "Sleep well!" She supposed it might have sounded sanctimonious, but she was perfectly sincere about it, and she hoped the man understood as much. He seemed to like her despite the difficulties of his training and his fish-out-of-water status in the world of American thaumaturgy.

He waved at her, nodded, and stepped through his door, already taking off his jacket. His shoulders were slumped with fatigue.

"Poor guy," she mumbled to herself. "He hasn't had sufficient rest during the day, and I don't think he's sleeping as well at night as he ought to be."

Shaking her head, she turned and headed off to find James. She needed to speak to him about things before she went home. Not only about Ezeudo, but about *him* since his mood, too, was growing dejected. The ravages of stress were everywhere lately.

Striding down the hall, Lauren spied a square of orange light emerging from the door of James' study, which was where she had expected to find him. If he wasn't there now, he would return soon.

She approached with gentle footsteps and leaned around the doorframe, peering in. James was slouching in the big leather chair behind his fine mahogany desk, and though he was facing the door, he did not seem to see her.

"Hello, James," she began. "We finished up, and Ezeudo went to his room for the night. May we talk?"

He looked up, blinking and seeing her for the first time. "Oh. Yeah, sure. Come in. Close the door behind you, please."

She did. It was a formality, of course. Shielding the room magically from Ezeudo's hearing could be done no matter what, but most thaumaturges found it mentally easier to cast the spell on a closed room than an open one.

"I'll soundproof the room," she offered, and James flapped a hand to give her permission. She was tired from instructing their student, but James looked the worse for wear of the two of them.

His shirt was rumpled, and he had not shaved in two days. His eyes had a dull and bloodshot look to them, and a lowball tumbler of bourbon on the rapidly-melting rocks was sitting untouched on a coaster before him. He barely seemed aware of her presence or anything that was happening in the here and now.

She came around the desk to stand beside him and he roused again, looking at her.

"James. What's the matter? It's been a long time since last I saw you like this. And you have not even had to handle the brunt of the teaching! Not that I mind, of course. It's only that I don't understand why you seem so down in the dumps lately. Let's talk it over?"

He blinked and made a sour face, his mouth contorting. It was obvious that he didn't want to converse, yet at the same time, the mood-vibe of his aura suggested he was probably admitting to himself that he needed to get things off his chest.

"Uh," he began, "yeah, I suppose you're right. I'm...distracted lately. I wish LeBlanc was here. She would know what to do."

Lauren pulled up one of the stools that lined the study and sat atop it, staying close enough to James that he could not pretend to ignore her if he changed his mind.

"Perhaps she would know what to do. About what, though? I haven't noticed any massive or glaring problems, though we're all growing tired."

James ran a finger over the rim of his tumbler, then picked it up and took a sip of the liquor within. Rather than answer her inquiry directly, he asked, "How is Ezeudo doing? Is he up to speed so far? Sorry, I should be taking a more direct role in his instruction myself, but I can't help that you're better at it than I am."

"Oh," quipped Lauren, "don't beat yourself up over *that*." She smiled at James. "And Ezeudo is, all things considered, doing fine. In fact, by the usual standards we apply to most students, I would rate the speed of his progress as 'above average' most of the time. He clashes with our way of doing things after being noticeably entrenched in his various self-taught habits for so long, but he's bright and quick on the uptake as well as dedicated."

After sniffing and taking another drink, James pointed out, "Your tone suggests that there *is* a problem, even though your words sound like good news. What is it?"

Lauren sighed. She was exceedingly patient, which was what made her such a good teacher. "As I said, he is progressing well by the standards we use most of the time. By the excessively strenuous and optimistic standards you have set, he is lagging a bit behind. I would estimate fourteen or fifteen months rather than twelve."

James set his glass down in a hurry so that he could safely

smack the desk, pounding its surface abruptly with the palm of his hand without spilling any of the bourbon.

"God*dammit*," he snapped. "I promised him we would be done inside a year, and if I have to break my promise, it isn't only that his feelings might be hurt. I don't think we have that kind of time. There must be a way to achieve a breakthrough that gets him up to speed."

Lauren squinted and smoothed her dress. The way James was reacting made no sense to her. She suspected there was something else he was angry about or afraid of that he wasn't telling her about.

The direct approach was often best. "Why the urgency, James? Do you know something I do not? I'm afraid I don't understand. Normally we would allow a year and a half. Rushing things along at this speed and keeping Ezeudo under so much pressure may backfire, you realize. If he ends up in a state of total mental burnout, he will need time to recover, during which we can expect no progress. That might stretch the timeline from fourteen months to, say, *sixteen*."

Looking into space rather than at her, James muttered, "Yeah, I know, thanks. You're right. I just...*shit*." He took a long swig of whiskey, draining everything in the glass except the last sip's worth. "I worry."

Lauren sighed and waited for him to talk himself into divulging the rest.

"I worry," he said, at last, "about where the world is heading and what the ripple effects through the pond of magic, so to speak, will be. After my *brilliant* fucking idea that led to this whole mess. After what happened in Los Angeles."

Some measure of clarity began to emerge, but there was still a lot of haze to cut through. Lauren queried, "What do you mean? I thought you and LeBlanc cleared things up there. Do you mean to tell me that you lied to the council?"

"No," James countered. "Not at all. It's more that despite our having treated the symptoms, so to speak, we never cured the disease, and now it's another pandemic. We opened Pandora's Box. Something in the world of magic has *changed*. After the entire city of LA started talking about good old 'Motorcycle Man,' I don't think there's any way of putting everything back in the box. Does that make sense?"

Lauren climbed down from the stool. "Somewhat. May I have a drink?"

"Of course," James replied. "You more than deserve one for doing my job so well. Anyway..." he inhaled, "let me rephrase things this way: our ability to track down individuals or small groups and blank their memories can only go so far. Can we mindwipe the entirety of LA? Or all the people on the Internet across the *entire goddamn planet* who started talking about what happened in LA? Sure, there are powerful mass rituals that can do things like that, but would it be morally justifiable? I don't know, Lauren. I'm in the dark."

As the small woman poured herself a nice gin and tonic, she nodded. The nature of James' crisis was becoming clearer to her.

Guilt was at the center of it. He blamed himself for the possibility that events might be slipping beyond the council's control, and it was likely all because of his idea that they publish that book and toss the ancient secrets of magic before the general public, just to see what happened. Just to recruit a couple of apprentices.

Lauren had to learn more, though. She opted to coax him into explaining further. "What do you mean, James? I heard your and LeBlanc's briefing, but I wasn't there in LA. So if there are pertinent details that I missed, well, you should tell me. And don't worry; I promise not to run off and tattle to Mary Mitchell."

James laughed. "Well, thanks for that, at least. But...yeah." He slurped the last of his bourbon and finished his story.

"Mother LeBlanc and I finally located the individual who had been roving around LA under the persona of the so-called

'Motorcycle Man.' Bizarrely enough, it turned out to be a tiny Korean-American woman your age rather than a young male, or possibly a young female, as we had suspected. Stranger things have happened."

Ignoring the vaguely implied dismissal of her abilities, Lauren nodded and kept listening.

"We cut off her power and her husband's since he had the gift as well. Their teenage son had only the slightest trace of it, so we left him be since it could not have been him. They didn't object much. I think they realized the little prank they were playing had gone too far, and being well into middle age, they no longer had the stamina to maintain it. They actually seemed to be looking forward to a life of normalcy."

Lauren tittered. "That is understandable. Our existence would be much simpler if we were not what we are."

James ran his finger around the rim of his now-empty glass. "So, for those two, the story ends there. But for a lot of other people, including us, it was only beginning. They set off a powder keg of chain reactions. Ugh, that's a mixed metaphor, isn't it? Wait, explosions can be part of a chain reaction, so I guess it makes sense."

Lauren, who sometimes taught English as well as magic, stated, "Yes, it does, mostly."

"Good," James continued. "So the Korean lady's little sojourn as LA's answer to Batman caused some *major* changes, and we are only starting to see the magnitude of them weeks after the fact. She broke the grips of multiple gangs, some of which were powerful enough to qualify as organized crime. I heard that even the official mob in that area took notice of her and were taking steps to rub her out if necessary. The cops don't like it when someone else does the job they're supposed to do for free, so they were trying to arrest her. Journalists were trying to expose her, the Internet couldn't shut up about her, and any bar you went into in Southern California, half the drunks would start spouting off about Motorcycle Man at the drop of a hat."

Listening to him rattle on about the details, Lauren felt something within her grow cold. It had become easier to imagine various branching possibilities, many of which were not good.

"Point is," Lovecraft went on, "a thaumaturge went public, so to speak, and normal folks fought back against her. There was a low-level street war, you might say, one that entered into urban legend before we could get there to shut it all down. Motorcycle Woman destabilized the whole power structure in the magical world, the criminal world, and the world of average law-abiding citizens. The only people who weren't heavily affected were high-ranking politicians and the super-rich, but that's to be expected."

"Of course," Lauren agreed. She had finished half of her drink without noticing, and her head began buzzing in a rather nice way. "It sounds, though, like you're trying to blame all of this on the lady in question. How could she have known what to expect when *we* have always been so secretive?"

Scowling, James muttered, "Good point. But it only takes a single match to burn the whole thing down if it's enough of a creaky old firetrap."

At that, Lauren narrowed her eyes. "Are you referring to the council?"

"In part," confessed James, "but we're not the only people on the planet who run an, uh, *official* magical organization, though the others are, if anything, more secretive than we are."

There was a moment of silence. Lauren chose not to speak but instead waited for James to say what came next.

"I am referring to the Orthodoxy, mainly. You've heard of them, right? A self-styled witches' coven in Eastern Europe. They claim to have been around since the Middle Ages at a minimum. There were reports that they went into remission during Communism since a boring, oppressive, and officially atheistic system isn't conducive to magic users, but after the fall of the Soviet Union, they came back with a vengeance. They again set themselves up as the 'shadow' of the Orthodox Church and consolidated their power after a series of bloody, nasty incidents that conveniently got blamed on the Russian mob or terrorists or whatnot. And they've only gotten stronger since then."

Lauren frowned. "The more senior members of the council do not acknowledge the existence of their organization, but..."

"Hah!" James interjected. "I'm so young that the first world event I remember is the fall of the Berlin Wall. Maybe that's part of it. You older folks probably knew about them all along, didn't you? Well, like I said, ripples in the pond. And the buzz online suggests Motorcycle Woman's personal crusade may have drawn *them* out of their base in Russia. Which, in addition to all this other crap, means that fun times may be ahead. All because you guys let me publish that stupid book. What the hell were you thinking? My worst idea ever, and you failed to stop me."

Sighing, Lauren finished her gin and tonic and returned the glass to the bar. "No one makes the correct decision every time, James."

He pushed his chair back from the desk and rubbed his eyes. "No shit. Between me, LeBlanc, and old Mrs. Kim there, we have inadvertently ushered in a new era of uncertainty and general fuckery. The world is changing. Having someone like Ezeudo in our court, keeping watch in Europe, would be useful since we *must* be prepared."

Lauren came over and put her hand on his. But before she could say something reassuring, he concluded his spiel.

"I don't know what to be prepared for anymore."

CHAPTER NINE

Kera had discovered something. To be more precise, she had *rediscovered* it since the evidence had been there in the past, but only now did it all click into place for her to make a truism out of it.

It was easier to make multiple big momentous decisions at the same time than to make one, wait a while, then make another. The brain became desensitized to them and adapted more easily. When things were too stable and "normal," any decision out of the ordinary was difficult and frightening.

She had reached the conclusion that with all the other crap going on lately, she might as well finally quit her job.

"Hey, Cevin," she said to her boss as she strode into his office ten minutes before her shift began for the evening. "Can we talk quick?"

Cevin looked up from the computer, where he had been going over invoices and order manifests and stock reports. "Uh-oh," he groaned. He had been more animated since he'd started dating that hot model-esque woman a couple weeks ago, but he was still Cevin. Moping came naturally to him. "What is it? I hope not a death in the family. Dammit, I shouldn't have said that. Sorry."

Kera bit her tongue to keep from laughing. "No, everyone's fine, but I suppose it might still qualify as bad news. My, ah," she cleared her throat and swallowed, abruptly wishing she had handled this the cowardly way via phone or email, "my two weeks' notice is effective as of Sunday. I'm moving on with some other plans I have. It's something I have been thinking about for a while, but certain chips had to fall into place before I could be sure. Financial stuff."

Her boss swiveled in his chair and looked at her, blinking his wide, bleary eyes. "Oh. Damn. Well, I'll be sorry to lose you since you've been a good worker. Business was down after all that stupid negative press we got, but it's picking back up again. I might have to hire two people to replace you." He sighed and gazed into the ether.

Kera blushed, unsure of how to react. "I mean, I might be able to make it more like two and a half, or possibly three weeks if necessary. But, yeah. I'm going to try and start my own business soon. I'll do a good job the whole time I'm still employed here, until the bitter end. In return, could you do me one favor? Don't tell any of the other girls. I'd rather tell them myself."

"Okay," he consented. "Fair enough. What kind of business do you plan to start? It isn't easy. I would know."

She smiled. "Yeah, I bet. I'm not sure yet. I have a few ideas. Give me a couple more days, and maybe I'll tell you since your advice might be helpful."

Deliberately, she did not mention that quitting was the only possible thanks to her parents finally agreeing to release her inheritance. Cevin probably suspected something like that, but it was better to leave it vague. Years ago, she had figured out that many people didn't enjoy hearing about how much money the rich had to throw at their children.

Stephanie, Jennifer, and the kitchen staff were people who had little in the way of savings, let alone investments or trust funds. They lived more or less paycheck to paycheck. Cevin probably had more, but only slightly.

Mentioning that her parents were simply going to *give* her a bunch of money—albeit on the condition that she used it for something ambitious and constructive—would have made things weird. She wanted her last weeks here to be good ones.

"Okay," Cevin said again. "Two weeks should be enough, and technically I have to let you go in that amount of time if you're officially quitting, but if I think I could use you for a couple extra days, I'll ask as early as possible."

He truly was a good man to work for. She recalled how he had paid to have Zee repaired after Mustang Guy had shot out the tank and tires, how he had given her time off when she needed it, and treated the staff decently in general. "Thanks, Cevin. I'll miss the place. But sometimes people have a calling, you know?"

"I do," he acceded. "Good luck. As for tonight, it's probably going to be busier, so make sure we're stocked up, and don't be afraid to yell for help if I'm not around and you think you'll need it."

Kera punched in and got started right before their usual rush hour. She found out quickly that Cevin's prediction had been accurate.

The crowds that began to stream in fielded considerable numbers, but they were mostly laid-back sorts Kera pegged as the type who wouldn't cause a lot of problems. One or two of them might start making noise if they didn't get their order fast enough, but none of them was the sort who'd have to be escorted from the premises or get into knife fights with each other in the parking lot.

There had been a brief period when the Mermaid had begun to acquire a reputation as one of *those* places, much to the staff's chagrin. Between Kera dampening the aggression with calming spells and the press losing interest in minor scuffles between the riffraff, things had begun returning to normal.

She liked the thought of the place continuing on a good course after she was gone.

Around an hour and a half after she'd started her shift, a quartet of good-natured lushes occupying her half of the bar asked for the nearest TV to be switched to a twenty-four-hour news channel. They wanted to hear about what had been going on lately.

Kera had a nebulous but unpleasant premonition that she knew exactly what they meant. All she said was, "Sure, just a sec. Knowing the world, I'm sure it's mostly bad news, right? Hah."

One of the two men gave a low, grunting laugh at that, though the other guy and the two women looked mildly concerned.

As Kera retrieved the control and changed from sports to one of the more objective and unbiased news networks, she saw at once that her customers would be in for five or ten minutes' worth of disappointment since the program was discussing high-level foreign policy. She made a show of flipping to a couple other stations, but there was nothing local there either, so she went back to her original choice.

"Sorry, guys," she told them. "They should hit local news shortly, though. Anybody need a refill?"

When at last the newscasters moved on to current events in the Greater LA area, the main subject of discussion was the recent surge in violent crime.

Dammit, Kera thought. *I need to know about this more than anyone, but I don't want to.*

The quartet watched in awe and consternation as a field reporter mentioned another homicide and a seeming influx of dangerous narcotics, which had all happened so fast that the police could not yet keep up.

One of the women at the bar quipped, "Shit, where's Motorcycle Man when you need him? Like, I heard he was still around, but you haven't been hearing as much about him lately, have you? I hope he didn't retire."

The others chimed in. They all seemed to admire their local superhero and yet were mildly disappointed by "his" inaction. Kera, pretending to be a regular neutral citizen, shrugged or nodded as need be, joking around but echoing their hope that something would be done soon.

She decided that it *would* be.

Toward the end of the night, as Kera was preparing to leave— an hour before closing time since Jenn and Steph had the honors this time—she finally had the opportunity to speak privately to Stephanie.

"Hey." Steph brushed past her and pulled her aside near the bathrooms. "There's more stuff going on with our friend the Barber. I heard some shit through the grapevine about him and what his game is."

Kera glanced around to make sure no one was nearby and sent out part of her expanded consciousness to try to discern that which was beyond what her eyes disclosed. If someone were hiding out of sight and intently focusing on her and Stephanie's conversation, she ought to be able to pick up on it.

They seemed to be in the clear, though. "Okay," Kera responded. "Shoot."

"Everybody in town who knows the first thing about the drug scene has been talking about that guy. Now, I don't do drugs myself—you know that, right?—but let's just say my sister knows a dude who knows a girl who knows a man who passed on what's coming down the grapevine. The word is that El Peluquero is an importer from south of the border, Mexico or Colombia or Brazil, probably, who's trying to become a distributor. *The* distributor, more like. And he's afraid of *nothing.*"

Kera nodded, her face stony. That half the city would suddenly be frightened of their own shadows didn't shock her since she had seen the Barber's handiwork. But the thing about him being an importer gave her an idea.

Especially in conjunction with the fact that all his hits on rival gangs had so far been on the west side of town. Closer to the ocean.

"Thanks, Steph. Have a good, uh, closing. I'm going to be out for a bit tonight, but we can talk more in the morning." Kera started toward her locker to grab her pack and leave the bar behind.

Her friend waved and called after her, "Hold up, girl. You aren't planning to...go after him, are you? By yourself? That would be nothing but trouble."

Kera frowned. "You're correct, but it's a variety of trouble the rest of town doesn't need either, and I might be the only one who can deal with it. I *have to* go after him. He's on a whole new level of terribleness from what I've dealt with before. But I'm not going to do anything hasty. Just, like, observe and gather information, then quietly leave. Okay?"

Stephanie still looked uncertain, but she calmed herself with a deep breath. "All right, but be careful. Later, we can talk about what comes next."

"Deal." Kera waved, grabbed her pack, and let herself out the back door into the well-lit lot where Zee waited for her.

She headed due west. There wasn't a shortage of Pacific coastline to search, and she had no way of knowing if El Peluquero had commandeered a large, seemingly legitimate shipping operation to act as a front business or if he and his men smuggled drugs in via smaller boats that snuck in on desolate stretches of shore where no one would notice.

Dammit. Okay, I need to think. Where were the murders? Can I triangulate them back to a specific place?

She gave it a try, calling up a mental map of Los Angeles and its surrounding suburbs and trying to recall the locations of any major wharves she knew about.

Venice Beach? Marina Del Rey? Those aren't the type of blue-collar dock locales where you would expect an operation like this to go down, but who knows? Long Beach would be the most obvious culprit, but that takes us way south of where the Barber's crimes have been concentrated. Dammit. I might end up having to cruise down the entire goddamn shoreline.

With logic failing to provide a clear answer, she would need to rely upon intuition—and magic.

Kera buzzed down the I-10 toward Santa Monica, uncertain so far if she would take any roads that forked off to the south or keep going straight to the sea. She cleared her mind, steadied her breathing, and reached out with her consciousness.

She had used a similar technique once to locate the hidden base of Pauline, the insane yuppie drug dealer who had wanted to blow up the Mermaid. It involved fixating on details associated with the person she wanted to find and then tracing the psychic ripples they made through the fabric of reality.

There was no specific spell for it that she was aware of. No such thing had appeared in *How to Be a Badass Witch* or in any of Pavla's teachings, though some elements of scrying were similar. Kera had taught herself.

Everything she could remember about El Peluquero, the chilling presence the man exuded and small bits of information associated with her and Stephanie's one-sided encounter with him, flashed in her mind. Then she listened for the vibrations.

It was like trying to locate a running chainsaw in a dark room filled with active power drills. As the news, the four people in the bar, and Stephanie had all indicated, talk of El Peluquero—and fear of him—was everywhere. For a brief and stupid moment, she wondered if people were discussing him more than they had previously discussed her.

Blotting out the mild jealousy the notion stirred up, she refocused on the task at hand. An exit led her off the freeway and to the southwest.

She stopped for a red light, nodded at some young guys in a battered car who whistled at her, and took another two turns.

The loudest of the psychic vibrations was centered around the marina after all...or was it the airport?

Logical thought returned and made the final decision, splitting the difference for her. She headed toward Playa Del Rey and the Ballona Wetlands. That would put her partway between the canals and docks to the north and the airport to the south, a good location for someone who might bring in merchandise via multiple venues.

The city seemed unusually dark and quiet as she wove through the streets, the air growing more humid and salty as the ocean drew nearer. She still had not fixed on a particular building or site, but her mind was filtering out distractions and guiding her. It had not failed her in the past.

Soon she approached a facility, the exact nature of which was hard to determine. It had waterfront property with noticeable docks and looked like it *could* be used for shipping and receiving. Possibly. The surrounding neighborhood was incongruous, and she wondered if some official had been paid off to ignore a zoning violation.

It was as good a guess as any. Kera drove back and hid her bike in the weeds near the Wetlands Preserve, then crept toward the compound. She cloaked herself from both sight and sound and cast a minor augmentation spell to improve her hearing.

As she prowled around the edge of the place, nothing overtly damning showed up. The facility would have made a fine hub for drug smuggling, but there was no evidence of it so far. If any ships or trucks from the airport had arrived recently, none were still around.

Crap, she scolded herself. *I should have gone home and then come back here during actual work hours. In fact, it seems like a criminal ring would have people working in the middle of the night to avoid detection, so maybe this place is legit after all. Did I make a mistake?*

The only personnel present were four security guards, three of whom slowly patrolled the periphery of the compound. The fourth sat in a low tower near the front entrance. There were also two random-looking guys loitering near one of the back loading bays. One of the guards passed them and did nothing but say hello, so presumably, they weren't trespassers.

Kera settled in to watch the pair and listen. They smoked and complained about the hours and how they had to be in ridiculously early to prepare for a shipment that would be coming in around five a.m., at which point the rest of the morning crew would arrive to help.

Then the next security guard in the rotation strolled by. Kera froze. She might be mistaken, but...

"Hey," the guard said to the pair, "ain't you guys supposed to be greasing the axles on the fuckin' door or something?"

One of the men snorted. "Not for another fifteen minutes, *amigo*. Have a donut and chill."

Shaking his head, the guard moved on. His face passed through a floodlight before he rounded a corner back into darkness.

Nope, Kera concluded, *I was not mistaken at all. That guy was one of the bodyguards at the house in Crenshaw the other night. I thought his voice sounded familiar. The face is the same, too. He took the Barber up on his offer, which means El Peluquero owns this place or has a partner in it.*

He doesn't seem like the type to share power, though.

She was about to put together a plan to observe the other guards and sneak in when the two advance workers opened the bay, but then she became aware of something else. Something more urgent.

Someone was watching her. Following her. She didn't know how she was sure of it, but she was. The information acted upon the subtlest part of her awareness but declared itself beyond any shadow of a doubt.

It's someone with magic. Or I'm being scried upon. Dear God, what does that mean? Please, please tell me the Barber doesn't have any thaumaturges working for him. That would be like hooking up a guided missile launcher to a Tyrannosaurus Rex. Just downright unfair to everyone else.

As she slowly circled back toward the front of the facility, doubt set in that the person trailing her had anything to do with the half-dozen men who worked here.

The epicenter of her anxiety was closer to the water. Without being too obvious about it, Kera wove away from the sea, continuously putting obstructions between her and the apparent location of her pursuer.

She ducked between outbuildings, then jumped over fences and floated back to the ground. She ambled past one of the guards, who didn't notice her, then crawled under an empty truck trailer. The skin-crawling sense of being observed lessened but did not vanish.

Next, as Kera began to move away from the shipping compound, she pretended to re-shield herself, but with an added deflection element in the rear where her pursuer's attention would be focused. It had been growing again. Now, it once more diminished without vanishing.

Kera was close to where she had stashed Zee. She reached out with her mind, with a light, probing touch. Too much intense focus would be visible to the other magic-user. It would be like accidentally bumping into someone in the dark.

Instead, her mind brushed past them and caught a whiff of their scent, so to speak. It seemed familiar.

Jesus! Kera exclaimed and tried not to gasp or freeze. *It's Pavla. It has to be. Her signature was so distinctive. She's got it partially masked, but I can tell it's her. What does she want from me? Did she have another change of heart and is coming back to finish me off?*

Kera had barely survived the last confrontation with the

Czech witch. It had solely been down to Stephanie's help and Pavla's own indecision.

Also, while it was difficult to be certain, it felt like there might be someone else, too. A second, perhaps a third witch, but that could simply be a diffusion of one person's aura. She would have had to get closer to be sure.

Kera stopped by her bike, waiting while making a show of checking Zee and trying to decide on her next course of action. She froze the image of herself standing over her bike and projected it as an illusion into the space she currently occupied.

Adding Zee into the visual and aural cloaking spell around herself, Kera climbed astride her motorcycle, started the engine, and drove off, leaving the illusion behind. A normal person or an amateur magic-user would think she was still standing there and fussing over her ride.

It was a simple trick. A thaumaturge of Pavla's ability might see through it instantly, but if it fooled her for even twenty seconds, that could be enough for Kera to get a head start and escape.

So far, no one seemed to be following her.

Still, she took a rambling, circuitous route back home. Pavla knew where she lived, but if Kera made it seem that she was headed elsewhere on business, she might lose her. She bore southeast toward Compton, then northeast into Monterey Park and Alhambra before cutting west toward Chinatown, intending to go all the way to the edge of Hollywood before doubling back southeast into downtown.

It was on a street corner in Lincoln Heights that Pavla caught her.

CHAPTER TEN

Kera was slowing down for a red light and thinking about stopping at the curb beyond to take a short break. She needed to drink some of the strong, sugary tea she had brought in her water bottle to recharge from the magical expenditures of cloaking herself and casting the illusion spell. She was getting better at managing her energy, but it was still far from effortless.

Pavla casually stepped out from behind a bench about fifteen feet away.

"Shit! Sorry, Zee!" Kera exclaimed, jumping off her bike and leaving it to lean against the curb. Adrenaline surged through her, and her brain shifted into battle gear. Her eyes and ears took in all the information they could in the second or less she had to react.

Besides Pavla's presence and image—the slim, unremarkable woman had wavy brown hair and a curiously magnetic vibe and demeanor and was dressed in clothes that seemed classy without drawing attention to themselves—one thing impressed itself upon Kera's keyed-up senses.

Pavla was alone. Either there had not been anyone else with

her at the shipping facility, or they had split up while chasing down their quarry.

Kera had no cover in sight, so she conjured a shield and ran straight toward Pavla, whose face showed mild surprise at her boldness.

"What do you want?" Kera shouted. As she asked the question, she summoned a wave of wind and sound that broadsided the other witch with enough force to tip over a tractor-trailer. In case she didn't like Pavla's answer, it was better to ask from a position of strength.

Pavla had a shield up, as Kera had expected, so the blast merely caused her to stumble back a few feet rather than crushing her to paste.

"Kera," Pavla snapped as she tried to regain her footing, "I am sorry, but this charade has gone on for long enough. You must either submit to our judgment and punishment, or you will be destroyed on the spot. Those are my orders. I cannot disobey."

Kera's gut clenched as though someone was twisting a knife in it. The anguish of betrayal, of love and friendship that had turned to hatred and enmity, flared back up and threatened to unhinge her from all discipline and restraint.

"Fuck that," she cried. "I'm not submitting to anyone. You'll have to kill me right here where anyone might see. Come and do it, unless you're afraid!"

Since it was late at night in a commercial district away from major highways, the area around them was silent and apparently devoid of people. Still, there might be security cameras that would pick up footage of two witches duking it out with magic. There might be a cop parked nearby, hoping to catch drunk drivers, who could not help but hear the commotion.

As soon as the words left Kera's mouth and the idea occurred to her, a faintly glowing dome descended over the intersection, just as it had during their battle in the alley. Pavla was still the more powerful and skilled of the two by a considerable margin. Preventing herself from being discovered was child's play.

However, she did not press her attack. Instead, she advanced toward Kera, glaring at her with eyes narrowed with menace and raising her fists as if she meant to fight the girl hand to hand.

She would rather I surrender, Kera induced. *She can't bring herself to kill me outright, so if I have to die, she would rather turn me over to her superiors and let them handle it so she can technically wash her hands of my death.*

The hypocrisy was so galling that for what may have been the first time ever, Kera wanted to be the one *doing* the killing. Her rage frightened her in the back of her mind, but for the moment, all that mattered was obliterating her adversary.

She drove toward Pavla with a frontal assault of brute force, paying little heed to her own safety beyond maintaining her personal shield charm. She threw localized fireballs into the air next to or behind the other woman, more blasts of wind and concussive vibrations, and punched and kicked when Pavla came close enough.

Nothing connected; the witch had come prepared to fight defensively. She used basic deflection and cancellation spells to swipe aside Kera's attempts at elemental attacks and augmented her own speed and jumping power to leap clear of Kera's melee strikes. Her counterattacks were weak or indirect.

In the part of her brain that was still rational, Kera thought her foe must be luring her into a trap or trying to bait her into overexerting herself too quickly. Pavla had taught Kera the importance of controlling her emotions, which meant there was no one who was better acquainted with Kera's weaknesses when it came to her feelings.

But she couldn't help herself. Kera had too many unanswered questions that began with the word "Why." The only answer she could think of was vengeance.

Kera conjured a cone-shaped mass of heat and flame around

her wrist and in front of her hand, effectively granting her a sword-like weapon of fire. She thrust and slashed it at her opponent while shouting and cursing, battering her with waves of force between strikes, and occasionally leaping into the air to try and flank Pavla when the woman reeled back in the process of defending herself.

"You fool," Pavla jeered, "do you not realize what is happening? You have created a situation where you cannot win, and neither can I! One of us has to die, even though I don't want it! Unless you can make yourself disappear. Don't you understand? The Orthodoxy will not permit you to exist as a rival."

She threw a lightning bolt, and Kera nearly panicked, but then she noticed that it streaked two feet over her shoulder. Either Pavla was getting sloppy in her exertion and the general chaos, or she had intentionally missed.

Kera pressed ahead, conjuring a pair of small Wind Shield spells on both sides of the woman to box her in and then seeking to beat the shit out of her the old-fashioned way. "Let *them* come after me, then!" Kera bellowed over the freight-train roar of the flattened tornadoes. "I'll take them all on!"

"You would," Pavla agreed, agitated but still holding back, still in control of herself. "And you would lose. You are not powerful or clever enough. You are abnormally good for one so new, but you cannot defeat us. You are nearly out of chances to submit in peace. They may let you live! Throw yourself on their mercy. It's your only chance, you stupid girl!"

Pavla shot straight up with the speed of a rocket and canceled Kera's mediocre Wind Shields at the same time, leaving the less experienced caster raging at another failed opportunity.

As Kera augmented her speed and strength again, Pavla drifted down from the sky and came to rest on the roof of a building across the street.

Then someone else appeared. Kera saw her out of the corner of her eye. It was a small blonde woman dressed in nice designer

European clothes, with a sly and arrogant expression on her otherwise pretty face.

Kera froze for an instant in indecision, not knowing who the newcomer was or what her intentions were. Pavla took the opportunity to hurl a cyclone of wind, force, and water that crashed between the two of them but closer to Kera, knocking her off her feet.

When Kera looked up, the blonde woman had shrugged off the miniature hurricane and was aiming a hand at her face. The look in the cold eyes of the intruder, who must have been an ally or the handler of Pavla, was unmistakable. She meant to *kill*.

"Hey!" a voice shouted.

All three women's heads snapped toward the sound, then a heavy blast of water, like the unleashed stream of a firehose, struck the blonde in the face and chest and drove her through the door of a nearby shop.

Kera sprang to her feet and ran toward the source of the deluge. "Stephanie! We need to get out of here *now*! Move, move!"

Her friend's face displayed her chaotic emotions: pride, fear, disbelief, and concern. Kera caught her by the shoulder and guided her toward Zee, pulling her onto the seat behind her as she fired up the engine.

"Dammit, girl," Steph commented, "I told you to be careful."

"Save it," said Kera. She scanned the area around her for gaps in Pavla's spells and found one corresponding to the smallest and darkest of the adjacent streets. Inhaling sharply and half-expecting to be shot in the back by either or both of the hostile witches at any moment, she gunned it. The bike streaked down the road and turned a corner. No blast came from behind.

CHAPTER ELEVEN

Kera jerked her head up from the pillow, her eyes ungluing themselves to open and her arms flailing about in a reflexive motion, looking for her phone or alarm clock.

"Yeah!" she shouted. "Yeah. I'm up. Uhh. What?"

She blinked, and the sound that had pulled her out of sleep registered again in her brain. It wasn't her phone or her alarm, though; it was the doorbell. According to her bedside clock, it was a bit after 10:00 a.m. To most people, that was a perfectly reasonable time to be up and about.

But most people didn't work at bars, particularly bars where she had the closing shift about half the time. She hadn't passed out until about five that morning.

Cursing and grumbling, Kera flung her sheets off and stomped toward the door. She peeked through the small window beside the front door, wanting to ascertain who was there. After she had spent a night at Stephanie's, she had returned to find no evidence that Pavla had been to her home. She wasn't about to jettison any semblance of caution, though; the Czech witch and her little partner were still out there somewhere.

No one was visible. Kera inhaled, the sound sharp and hissing.

Her immediate suspicion was that someone had cloaked themselves.

"No," she muttered, "probably it's a normal person who just left before I could get to the door. A delivery, maybe."

She hadn't ordered anything recently, though.

Readying a shielding spell in case the dreaded attack should come, Kera flung open the door. No one was there, and she sensed no magic. The only thing in front of her was a thick envelope made of light cardboard, the kind people shipped books and magazines in. Her address was handwritten on the front in ink, but her name was not. There wasn't any sender info, either.

"This has to be a trap. Or a mistake." She looked at it, focused on it, and tried to sense if anything was amiss.

When nothing flared up in her brain, she absentmindedly pulled out her phone and saw that she had a text. It was from Chris. She swiped it open and read.

Hey, Kera, I know you won't be up until later, so just respond to this when you can. Wanted to check in and see how you were doing. I trust your judgment, mostly, but if you're planning on doing anything dangerous, please at least let me know beforehand, and don't be afraid to ask for help. On a more pleasant note, want to get some food and coffee soon? Maybe today?

She smiled to herself. "Do I want to get some food? Stupid-ass question, but still thoughtful of him."

She wrote, **Sometimes danger shows up even when I don't go looking for it. I'm fine for the moment, and so is Steph. But yeah, let's consume an unnecessarily massive number of calories soon. Maybe later today if I have time, otherwise tomorrow.**

She returned her attention to the parcel.

A piece of information, long forgotten, surfaced amidst her

thoughts. It was a federal offense to open mail that was addressed to someone else.

The problem was, the thick cardboard envelope wasn't addressed to *anyone*, and she was not certain it had been sent via the Postal Service anyway. It looked as though someone had dropped it off in person on her doorstep.

Kera wracked her brain for a spell or charm that could neutralize any hazards, magical or mundane, that might be attached to the package. She recalled one, a containment spell that could keep the effects of any curse or delayed-action attack spell suspended in one place for an hour or so unless it was cast by someone of exceptional power.

Taking a deep breath, she waved her hands over the envelope, which was still lying on the pavement before her door, and muttered the incantation. A passing cyclist looked at her with a squint of amusement. He probably thought she was off her rocker.

She ignored him. The air around the parcel shimmered, forming an oblong field that encased it.

Satisfied, Kera went back inside, got her riding gloves in case the cardboard was laced with anthrax or something, and knelt to pick up the package. Since the containment spell was centered on whatever was within, the faintly shimmering field moved with the envelope. She closed the door with her foot and brought the object in to set on her kitchen counter.

Thus far, there was no indication of anything malevolent. Kera conjured a light shield in front of her face and torso, then reached around its edges to carefully tear open the edge of the envelope. She peeked in. It looked like nothing more than a stack of papers, about the thickness of a modest-sized book.

"Weird," she mumbled and let the torn cardboard fall back into place.

Next, she cast a purification spell, which ought to identify and destroy any diseases, poisons, parasites, or lingering hexes that might have been laid on the parcel. It took a moment; she had only a couple practice sessions with the spell under her belt. But after some concentration and finagling, the charm worked.

Her eyes, seeing on behalf of her magically expanded consciousness, detected nothing dangerous on the papers except the usual minor everyday bacteria that swarmed over everything humans or other living things had touched.

Still, it was difficult not to remain suspicious.

Kera kept the containment spell in effect in case there was a curse that had been well-hidden and might trigger after the fact. It occurred to her also that it might have a tracking beacon on it and might be used to pinpoint her location for a discreet lightning strike. She took it to the farthest, emptiest corner of the warehouse from her living quarters.

"I need a shower." She sighed. "And then a pot of nice strong coffee." She didn't see herself going back to bed.

Not two minutes after she had emerged from the shower and dressed, someone knocked on the door.

"Goddammit," she muttered, striding across the broad floor of the warehouse and jumping over her bed. "Now what? It can't be the same person who left the package since they're knocking instead of ringing the doorbell. I think."

When she looked out the window, the sudden buildup of tension she had suffered melted. It was Chris.

"Hi," she said, opening the door. "Wish you'd warned me, but I'm not complaining that you're here. Sorry, I just got out of the shower, so I'm a little raw. But, you know, fresh."

He laughed and hoisted a massive paper cup in his hand. "My apologies. I figured if you were actually up at this ungodly hour— hell, it's not even noon yet—I might as well stop by. I have the day off, weirdly enough, and I brought you this. It's technically coffee, but mostly it's a dessert in liquid form. I got the one with the largest possible number of calories they could fit in one cup."

Kera gazed at her gift with longing and admiration, then

hugged Chris with one arm around his neck, accepting the coffee with the other. "Aww, thanks! To be honest, I needed this. Only got maybe five hours of sleep. I thought about going back to bed, but something's been occupying me, so a bunch of caffeine and sugar and dairy fat will help me focus on it."

"I'm curious," he replied, stepping in and pulling the door closed, "about whatever that is. And what you said in your text about 'danger finding you' or whatever. Tell me when you're ready."

She frowned, not in the mood to discuss what had happened when she had gone to El Peluquero's shipyard and then had her violent run-in with Pavla, but she supposed she owed it to her boyfriend to tell him. "Okay, but let's wait on that part. First, I'm more interested in...this."

Kera flourished her hand toward the parcel she had received. It still lay in the far corner, and both of them walked toward it.

"Who's it addressed to?" he asked, squinting.

She grimaced. "No one. No sender, either. I don't think it was actually mailed, just dumped on my doorstep. I've been carefully scanning it for any curses, poison, or anything like that, but so far, nothing. So I *think* it's safe to open the rest of the way."

Chris took a step closer and looked it over. "A magazine or some papers, from the looks of it. You might as well have a look. It might be important, and if it was sent to you by accident, you can claim innocence based on the lack of a name or proper postage."

He was right, Kera decided. Steeling herself, she ripped open the remainder of the cardboard.

Of the sheaf of papers within, some were contained in basic office binders. Perplexed, she looked them over and was befuddled. It seemed to be personnel files for a company, but she had never heard of any of the people described in them.

She sighed in annoyance. "For fuck's sake. Must be business mail for the people who owned this warehouse before I rented it and converted it into a one-woman residential facility. I should have known."

Chris moved closer and peered at the documents. "What's the address on that file? Doesn't look like yours."

Annoyed with herself for not having checked, Kera turned back to the paper he was looking at and examined it more closely. The business seemed to be located at an address in, or at least near, Playa Del Rey.

"Wait." She gasped as it dawned on her. "Holy shit."

Chris stiffened with concern. "What's the matter?"

Kera raised her hands and rubbed her temples, closing her eyes while the gears of her mind turned. "Playa Del Rey is where El Peluquero owns a shipping facility. I scoped it out the other night. Long story. Still, I can't say for sure that this is related."

She examined the address again. The business was called "N-Safe Solutions," which provided no clue as to what type of firm it was. And other documents mentioned a bevy of other addresses all across the city, though mostly in its western half, as well as adjacent suburbs.

Rubbing his ear, Chris remarked, "Huh. Interesting. I imagine we would have to look all those documents over to get a better idea of what they are, which sounds tedious. If you're comfortable doing it in public, want to save it for when we're waiting for brunch? There's a place nearby that serves amazing breakfast food until 1 p.m., so I'd say we have plenty of time."

Instantaneously, Kera felt better. "Yeah, I'll have to give the green light to that. I would offer to drive since you already drove here and all, but I don't want my bike associated with the possible image of me looking at all these dossiers or manifests or whatever they are."

"Sure, I can drive," Chris shrugged, then smiled. "If you pay."

"Deal," replied Kera. Her inheritance would be available to her sooner with every passing day.

The drive to the restaurant only took ten minutes. Kera

hadn't heard of the place and was suitably impressed that Chris had. She would have to tap him in the future for new places to get food.

Within, they found the place basic and cozy but unremarkable. It was moderately busy, but they seemed well-staffed enough that people wouldn't likely have to wait too long to get their orders.

The pair took seats, greeted the waitress, and ordered three meals, with Kera saying something about a friend who might be joining them.

Their attention drifted toward the nearby TV screen that faced toward their booth from the ceiling. A local news report was repeating the main facts of the recent crime wave, adding details about how a tense mood was settling over the city and lesser crimes were starting to proliferate as the police directed more of their attention toward stopping further gangland homicides.

While Kera focused on the broadcast, Chris flipped through the dossiers and checked some things on his phone.

An idea had begun to form in his head about ten minutes ago, and the more he investigated it, the more likely it seemed to be correct. His first destination was local crime watch groups from around LA, particularly in the western part of the metro area near the ocean, as well as police reports and conspiracy theory-oriented message boards related to strange incidents and illegal activity in the same areas.

It did not take long for a pattern to emerge.

"Kera," he piped up, "have a listen to this. Might be important, though you would know better than I would."

She turned toward him, her eyes bright with interest. "Shoot."

He took a deep breath. "Okay. The correspondence isn't always perfect, but a *lot* of the addresses I'm seeing in these documents correspond closely to places where there have recently been major crimes. Everything from murders to break-ins and larcenies to white-collar crime. There's even a few people saying that the shipyard in Playa Del Rey is where most of the corrupt and dangerous assholes tend to congregate. Does that sound like a coincidence to you?"

The muscles in Kera's face tightened, and her eyes were grave and intense. "No," she murmured. "No, it doesn't. The question is, who dropped that stuff off at my door, and why?"

Chris was about to offer some suggestions—a disgruntled employee, a concerned neighbor—but he hesitated upon realizing there was no way to answer how people like that would know who Kera really was. While he thought it over, their waitress came up with their food.

"Hey," she announced, "here you go. Oh, did your third person not show up yet?"

Kera smiled. "No, I guess not. Don't worry, though, we'll pay for everything. And maybe take their portion home in a box."

The young woman set two heaping platters of breakfast food before Kera and one in front of Chris, asked them if they needed anything else, and excused herself.

Once they were alone again, Kera muttered, "I haven't eaten in public much since I...you know. It's embarrassing for girls to be seen eating this much. Normally I don't care about shit like that, but I guess I'm not impervious to it after all."

Chris laughed, but in a warm and understanding way. "No one's watching," he pointed out. "And if anyone asks how or why we eliminated the extra plate, you can pin the blame on me."

"Thanks." She sighed, her face relaxing with relief. Then she dug in.

Forty minutes later they returned to the warehouse, though not with a leftovers box since Kera had managed to polish everything off. More importantly, they had both had time to think about the information they had drummed up on the sheaf of dossiers.

Chris settled into a chair. "I wonder if the person who delivered that stuff to you is someone else in the criminal underworld who doesn't like El Peluquero? Maybe it's someone you, um, had a run-in with before."

Kera nodded. "Yeah, that occurred to me also. I feel like there's something on the tip of my tongue or a revelation that's going to break out in my mind soon, but it hasn't yet." She gritted her teeth. "So frustrating. I'm going to take a shower, okay? You can wait. I won't be too long."

He agreed but wrinkled his brow in perplexity. "Didn't you take a shower this morning before I showed up?"

"Yes, yes." Kera waved a hand. "I smell like bacon, though, and it seems like stuff you're trying to remember or think of always comes to you when you're in the shower, right?"

Chris smirked. "Good point."

Five minutes later, as the hot water in the bathroom began to run and Chris sat half-watching the television set and flipping through the papers again, someone knocked on the door.

He got up, then halted, wondering if he should ask Kera's permission before letting anyone in or what he would do if it was someone strange or hostile. He went to the window and tried to get a sneak peek at who it was.

The tension dissipated at once. It was Stephanie.

"Hi, Steph," he said as he opened the door. "Kera's in the shower. Come in."

Their mutual friend stepped in and stretched her arms. "How you doing, Chris?"

"Fairly well," he answered her. "Unfortunately, you missed brunch, but we'll make it up to you some other time."

Stephanie pouted. "Damn. Brunch sounds good. I had a big breakfast, though, and was planning to get lunch after I left here. I think what magic does to your appetite is the worst part. I spend twice what I used to on food. Can't afford this shit forever."

They spent a couple of minutes discussing tips for eating on a budget before the conversation drifted to the subject of Chris' friend and Steph's sibling.

The latter asked, "Has Ted said anything about my sister? They still together? Honestly, I haven't heard much from either of them lately."

Chris was curious about the subject as well, but he probably knew as much as she did. "I haven't really heard from them either. Ted and I have both been busy at work—he's trying to get promoted, so he doesn't slack off and sneak over to my cubicle as much as he used to—and we're preoccupied with other things in our free time. As far as I know, the main thing he's preoccupied with is Regina. I guess they hit it off."

Steph helped herself to a soda from the fridge; they both were aware that Kera wouldn't mind. The sounds of the shower continued from the bathroom.

"Well," she commented, "as long as she's happy."

Chris added, "Probably. She seems cool from what little I've seen of her, but she and Ted mesh well, weirdly enough." His smile drooped. "He's confused why I'm still dating Kera, though, after all the turmoil. And, of course, part of why I haven't talked to him as much is because of, well, Kera."

Stephanie laughed out loud. "'Turmoil' is an understatement, my friend. Never a dull moment with Kera around. We love her, though."

After they concurred, sharing a warm moment, the mood turned more serious.

"So," Chris began, "what's your take on the developing situation with this Hairdresser guy and his criminal empire? You heard anything new?"

Stephanie had not, and most of what she had to say was what everyone was aware of so far, along with her personal experiences. Unlike Chris, she had seen the man.

Nodding, Chris showed her the packet of dossiers and summed up what he and Kera had been puzzling over.

Stephanie put her arms around herself as though she were cold, though it was a warm summer day. "Damn," she murmured, "what did we get ourselves into? What is *Kera* getting into, with people delivering stuff like this right to her? I wonder if Pavla did it to lure her out? Seems like everything gets nastier right when we thought it was nasty enough. Who knows, though?"

The shower stopped running, and they heard the sound of the curtain rings scraping on the bar as it was sharply drawn across the stall.

"Well," Chris observed, and again they bonded in a mutual feeling about the same subject, "like you said, never a dull moment."

CHAPTER TWELVE

After emerging from the shower, Kera was pleasantly surprised to find Stephanie there. They talked for a short while, making plans to go to the gun range again soon and checking up on one another.

Steph concluded with, "I can't stay, sorry to say. Got to see my mother after neglecting her for too long, then I work all evening. We'll talk more again soon, though, okay?"

"Sure," Kera agreed, hugging her. Chris did the same.

After she left, the couple sat down and contemplated what to do next.

Chris, folding his hands and gazing vacantly at the wall, said, "I've been thinking. We ought to attempt a third-party verification of the info in that bundle."

"What," Kera responded, squinting, "you mean, send it to an analyst or some reporters or something? I'm not so sure that would be a good idea. Outsiders have a way of blabbing to other people or otherwise drawing attention that we don't want or need."

Chris' eyes refocused, and he shook his head. "No, no. Why

hire someone else when we can do it ourselves? We're computer scientists!"

Kera laughed, partially at herself; she felt like a dolt. "Of course. I'm a bit out of practice after slinging drinks for the last several months, is all."

"No problem." He stood up. "If you would be so kind as to let me use your laptop, I'll simply pick up where I left off at the restaurant. Message boards and discussion groups, police reports, news stories... If we can cross-reference and triangulate all that stuff with the data in those papers, we can assume it's mostly legitimate. If not, then someone is fucking with us, trying to lead us on a wild goose chase."

Unable to disagree, Kera started her computer and allowed Chris to sit behind it on the condition that he didn't rummage around in her personal files.

"Ahh," he remarked. "Wouldn't want me to find your porn stash, right?"

"Ha, ha," she grumbled. "I don't even remember half of what I have on this thing, but that's part of the issue, I guess. Anyway, get to work. I'll observe and assist."

They barely talked for the next thirty or forty minutes as Chris delved into a cluster of subreddits and channels on Discord and Slack devoted to discussing true crime instances, localized conspiracy theories, renting and moving advice, and anything else that might shed light on shady events in their target areas.

At the same time, Kera conducted searches on her phone for criminal reports corresponding to similar topics. Her boyfriend entered the results in a rudimentary spreadsheet to keep track of things that did or did not add up.

Chris broke the monotony of silence with some much-needed commentary, though what he had to say was only half-comprehensible to his girlfriend.

"I have to admit, this is kinda fun." He allowed himself a sly little smile, but his eyes remained fixed on the computer screen.

"It's not too difficult as far as the basic nature of what's required. Sifting through information, noticing patterns, logging anomalies, and stuff like that. Basically the same as what I do at work."

Kera balked at the last line. "You think your job is fun?"

"Eh," he countered, stiffening a tad in self-defense, "not particularly. What I mean is, it's a type of thing I know how to do well, only in this case, the details are way more interesting than the crap I do for the company. Sort of like if your job was to take people's requests for liquid bombs from behind a bar, and after you mixed them, you threw them as hard as you could and watched shit blow up in multicolored explosions.

At that, Kera cracked up. "Oh, man. That's a mental image I will never, ever get rid of for as long as I continue to work at a bar. Which is, uh, only another week and a half, but still. Thanks, I needed that since to be honest, I'm starting to find this all boring as fuck."

Chris looked at her. "Really? I thought it would be right up your alley. We were both educated in the same stuff and have some of the same strengths and interests. Then again, you spend a lot of time running around town casting spells and beating people up, so I guess after *that*, mere data-crunching would seem pretty underwhelming."

Five more minutes passed.

Outside, the noise of one particular vehicle's grumbling engine and spinning tires detached itself from the general cacophony of LA traffic and grew closer to them. It was too close to be incidental. Someone had pulled in next to the warehouse.

Kera sprang to her feet, holding up a hand toward Chris. "Just stay where you are. Probably someone turning around, but I'm going to have a look. If I tell you to hit the floor or get out of here, do it, okay? Because if you hear that from me, it means it's a matter of life and death."

Chris swallowed. "Okay. Be careful."

Moving cat-like across the floor, Kera cast a cloaking spell on herself before reaching the window nearest the sound. She heard the car come to a stop and one of the doors opening. Footsteps clattered across the pavement.

Kera looked out the window, bracing herself for anything.

Then she exhaled with such speed and force that the window briefly fogged up. Relief overwhelmed her. It was the Kims.

Mr. Kim had gotten out of the car on the driver's side to help his wife out the passenger-side door, and now both of them were approaching her home. Kera gave a final glance around, combined with a brief magical scan to determine that nothing was amiss. Satisfied, she flung open the door.

"Hi!" she greeted them. "Wish you had called so I could have been ready, but of course you're always welcome here."

The older couple waved, then moved into hugging distance and embraced her.

Mr. Kim opened with, "Ha, sorry. We meant to come over but could not decide whether to surprise you or not and the time we wasted deciding meant we had to leave before we *could* call. How are things?"

"Kera," Mrs. Kim added, "it is good to see you."

She thanked them both and told them things were mostly well, which was more or less true. "Also, are you feeling better, Mrs. Kim? I'm somewhat surprised you made the trip here."

She looked better, Kera thought. No, her appearance was largely the same, barring the relaxed and pleasant expression on her face. Her mood, her vibe, her emotional aura had undergone an improvement. There was a glow of hope and vitality to her the girl had not noticed in a long time.

Kera burned with curiosity about what had happened to cause the change, but Mr. Kim was rambling about business at the store, what Sam was up to in school, and the weather, and she didn't want to interrupt.

During the whole of their conversation so far, a bag loaded with what looked like aluminum-covered pans and trays had rested between the Kims. Kera tried not to glance at it, but it was difficult. Comestibles were perhaps the one thing that could distract her from her suspicions.

Finally, Mrs. Kim said, "We brought you food. You do not eat with us as much anymore, so we have to bring you leftovers."

Kera picked up the bag so neither of them would have to carry it. It was surprisingly heavy. "Aw, thanks. I don't mind leftovers in the slightest. In fact, sometimes I think a lot of foods marinate over time if you leave them in the fridge for a day or two. Like, it actually improves the flavor."

"Yes," Mr. Kim agreed. "Soup in particular. I always seem to have one bowl the first night and two the next night. Ha!"

Kera suddenly felt awkward about forcing them to stand outside her home. "Please come in. Things are a little messy, but nothing too terrible. Chris is here, also. We were working on something, but it can wait a little while."

As she guided them into the warehouse, it occurred to her that Mrs. Kim had never been here before, and abruptly she thought about the prospect that the older woman might disapprove of her minimal decor or careless lifestyle. The Kims' home was always so neat and cozy and well-maintained.

Chris rose from his seat at the computer while Kera helped Mrs. Kim to the couch.

"Oh, hey," he greeted them. "Nice to see you two. Oooh, and is that food? Sorry. I didn't have breakfast. It's weird to think I would manage not to eat anything with Kera around." He would lie about having eaten to take one for the team, especially for Mrs. Kim's food.

Mr. Kim chuckled. "There is plenty for both of you. Ye-Jin made even more than usual because she is feeling great."

Mrs. Kim smiled and nodded.

Kera blinked, not daring to believe her condition was improving. "Really? That's fantastic, if so. Wait, did you start cancer treatment yet? Ugh, I'm sorry, I've been so busy lately that I forgot exactly when that was supposed to happen."

"Yes," Mrs. Kim confirmed. "It will take a long time, but I am better from knowing that we have begun."

Her husband moved closer to her and put his hands on her shoulders. "To be honest," he clarified, "her first treatment is this evening. She has not started yet. But like she said, just the knowledge that it is finally happening has improved her mood, and I think given her strength. We're all happy."

Kera bit her lip and tightened her abdomen, struggling not to embarrass herself by crying in joy. For *months* they had all been worried. Kera herself had expended tremendous effort in trying to fight the cancer with magic, exhausting herself badly and risking her own health while simultaneously trying to avoid screwing anything up and making the disease worse.

But with her help, Ye-Jin had persisted until today, and now things could be turned around.

Kera embraced them both again, and she got misty-eyed but avoided outright crying. "Oh, God. That's great. You don't even know how much of a relief it is. Is the prognosis good?"

"Yes," Mr. Kim affirmed. "They did not say it was certain, but they mentioned something about how it is, haha, *miraculous* that her condition stabilized over the spring and summer. We got this far. Now the pros will deal with the rest. We cannot thank you enough, Kera. Without your help, she may not have made it."

Kera held Mrs. Kim's hand and the two looked into each other's eyes, not bothering to speak but sharing the moment in silence.

Chris meanwhile spoke to Mr. Kim. "I didn't know all the details, but I'm glad to hear that. Congratulations."

"It is better that you don't, probably," Mr. Kim shrugged. "This way, you don't have to go through many weeks of anxiety like we did. You get to skip straight to the good news. Much nicer."

The four of them talked for another five minutes about other things going on in their lives, and Kera's joy turned back to anxiety. It was difficult to keep things from the Kims since they were good at asking the right questions to pry more out of her, and she felt bad keeping things from them, anyway. But she worried that they would try to interfere and talk her out of her current course of action.

Again.

Chris hesitated to spill all the beans. He could tell Kera was nervous and trying to avoid divulging everything. After a couple of minutes, he excused himself to the computer to resume his work.

Kera meanwhile paced across the open floor between the living area and her personal gym. Mr. Kim must have noticed that she was agitated.

"Remember, Kera, you can tell us about anything that is bothering you. We know you sometimes take too much on your shoulders at once, but we believe in you and in your ability to deal with things beyond what most people are capable of. Don't ruin yourself with too many cares and worries."

He exchanged a glance with his wife, then they both looked at her.

She paced faster. "Yeah, you're right. I just haven't gotten over what happened with Pavla. And now I'm worried about what's going on in the city. All these murders. It's like the progress I made before to clean things up was all for nothing, and we're sliding back into dark times again."

Her footfalls were more like stomps than steps by this point.

Chris rubbed his eyes and leaned away from his chair. "Kera, sorry, dear, but I can't concentrate with you basically kicking the floor like that and prowling around behind me. Do you think you could either go train with Stephanie or at least switch to attacking your punching bag instead?"

She stopped and sighed raggedly. "Okay, fine. I'll take Option Number Two." To the Kims, she commented, "My apologies. I can still talk while training, mostly. Besides, this way, you two can critique my form. If, um, you have time before you need to head off to treatment."

Mr. Kim replied, "We have five minutes or so. Do what you need to do."

Kera stretched, then launched herself at the bag, putting more of her energy into moving for the sake of movement, dodging and repositioning herself, than she did into striking it, though she segued quickly enough into kicks, punches, elbow strikes, and pantomime takedown moves.

During a lull in the noise and activity, she remarked, "I'm trying not to overload myself with difficult stuff, but I'm in too deep." Her fist, piston-like, struck the bag near the top and retracted. "I don't want too much trouble, but trouble keeps finding me after what I've already done."

The Kims took a short period to digest what she'd told them. Then Mrs. Kim answered her. "Then you must face it. But be smart. We do not want you lost."

Kera stopped for a break, turning toward them. "I will. If I can't avoid the storm, I'm going to weather it."

Mr. Kim smiled and gestured. "There's more of you to weather it, anyway. You're gaining weight again! Still skinny, but looking healthier now. Anyway, we must go."

She relaxed, chuckling at the realization that they were right. With all that had happened lately, her mind had barely registered that she had gained about five pounds, lifting her into the thin side of the average range.

"Thanks," she told them and joined Mr. Kim in helping Ye-Jin to stand, though she seemed capable of it on her own. "I'm getting more efficient at managing my energy when casting, so that's part of it. But it turns out that even the voracious effects of magic are no match for a steady diet of pasta and McDonald's."

Mrs. Kim made a vague hissing sound. "Do not eat that stuff too much. Bad for you. Not real food!"

"Well," Kera observed, "I have plenty of real food from you to last me a couple days, so that's a start. Anyway, goodbye and good luck."

She saw them back to their car and waved as they drove off. Her ruminations turned back to the good news they had unveiled.

Whatever Higher Powers might exist in our universe, whichever ones are responsible for the miracles that people like me work when we perform thaumaturgy, thank them, praise them. Mrs. Kim is going to make it. Everything I did to help her wasn't in vain.

When she reentered the warehouse, Chris wasted no time in grabbing her attention.

"Hey, Kera, check it out." He motioned her over with a sharp movement of his hand. His widened eyes were fixed on the screen, and there was an excited tension to him that suggested he'd struck gold.

She hurried over. "What?"

"Thiiiiiis is interesting," he quipped and turned to face her. "Tonight. It's going down tonight."

CHAPTER THIRTEEN

Mr. Kim had never liked hospitals and clinics. He understood it was a common feeling within the general populace. The cold, bright, antiseptic nature of the interiors, the rambling layouts and reams of official posters everywhere, and the simple fact that one only went to such places when things were bad.

But it was worth it since sometimes going to a medical facility meant there was an end in sight to people's woes and suffering.

It was well past dark when the couple left the treatment center. Mr. Kim had remained in the waiting room the whole while. It was the least he could do for his flower, being there if there were any disturbing developments. And he wanted her to know that he was present in the next room or two over, cheering her on, and would be there for her when it was over.

She had emerged shaky but optimistic. Later, she complained of the humming machines, the tubes, the invasive and impersonal procedures, and the strange doctoral jargon, though the staff had treated her with care and politeness and respect.

She was obviously not looking forward to the numerous sessions to come. But she was strong and smart enough to realize that if she made it through this, they could look forward to years more together and years more with Sam.

Mr. Kim guided his wife out of the lobby and to their car. He thought of their son, who they had left in charge of the shop while they were gone. It was rare for him to screw anything up these days, though he did have an annoying habit of closing the store five or ten minutes early if there weren't any customers.

Today, though, Mr. Kim didn't care, as long as the boy handled the money correctly and didn't accidentally burn the place down.

When they pulled into their standard lot, which wrapped around beside and behind the store and their attached home, there were more cars than usual parked out front. Mr. Kim pulled into one of the spaces far in the back, mildly annoyed at the prospect of Ye-Jin having to walk farther in the relative dark after what she had been through.

As if sensing his thoughts, she piped up, "I will be fine. There must be extra people at the cafe across the street."

Mr. Kim grunted and climbed out, scanning the lot before he helped Mrs. Kim out of her seat. The back of the lot opened onto a narrow alley that was always dark. The lights of the various nearby businesses never seemed to penetrate its gloom.

As they two left the car behind, a black silhouette emerged from the alley and stopped about seven paces from the couple. They could see none of its features, and it did not speak, but they could feel they were being stared at and compelled by some obscure urge to remain and speak.

Despite the preternatural force keeping them from fleeing, Mr. Kim instinctively stepped in front of his wife, placing a hand on her arm and gently urging her into the safe spot behind him. His muscles tensed, his senses sharpened, and a primitive mechanism in his brain converted the acidic fear that pooled in his stomach into fuel for action if necessary.

For the first time since the strange thaumaturges had come

and removed his and Ye-Jin's powers, he found himself missing them. Magic was more a burden than a gift, but in times like this...

"Can I help you?" he asked, his tone firm and steel-edged despite the politeness of his words.

"Better than that," the figure replied. "You can help yourselves."

The Kims froze, both chilled by the voice. It was distorted somehow, as though it had been passed through an electronic filter that altered its pitch and tone and disguised whether it belonged to a man or woman, along with adding a slight echo effect. There was also the trace of a slight though unidentifiable European accent.

Mr. Kim wanted to move closer to get a better look, but that might well be the height of stupidity. He stood his ground, protecting his spouse.

The dark figure went on. "You two should stay out of matters that do not concern you. Your help is not needed. The business of other people is not your business, and there are certain troublesome individuals to whom you should not give your friendship."

Though he did not say it aloud, Mr. Kim knew who the shadow meant by "troublesome individuals."

For the next few seconds, he could think of little except the ridiculous gall of someone telling him who he and his wife could or could not befriend. He felt Ye-Jin's anger, too; it was palpable.

"Who the hell are you?" he demanded. "And what makes you think you know anything about us or have the right to tell us what to do?"

"Oh," the voice responded, "I am merely a bystander, one who sees everything and can often predict the course of events. I know a great *many* things about you, and I can tell when things are about to become...ugly."

In Korean, Ye-Jin whispered, "They are not directly threatening us so far. They are warning us about Kera."

Mr. Kim patted her arm to show that he had heard, though he kept his eyes on their mysterious visitor.

"Think," the shadow continued. "Think hard about what you do next. You must ask yourselves certain important questions, such as what is best for you? What is best for your son Sam? The three of you seem like a very nice family. It would be terrible if something bad were to happen to any of you, all because you spent too much time close to fools."

Mr. Kim suddenly wanted to be sick, but he held firm.

The dark figure concluded its spiel. "If I were in your position," and at this, the head turned to look at the convenience store, "I would close up my shop and take a long, pleasant vacation to somewhere far away—Nova Scotia or Dubai, or back to Korea. Please, think it over. But decide quickly."

Then the shadow retracted, shrinking as it stepped back into the alley and vanishing amidst the darkness as though it had never been there.

The spell holding them in place—and both of them were increasingly sure that a spell was exactly what it had been—dissipated, and they were free to act and move. Without speaking to one another, they hastened to the front entrance of the convenience store. They could have gone directly into their living quarters via the side door, but somehow it seemed more appealing to circle around the building to where the lights and cars and people were.

A quartet of young people strolled by, chatting among themselves and blissfully unaware of anything amiss. Motorists passed. Traffic lights changed from green to yellow to red and back. Everything seemed normal away from the dark alley.

Mr. Kim unlocked the front door. Sam had closed up and left the security lights on, so all was well. He wanted to kick the door down and run up the stairs shouting Sam's name, *needing* to see that he was all right.

But his wife had been correct. At this point, the dark figure was only delivering a warning. Trying to intimidate them with the *possibility* of harm to them and their son.

When they moved beyond the shop into their home, they found Sam sitting at the kitchen table, casually doing his homework while listening to music on his phone. When he looked up at them, he paled and tensed.

"Is everything okay?" he asked. "Mom? How did it go?"

His parents exhaled in relief.

"Yes," Mr. Kim stated. "The treatment went well, and your mother is fine. Still, the stress lately is getting to us. Maybe we all need a vacation. I...I will think about it."

Sam's brow furrowed at the same time Ye-Jin's did. The boy asked, "Um, isn't the treatment something that needs to be done continuously over a period of time? We can't go anywhere, can we? Wait, you meant just closing the shop and taking a *staycation*. Ha."

Frowning, Mr. Kim replied, "Something like that. As I said, I need to think it over."

"Thank you, Sam," Mrs. Kim added, "for watching the shop." Then she went to her son's side and embarrassed him with a long, tight embrace. At the same time, her husband looked out the window, toward the shadowed alley.

Out there, the figure that had approached them was out of sight but not gone. It had backed into the darkness, out of normal human sight, and then, for good measure, had cloaked itself magically from *any* sight save that of the most skilled witches.

Pavla continued to watch as new lights came on in the second-floor living area behind the little grocery store. She listened to the sounds of people moving through the house and felt the emotional vibes emanating from within—the fear and anxiety and worry, the relief when the older couple was reunited with their son.

And the love. The Kims were a close-knit family, and she

suspected that whatever bonds they might have with other people, nothing and no one would come before their own blood.

She nodded, satisfied. It was better for everyone this way. Many times she had done her duty even when it seemed morally distasteful to her, but she loathed the thought of innocents coming to harm unless strictly necessary. There was still time for these people to detach themselves from Kera and live in peace.

She turned and walked away, emerging from the alley into a less busy street where she could amble for some time, invisible, before uncloaking herself at the proper moment. She had done it in public before with such deftness that no one noticed when she suddenly appeared out of thin air.

Earlier in the day, Pavla had watched as the Korean couple arrived at Kera's warehouse; Pavla had spent much of her recent time staking the place out. She had not moved against her target or done anything else so far.

Olina, meanwhile, was no longer glued to her side as much, mostly because she spent half her time running to Anezka to complain and tattle. But she would be back, and unless Pavla intervened, Olina might find out about the Kims too and think of a devious and ruthless way to use them against Kera.

In fact, Pavla was fairly sure she sensed Olina's aura growing closer to her by the moment. The loathsome little witch would start shadowing her again before the evening was out and quite possibly within the hour.

She pulled out her phone and did a quick search on certain types of local establishments. There was one that looked suitable about a mile away, and Pavla didn't mind walking. The city was oddly pleasant at night, and the weather was mild and balmy. She imagined that Los Angeles would be lovely much of the year. The summer days were too hot for her taste, though.

Pavla cut across two streets, doubled back at an intersection, cut through an alley, went down a further street out of her way around an unnecessary pair of blocks, turned back in the correct direction, then waited five minutes near a street corner, pretending to look at something on her phone.

Olina was still getting closer, though she had lagged behind for a brief period. Her pace was picking up now.

She must be getting irritated with me for wasting her time and randomly moving across half the city, Pavla thought, and an evil smile played across her lips. *I do believe I have turned a single mile into more like two and a half. Poor, poor Olina, having to devote so much effort to find me again, only to discover me...here.*

The establishment she had selected for the evening was a Thai restaurant that was open late. Pavla could use a nice dinner.

Inside the place, as she was in the process of telling the hostess she required seating for only one, small footsteps stomped up behind her. "No. Make it two, please. I am with her."

Pavla turned around, making a show of widening her eyes in surprise. "Olina! So nice of you to join me. I did not think you would make it in time for dinner."

Olina smiled in a way that might crack a mirror. "Yes, I barely managed." She wrinkled her nose. "It smells so *spicy* here."

The hostess led them to a table in the far corner of the floor and a waiter took their drink orders, then left them to peruse the menu. After he returned with their tea and water and left again, the two women spoke at last.

"This," Olina snapped, in Russian, "is *another* demerit against you, Pavla. You had reported that you would remain at the girl's...ugh, apartment...to keep watch on her and inform us if there were any developments that required you to go elsewhere."

Pavla shrugged and spread her hands, wearing her best expression of innocent confusion. "Oh, forgive me. I did send you a message, but you must not have been paying attention closely enough to receive it. Perhaps it got tangled up somewhere in all the smog in the air. In any event, now we can have a lovely meal together, so all is well."

Sadly, Olina did not get more irritated. Instead, a slow, fiery, gloating smirk spread its way across her face.

Whatever that means, Pavla surmised, *I am sure it's bad.*

"Yes," said Olina, "a nice friendly dinner. Oh, but that reminds me, I had a chat with Anezka, and while she considered this obvious, she wanted me to emphasize it to you since you seem to have had so much trouble grasping it thus far."

Pavla raised an eyebrow as she sipped ice water from her glass. "Yes?" *She may be bluffing. She is such a dishonest person that it is unusually difficult to tell when she is or isn't lying.*

Olina twiddled her finger around on the tablecloth. "The Grandmistress has declared that the next time you meet Kera, she must die. If she does not, you will be considered to have been compromised, and her intended fate will become yours. It is you or her. Make your choice, Pavla. We have all had enough of your little games."

Pavla smiled. "Of course. I understand."

Yes, she thought, *I was right. Olina never smiles when she has something good to say, after all.*

CHAPTER FOURTEEN

Kera could feel the coming dawn. She could not see it yet, but she knew it was coming. Stephanie, who crouched beside her, probably could as well.

Both of them worked late shifts as a matter of course and were sometimes up until the sun finished its revolution around the other side of the planet. After a certain amount of time working nights, one became highly sensitive to the revolving patterns that distinguished darkness from daylight.

The silvery haze would soon form on the eastern horizon. At present, they were up in the San Fernando Valley, specifically the Raymer area north of Van Nuys. They hid in a narrow strip behind a line of shrubs across the street, a wooden fence at their backs, struggling to stay comfortable on the rough sod in which the foliage had been planted.

The business they were keeping watch on was purportedly a legitimate shipping-and-handling facility that mostly dealt in sporting goods. Word on the street and in certain corners of the Internet, though, was that the owner also peddled lower-end drugs and occasionally random stolen merchandise on the side.

None of the activity they had seen from the place was overtly suspicious. The man who was the apparent owner was staying there overnight and had received a small shipment in the back of a flatbed truck of crates that might conceivably contain anything. But busting *them* wasn't the goal. The ruthless people who were coming after them were the true problem.

Stephanie sighed. It was a loud, rough-edged sound of annoyance and fatigue made by someone who wasn't even trying to hide their feelings. They were behind a magical sound shield, so there was no need to fear that anyone had heard them.

"Was Chris *sure* about this?" Steph asked. "I mean, he seems like a smart man and all, but I'm fixing to think he got his information wrong. He told us 'tonight' when it's seeming like what he meant was 'tomorrow morning.'"

Kera managed a dry chortle at that. "I know what you mean. Being a vigilante *after* working on 'bar time,' the two kind of blend together, don't they? Chris is on a nine-to-five schedule, though, so you'd think he wouldn't make that mistake."

As per her boyfriend and the reams of data he had managed to collate and analyze, it was extremely likely that El Peluquero was planning a hit on the small warehouse she and her friend were now staking out. If that was the case, Kera had no intention of allowing the foreign drug lord to succeed.

But she could not be certain that Chris had been right. It wasn't as though they had found a memo explicitly stating something like, *Okay, all my fellow criminals, El Peluquero here. Tonight at exactly such-and-such time, we're going to illegally attack this location —here's the address—and commit the following laundry list of felonies. Oh, and here's how many men we'll have, how we'll be armed and equipped, and the exact tactics we'll be using.*

Kera so wished underworld bosses were that stupid; it would make her life far easier. But the Barber was not. Chris had run his spreadsheet data through a couple of probability algorithms, then both he and Kera had concluded that this place was likely the target. El Peluquero was definitely planning something for tonight, and he was definitely interested in taking this place over.

But they did not have a total lockdown on the time, nor could they be positive that this warehouse was the subject of tonight's activity.

Kera's phone buzzed in her pocket. Grimacing and wondering who would be texting her at such a ridiculous hour, she pulled out the device.

"Is it Chris?" Steph wondered. "Oh, please let it be Chris. Though I could see it being Jenn if she had a long night and is still up."

"Right," Kera agreed. "Hmm. Nope, it's Chris. He must have gotten up early to check on us. Good thing, too, since I was about to text him anyway and wake his ass up."

She swiped open the message and read it. Her grimace drooped into an outright frown. "Well, shit. Shit, shit, shit." She was starting to feel like a fool since if what Chris had just told her was the case, it was as much her fault as his.

"Oh, no," Stephanie quipped. "He put too many zeroes after the decimal point or something, didn't he? I knew this seemed all wrong."

Kera kept her eyes on her phone. "Well, no, not exactly. All he said was that he popped into a gossip board and didn't see anything about weird shit going down tonight. If we haven't seen anything yet, then maybe he was wrong after all, and we were looking at the wrong facts or processing them incorrectly, et cetera. He says he may have gotten overexcited earlier and not thought it out enough."

Steph put a hand to her face and sighed again.

"Although," Kera clarified, "I'm the one who jumped all over it right away. In fact, if I remember correctly, I was more sure than he was. Think about it." As she spoke, her confidence that they had been correct swelled. "This place is strategically located in the northern part of the city. The Barber's operations are mostly based in the west, right? If he takes over two of the four cardinal directions, his turf will mostly encircle the center of town, and he'll be well on his way to controlling the whole southern part of the state, with a nice avenue to ship drugs up to NorCal, too. And it's been, what, two days since the last hit? He's been consistently taking out rivals every two to three days since he arrived in LA and began his conquest. And Chris is smart and reliable, or I wouldn't be dating him."

Her friend's eyes moved sideways as she hashed it out in her mind. "Okay, great. But who says he isn't looking at some *other* place in the Valley? Or that it isn't going to be *tomorrow* night?"

Dammit, Steph, I was on a roll!

Out loud, all she said was, "I'm not sure. Let's give it another hour, like until the sun is fully up, then we'll call it a night if nothing happens."

They only had to wait another ten minutes.

Kera had fallen into a mental trap, devoting too much of her attention and mental energy to pep-talking herself, so Stephanie noticed it first.

"What's that?" she whispered. "Cars or trucks coming up. Uh, vans, to be precise. Damn. Do those look familiar to you? I could have sworn we seen one of those at that gangster's villa last week. But I could be wrong."

Kera perked up, her eyes flicking toward the approaching vehicles. Two black vans, unmarked and cryptically sinister, approached their position, one in front of the other. As they entered the lot where the warehouse lay, they split apart, each driving to an opposite side of the building. Flanking it.

Hoo boy, Kera thought. *If this is what I think it is, things are about to go south and fast.*

A commotion rose within the building as the people inside—Kera wasn't sure how many there were besides the owner and one other worker they had seen—noticed the vans and stirred to action.

Kera turned to Stephanie. "Okay, review of our preexisting plans combined with a slight change of plans since we always left some of it open to, y'know, adapt to an evolving situation or whatever. Those two vans *might* be here for innocuous reasons. Maybe they're part of the normal business the place does. Maybe it's the cops, even, in which case we can't get involved. But somehow, I doubt it. This feels all wrong."

Her friend nodded. They could both sense the mood of dread and tension emanating from the warehouse and the vehicles, a generalized sense that something terrible was about to happen.

Steph replied in haste. "First step is still cloaking the owner guy and anyone else in there with a bunch of protection and luck spells, right? I can handle the luck part, but you have more experience with shields."

"Yes," Kera confirmed. Out of the corner of her eye, she watched as a silhouette moved across one of the warehouse's windows, and the side doors of the vans opened. "We shield ourselves too, obviously, and stay invisible if we can."

It was difficult to maintain multiple spells that had a consistent and ongoing effect. She lacked the training and experience to manage more than two or three, and that required enough effort that she couldn't fight at the same time.

"We get the owner out of danger," Kera went on. "Based on what we've seen the Barber do previously, he tends to kill the leaders of rival outfits but then tries to recruit their underlings into his organization. So the owner is the priority. We take out the assassins with nonlethal attack spells and forgetfulness spells. Then we bundle our guy into one of those vans and drive it far, far away from here. Once we're somewhere safer, we hit him with an amnesia spell, too, then leave him and go home. The news won't even have much to report, except maybe a noise disturbance or some reckless driving."

She also had a backup measure of her own but decided not to mention it. It might not be necessary.

The very instant she concluded her brief spiel, five men, three from one van and two from the other, jumped out.

All were dressed and geared up for battle in black fatigues, body armor, helmets with visors and gas masks, and an assortment of fearsome weapons. Two had military-grade carbines, two had submachine guns, and one had a semi-automatic combat shotgun. All had plenty of spare magazines or shells as well as pistols and knives.

The speed and professionalism with which they fanned out to encircle and secure the building, with three of them at the main entrance while the other two watched the sides and rear, was almost shocking. For a moment, Kera wondered if the men were SWAT or DEA or something, and they had made a terrible mistake.

But as she understood it, government paramilitary usually wore their logos on their uniforms. The hit squad had no insignias visible anywhere. They could have worked for anyone.

"Now," Kera said.

Both young women jumped up. For the moment they were cloaked from sight, but the invisibility spell would undoubtedly weaken as they turned their energies toward other enchantments.

From within the warehouse, a man's gruff voice shouted, "Hey! I don't know who you fucks think you are, but you got no business here. Identify yourselves or get the hell out! We'll defend ourselves if we have to."

There came a distinctive double clicking sound that Kera was pretty sure signified a pump shotgun being cocked.

Oh, crap, Kera thought. *If he shoots back, he and his employees will get slaughtered, though that might have been on the agenda anyway. A shotgun can't penetrate full-strength body armor, and these five assholes mostly have automatic weapons. We need to do this fast. We need to have done it ninety seconds ago.*

"Steph! Luck spell on everyone in the building!"

Her friend had already begun casting the charm. "Way ahead of you," she murmured, then lapsed into the necessary incantation.

Kera, for her part, focused on the people within. It took a couple of seconds to locate the auras of the individuals who were trapped there since she had not been able to observe them properly beforehand. There was an older man whose vibe was fearful but defiant and two younger men who were just terrified. The first must have been the owner-operator.

Concentrating, Kera detected the approximate edge of his main aura and conjured a shield at that point, surrounding him with an invisible barrier that would protect him from harm. It might also hamper his movement, though, and an attacker could slip inside it with a knife if he moved smoothly enough. Shields mainly deflected fast, violent foreign objects or energy blasts.

As she moved on to the other two men, one of the black-clad attackers raised a fist, signaling the others.

Then they opened fire. The air split open as though bolts of lightning had struck as muzzles flashed and dust-puffs erupted from the walls. The hitmen weren't going to risk letting their target escape. They were peppering the whole building with bullets and buckshot, probably as first maneuver to soften up the resistance, followed by forcing their way into the warehouse.

"Fuck!" Kera cried, and she diverted all her attention to calling up shields around the other two people within. She succeeded, but she could feel their cloaking spell flickering. She and Steph would be visible to the assassins in a few more seconds.

At the same moment, Stephanie completed her luck enhancement charm. Random, chaotic events that affected the three individuals within the warehouse would now be far more likely to play out in their favor.

Kera only hoped they hadn't all been killed by the first volley of fire.

As if in answer to her concerns, two of the three defenders

opened fire. The booming roar of the owner's shotgun sounded from the front of the building, and one of the hitmen ducked and rolled out of the way. Closer to where the two witches advanced, a hand holding a pistol knocked the glass out of a windowpane and fired four shots in a blind-spread pattern before retracting.

What about the third guy? Kera wondered, starting to feel sick. *Why isn't he joining in?*

Two of the paramilitary goons turned toward them, staring dumbly for a second or two before raising their guns.

"No!" Stephanie called and threw up her hands, casting a quick and moderately powerful if rather sloppy confusion spell in the same motion. The men staggered, and one's carbine drooped in his hands.

Kera finished them with a blast of sonic-concussive force. Both were knocked off their feet, dropped their primary weapons, and flew ten feet through the air to crash into the pavement or the side fence. There was no way to tell yet if they'd been struck unconscious, but they would be out of commission for a moment or two.

One of the other three hitmen was coming around the corner toward them.

"Steph!" Kera barked, "hold him off. Do whatever you have to. I'm going in."

Stephanie shouted something that sounded like a confused amalgamation of every known swear word, then steeled herself and prepared to attack and defend. Trusting her to handle herself, for now, Kera summoned a shield, augmented her speed and jumping power, and launched through the nearest window.

Glass crashed around her, deflected by the magical barrier, and she careened toward a heavy wooden shelving unit. Rather than trying to dodge it in midair, she took the hit and latched on with her hands, though the impact of her and her shield threatened to tip the whole thing over. She performed a rapid visual scan of the interior.

The warehouse wasn't much bigger than hers, and in a brief flash of stupid whimsy, she wondered if it had been built by the same people who'd designed her home. There were only shelves on one side; otherwise, most of the cargo was stacked in crates and boxes on the floor or against the far wall. The three inhabitants had taken up positions in the center, which was not far from the windows.

Two of them were standing, unhit and bristling with violence. The third, one of the two younger employees, had taken a bullet or two but was still alive. It looked like he had been hit in the thigh and grazed across the side above the hip. He lay squirming in a puddle of blood, his hands grasping at the air.

Nearest to her was the guy with the pistol. He looked at Kera and blinked, then his jaw dropped open.

"Jesus!" he gasped. "That dude is flickering in and out of sight!"

Oh, hell, Kera lamented. *We're going to have to memory-wipe these poor bastards pretty hard. If we all make it out of this alive, that is.*

The wounded man was too preoccupied with the pain of his injuries to notice, but the stocky, bearded, furious-looking owner swiveled toward her and raised his shotgun.

Kera held up a hand. "No, no! I'm on your side! Come on, we can get out of here if we move now. We're going to take one of their vans. We can help your friend into it, I think."

A loud rushing, crashing sound echoed through the windows. Kera, still clinging to the top of the shelves, had a better vantage point than the men did, and she saw two of the three assassins falling over themselves under a torrent of water. The third, though, managed to sprint clear of Stephanie's aquatic blast and was repositioning himself to fire on either her or the building.

The owner's head spun toward the noise outside, then back to Kera. "All right then, start helping! Clear us a path to the vans out there!"

Kera fixed on the hitman who had dodged Stephanie's attack. He had caught sight of her and raised his SMG. She threw a mobile shield shaped into a blunted spearpoint with a substantial amount of forceful wind behind it at him. His burst of fire ricocheted off the projectile.

Then he tried to dodge and half succeeded. He avoided the full force, but it brushed him hard enough to throw him off-balance, at which point a sphere of water smacked him in the face and knocked him to the ground.

Kera hopped down from the shelf. "That should be all five of them on their asses. Come on!"

She ran to the front door and flung it open, reinforcing her personal shield to be safe. None of the five assassins were back in the fight yet, but one of the vans had pulled closer to the building, and the driver was climbing out. He too was dressed in black combat gear, and he was taking a bead on her with what was either a large pistol or a small submachine gun.

With no time to think, Kera cast a Firefly spell, targeting the man's legs. His pants right above the tops of his boots burst into flame. But he did not react, only finalized his aim and squeezed the trigger.

His gun released a three-round burst, which her shield stopped, but she still froze, balking at the man's discipline. He fired again, and only after the second volley did he start running away while beating out the flames that were engulfing his pants.

Holy living crap. Kera's spine went cold. *These guys are incredibly disciplined and motivated. They must be ex-military contractors or something. El Peluquero is playing for keeps if these are the sorts of people he has running his operations.*

Behind her, the warehouse owner rushed up, his weapon held across his chest, eyes darting around for adversaries. He saw the driver with the flaming legs and fired his shotgun once at the man.

Kera ducked, covering her ears and wincing in pain as her

tinnitus flared up horribly. The driver, meanwhile, cried out and fell over. He probably wasn't too badly injured thanks to his armor, but getting blasted with buckshot could not have done him any favors. As he rolled across the ground, the flames winked out.

Good. I didn't want to burn him to death, but we can't let these assholes win no matter what.

Kera ran to the van. There were no keys in the ignition, so cursing herself and sucking in air, she sprinted to the driver, who was struggling to get to his feet. She kicked at his head, and to her shock, he caught the blow with a fast, sharp motion and punched toward her knee, aiming to break her leg.

Crying out in alarm, Kera jumped straight up, wrenching her leg free a quarter of a second before his fist struck. She sailed over the man's head, and from her airborne location, she saw three things happening at once.

First, the owner was hustling the uninjured employee out of the building and directing him to secure the empty vans. Second, Stephanie was coming back around the corner of the warehouse. And third, four of the five initial attackers were back on their feet, though two looked battered and wobbly.

Stephanie would not be able to deal with them in time. As she drifted back toward the earth, Kera summoned a net of static electricity that engulfed the three men in the rear—the ones whose clothes were drenched by Steph's water magic.

They screamed in pain as sparks and steam rose from them and their muscles seized up. Not wanting to torment or kill them if she didn't have to, Kera released the spell a second later as her feet touched the ground. The hitmen collapsed in unison.

"Kera!" Stephanie called. "There's another guy in the warehouse. He got shot! We got to get him to a hospital."

"Stop the bleeding," Kera instructed her. "I'll deal with—"

A blur of motion to the side caught her eye. The driver, the man she had just escaped from, had retrieved his machine pistol and was aiming it at the owner, who was starting to pivot but was too slow to shoot first. He was still shielded, but Kera couldn't be certain how much strength the barrier had left.

Amidst the chaos, Kera acted on instinct. Her right hand shot down to her side, yanking free the Glock 19 she had concealed under her riding jacket, and in a flash, the pistol was gripped in both hands and aimed at the assassin.

The black-clad driver fired an eye's blink sooner than Kera did. His three-round burst spattered uselessly against the beefy owner's shield, though the man stumbled back in alarm.

Kera's aim was true, however. A single shot rang out from her pistol, and the nine-millimeter slug found its way into the side of the man's head half an inch below the rim of his helmet.

He let out a brief, sharp choking sound and toppled to the ground, lying still except for the twitching of two fingers on his gun hand.

Oh, no, Kera thought. *What the fuck did I just do? Why didn't I use magic? I'm getting tired after all these spells, but...*

Stephanie froze. "God damn, Kera, where and when did you get that thing?"

"Not now," Kera countered. "Go stabilize that wounded guy. I'll be right in."

They still needed the keys. Which meant that she would have to get them off of the man she had killed.

Squirming and trying not to look at him—at least his face wasn't visible under the helmet, visor, and mask—she darted her hands into two pockets before finding the keys and pulling them out.

The fifth man popped up behind her at the same instant the owner came up at her side, blasting his shotgun and driving the attacker back behind cover.

"Lady, or guy, whatever," the man said, "I dunno who you are, but we owe you one. Who are these guys, anyway? Feds?"

She swallowed, horrified by the prospect that they might be

but strongly suspecting otherwise. "They work for El Peluquero," she replied in a flat monotone. "He wants to take over your business."

The man snorted. "Figures. I heard about that son of a bitch. Hey! Look!"

Kera sprang up, already running back toward the nearest vehicle, and saw a third black van coming around the corner toward them. "Oh, fuck!" she snarled and jumped behind the wheel.

The engine started easily enough, and the young man with the pistol stared at her dumbly, then ran back toward the warehouse to join his boss in keeping the one active man among the initial five hitmen occupied with suppressing fire.

Kera drove right up to the entrance, backing toward it so they could load the wounded man in the rear without disturbing him more than necessary. She thought back to the hostage she had rescued from the burning apartment complex months ago, shot by Vincent Anastidis. She hadn't tried to move him. Moving a person who was badly hurt was really, really stupid.

But leaving him here with hostiles pressing in would be even worse.

Fortunately, as Kera opened the back doors of the van, Stephanie appeared, pulling the young man along. He kept moaning and yelping in pain as his body tried to resist the movement, and though Steph had wrapped his wounds to staunch the worst of the bleeding, it appeared they were breaking open again. One whole side of his shirt and much of his pant leg was stained red.

Kera came up beside the pair and cast a lower-middle-powered healing spell on the employee. Instantly, she felt as though she had lost three hours of sleep and two entire meals. Healing was the most taxing of all forms of magic.

But it ought to keep the man alive.

"Come on," Kera urged, and they secured the man in the back.

"You stay beside him. Do you know that relaxation spell? Use a weak one on him if you have to. I'll deal with the rest. We need to get those other two guys out of here, too."

She sprang out of the vehicle and turned to face the approaching third van. A man was already leaning out of the passenger side and aiming a rifle at them.

Kera conjured a shield-barrier that was ten feet across halfway between her and the van. It absorbed the shooter's first volley of bullets, and the driver seemed to grasp that something was in their way, so he hit the brakes.

Kera centered a heat spell on the axle of the front right wheel. White and reddish-orange light flared up, and the rim melted as flames rose into the engine. The driver frantically attacked the wheel, but the van swerved to a rough halt, dead in its tracks.

Mere seconds later, the four men within piled out. All of them were armed and armored.

By now, the warehouse owner and his other assistant were running toward the vehicle Kera and Stephanie had commandeered. Kera motioned them in and, breath heaving, they hurled themselves through the side door. Kera slammed it before crawling behind the wheel again.

They only escaped by a hair's breadth, and it was solely because the new batch of hitmen found themselves slowed and confounded by the still-extant invisible barrier. It took them about three seconds to work their way around its edges, but those few precious moments were enough for Kera to slam on the gas and drive past them, knock over one man who got too close, and start down the street.

She zig-zagged and kept her head low, shouting at the others to do the same. Gunshots rang out and holes appeared in the sides of the van, but no one got hit. The warehouse and the small army of assassins dwindled behind them.

"The other van," Steph pointed out. "We got one, you toasted the third, but there's still that second one. They're gonna figure it out real quick and be after us."

Kera gritted her teeth. She was incredibly tired and strung out. The whole battle had probably only lasted a couple of minutes, but it had felt like hours of strain. "You're right. Can you cloak us? I'm, uh, running out of energy."

Stephanie closed her eyes and spent a moment calming herself. "Yeah, I can." She raised her hands and mumbled something.

The younger guy with the handgun, the one who wasn't hurt, stared at her. "*Cloak us?* By praying? Who in the name of Odin's goddamn hangnail *are* you chicks?"

The owner looked at Kera from the backseat. "I'm kinda wondering the same thing. I ain't never seen a single human being do some of what you just did. Unless, of course, all those stupid 'Motorcycle Man' stories were true after all."

It occurred to Kera that she had left Zee behind. He was parked a full block and a half from the warehouse, so he was not in immediate danger, but once the cops showed up and started sweeping the area, he might be captured. She would have to go back and soon.

She muttered, "More things in heaven and earth..."

"What?" The owner scoffed.

"Never mind. Steph, sorry to keep asking you to do so much of the work, but can you find out where the nearest ER is? That guy needs treatment, and the Barber's men won't dare assault a hospital. That only happens in Hong Kong action movies, I think."

Before her friend could respond, the owner protested. "Don't take us to a hospital! They ask too many questions. We ain't entirely legitimate businessmen. Hope you're not too disappointed or whatever. But I know this guy..."

Kera ignored him and subtly hit him with a combined charm

of confusion and relaxation. His words dribbled off, and he stared into space.

"Steph," she added, "after we drop these guys off, we need to go back for my bike. If they find it—and, uh, by 'they,' I mean either EP's boys *or* the cops—we could be in a world of shit. Actually, you go somewhere else separately on foot and cloaked, and I'll catch up with you a little later? It's safer that way."

Stephanie nodded. "Okay, yeah, that works, but be careful. You need a recharge?"

"Yes," Kera admitted, "but I'll manage."

The guy with the pistol wasn't paying attention to their conversation. Now that the adrenaline was wearing off, he seemed to be in shock. "Shit," he remarked. "This is all like a frickin' nightmare. Like I drank too much last night and then dropped acid right before bed."

Kera knew how he felt. "Don't worry," she reassured him, "I promise you won't remember any of it later."

CHAPTER FIFTEEN

James Lovecraft felt the mental tripwire alarm going off a good five seconds before, confirming what the alarm suggested, he also heard footsteps approaching his study. He sighed, minimized the windows he had been looking at on his computer, and tilted the screen a tad to make it less visible from the doorway.

"Is it really *that* difficult," he asked with a soft sigh of exasperation, "to practice stuff you've already learned on your own after being specifically instructed to only seek help if something weird happened? Come on, man."

No one was present to hear him. He simply felt better when he said stuff like that out loud.

A fist banged on the door. "May I come in?" Ezeudo's voice asked. "I wish to ask about something."

"Yes, yes, come in." James took his glasses off and rubbed his eyes as the door opened.

The tall Nigerian took two steps and then stopped. "James," he began, "I will cut to the chase. I do not think I can reach the milestones you have set on this schedule. I have not had any new lessons for over two days now. This means I am falling behind and will have to learn more spells than I am capable of mastering in the days to come."

His jaw was set, his eyes glimmered, and his hands shook, though he had folded them behind his back. He was tense, anxious, irritated, and defiant in spite of it all. James could feel it in the man's aura. He had come here knowing he would probably be rebuffed or perhaps threatened, but he had come regardless.

James folded his hands, opting not to answer right away. "Your progress has been pretty good so far," he pointed out after a moment had passed.

"Good," Ezeudo acknowledged, "but difficult. So very trying. Only barely have I passed the tests you people have set for me so far. Now you are neglecting my lessons, leaving me to 'practice on my own,' as you put it, with the expectation that I will somehow be able to work even harder next week to make up for it."

He was technically right, James realized. He waited, continuing to listen.

Ezeudo went on. "Not only is this not fair, it is not smart or efficient. As your expression goes, something has got to give. Either the load of courses coming up must be lightened, or we must resume my lessons in new spells and procedures at once so too much is not expected of me at one time. I have struggled with stress and exhaustion. Now I struggle with boredom and dread."

James frowned and rustled his shoulders, covering it by seeming to adjust his position in his large, comfortable chair. He felt put-upon, largely because Ezeudo's words meant he could no longer get away with stalling the man while he pursued other things.

"Well," Lovecraft began, "you raise a valid point or two. What we were hoping was that your, ah, self-directed practice session would give you time to relax and recharge, and then you would be ready to tackle an even larger course load next week. But if you work better under a steady stream of middling pressure, perhaps we can arrange something."

"Yes," said Ezeudo, "I do. And it would be best to arrange it soon."

The man has cojones, James noted, with approval. *After all the scary implied threats of what we'd do to him if he defied us, and he still ends up trying to make demands about how we teach him. I guess that's to be expected with a grown adult—he's older than I am by a few years, after all—who has lived a highly independent lifestyle.*

But I'm busy, dammit. Where the hell is Lauren? Yes, she handled most of the first portion of his training, but it wasn't fair or smart or efficient of her to leave me to do all the teaching just when things back in Los Angeles are getting so interesting.

"All right, then," James told his student. "We will resume your lessons tomorrow morning, so a day and a half earlier than planned. That should be enough to balance things out. For the rest of today, though, please continue as previously instructed. It will be good for you to affirm your ability to do everything you've learned up to this point. And I have some things I have to finish before I can start instructing you again."

Ezeudo paused, wrinkling his mouth and seeming to think it over. "That is acceptable. Resuming my lessons tonight would be better still, but I imagine that your business with the council offers up many tasks that are more important than teaching me."

The sarcasm was not lost on James. "Oh, more than you realize," he quipped.

The other man asked, "When is Miss Jones coming back? Both of you are good teachers. But she is more...available."

James shrugged. "She isn't available *now*. She has other things to do, too. But I know what you mean. I'll see if I can prevail upon her to make extra time and return sooner than planned. LeBlanc, too, will be back before long. Then she can take a hand in things as well."

"So be it," Ezeudo declared. "Thank you." With a nod, he turned and left, shutting the door behind him.

Once he was gone, James allowed his face to sink toward the surface of the desk and smacked himself on the back of the head, groaning at the agony to come.

Until their guest had arrived here alongside him and LeBlanc, and until the lessons had begun, James had forgotten how much he loathed teaching. His subconscious mind must have repressed the memory, making it seem less terrible than it was.

Still, to a large extent, bringing Ezeudo home to train him had been his idea and the logical outcome of his plans to expand the council's reach.

He pushed his chair back, got up, and went over to the bar to mix his third drink of the day, though it was not even dinner time yet. He vowed to limit himself to one more adult beverage that night. Being plastered tomorrow while instructing Ezeudo would only make things worse.

As he poured brandy over a trio of ice cubes in his usual tumbler, he reflected on all the new information that had come up over the course of the afternoon. Physically, he was in upstate New York, training a new thaumaturge in his ancestral home. Mentally, he was still in several other places, mainly LA.

Things in the City of Angels had not quieted down much since he and LeBlanc had left, despite their having depowered the troublesome Korean couple. It was difficult to sift the truth out of all the grains of rumor-mill bullshit, but the impression he was getting was that "Motorcycle Man" had set an example other citizens were trying to follow.

There had been a mysterious rise in vigilante activity, he'd found, though it seemed to have correlated most recently with a surge in crime. The latter seemed to be connected to some new crime boss moving in and setting off a generalized turf war among the gangs, mob factions, cartel offshoots, and so forth.

As for the former, there was no consensus on whether or not

it was all the work of Motorcycle Man still, or if it was due to various copycats trying to inherit MM's mantle and bask in his—her—dubious glory.

"Ugh." James grunted, tossing back half of the chilled brandy in one swig. "The ripples in the pond we sent out turned into more like a tidal wave moving across the ocean."

They'd shut down the original Motorcycle Woman, but there was still magic in LA. Far too much of it, in fact.

James sat back down. As worrisome as everything else was, what scared him most was the Orthodoxy. He was now ninety-nine percent sure that not only were they real and not merely an urban legend, but that they were far more powerful and dangerous than he had suspected.

The American Council, he had concluded, was sheltered and vain, including him. They had never truly believed there were other organizations that could rival them. Sure, magic had a longer history in the Old World than in the New—aside from the various Native traditions, though sadly many of those had been lost to time—but it had decayed and was unable to assert itself as forcefully as it had centuries ago.

Or so they had thought.

Reliable information about the Orthodoxy was difficult to come by, but most of what James could reasonably confirm disturbed him. Their members tended to be inculcated with fanatical loyalty and were taught a wide range of magic, including via methods the more "modern" American council had left behind in favor of a relatively scientific approach.

Worse, the way they operated reminded him more of an organized crime group or a violent cult than an august, scholarly body. The Orthodoxy sought expansion—craved it. They wanted to accumulate wealth and power.

And they were willing to kill for it. The council considered killing to be of the utmost gravity and never sanctioned it except in matters of the direst need.

Thus, in a way, James had been proven correct, after all. The council needed new blood. It had to be prepared for what might well be coming, especially since the Orthodoxy had slipped its tentacles into the Los Angeles underworld.

"Oh, Ezeudo," James muttered. "Be thankful you don't know the half of it yet. If you think things are stressful *now*? Ha. You'll have some fun surprises coming, to be sure."

He finished his drink in another long draught, relishing the icy fire in his throat. It perked him up, at least in the short term. In the longer term, he might well need to ease back into total sobriety.

He wasn't looking forward to it much.

Ezeudo stood between two fountains in the estate's beautiful back garden area, staring straight ahead; he could partially see both fountains out of the sides of his eyes but was not looking directly at either. His hands were extended in front of him, palms facing outward.

He made a low humming in the back of his throat, "charging up" the spells the way his people had taught him, then shifted as the powers of the universe descended to aid him. The humming became an incantation, the words taught to him by the Americans.

And though the flow of energy experienced an instant of confusion since it was unused to being commanded by methods from two different traditions in such quick succession—it was not disrupted. It did not halt. It moved forward to perform the tasks requested of it.

In the fountain to the left, the water rose up in a foaming wave. First it was a straight ascent, then it began curling around the central column of carved marble in an aquatic cyclone.

In the fountain to the right, the water did not move at all. In fact, the molecules that made it up slowed down. A frosty mist appeared above it as all the heat was squeezed out and the water changed from liquid to solid, rising above the stone rim as it expanded. Ezeudo had made certain to allow it to move upward as he did not wish to crack the fountain.

Then, maintaining his hold on both spells according to the techniques James and Lauren (mostly Lauren) had shown him, he cast a third.

A magical shield, impervious to most violently moving objects as well as heat or electrical energy, shimmered into existence in front of him, wrapping around him on three sides to provide greater protection.

Then he summoned the foaming, angry water from the left fountain to spray at him with the force of a firehose. It turned white from the churning disturbance and dashed itself against the shield, scattering droplets across the lawn.

Ezeudo continued to look straight ahead. Next, he summoned the water from the other fountain. It cracked apart and the ice shards rose, flinging themselves at his body in a mass of crystalline knives and jagged, frozen boulders. They shattered against the barrier with a loud crashing report, and the snow-dust and shining fragments fell to the grass.

Ezeudo inhaled slowly, then breathed out at a sharper speed. He dismissed the shield and watched it dissipate.

Next, he gathered all the water from the fountains, or at least most of it, whether in liquid or solid form, and commanded it back where it belonged. Soon both of the stone basins were refilled to the proper level, and the marble columns in the center burbled again with activity.

Finished, the man closed his eyes and trudged to the nearest wall, leaning against it in his fatigue. "So much work." He sighed. He was trying to keep speaking English, even when alone, to make life in America easier. It would not be constructive to lapse into his native tongue or even into French.

He had done it, though. The difficult way to multi-spell manipulation was opening up to him, and though it sapped much of his energy, it hadn't exactly killed him. He would be well again after a hearty meal and a short rest.

Otherwise, there was little for him to do the rest of the evening except go through the motions of the other simpler tasks he had learned over the past weeks. He grasped that repetition helped to code such things into his reflexive memory, but it was so, so *boring*.

Tomorrow, he would no longer be bored, though. He would be overwhelmed again.

Ezeudo strolled around the side of the mansion, intending to take his practice to the front lawn, largely because it gave him an excuse to take a short walk and clear his mind.

There was a table set up nearby with drinks in bottles and snacks under covered trays, as per James' orders to his house-keeper. The man paused at the table for a couple minutes, eating and drinking to recharge himself.

To his surprise, James appeared, moving across the grass at a leisurely though not reluctant, pace.

"How's it going?" he asked.

"Well," Ezeudo reported, and it was the truth. He explained his breakthrough with the fountains, adding as an aside that he'd managed to avoid unintentional property damage to boot.

James smiled and clapped his hands in front of him. "Excellent! See, sometimes being able to work things out by yourself is the best way to take it to the next level. How are the sandwiches? They look kind of small, but we're used to making little hors d'oeuvres-type things for fancy parties, shit like that. I should have ordered a sub tray instead, given the number of calories you're probably going through."

The Nigerian shrugged. "They are fine. Very tasty. Grape soda would be better than lemon-lime, however."

"I'll make a note of it," James said. He gazed across his property. "Did you know," he mused, "that there was a time when thaumaturges with a *lifetime* of experience would be considered grand high poobahs—masters—of their craft if they attained only what you have learned so far?"

Ezeudo was not sure how to respond to that. He was still acclimating himself to the cultural differences in how Westerners approached magic, and he was uncertain if James was including the elder mages among his own people in his presumed lauding of modern practitioners.

"I did not know that," he stated, his tone neutral.

"Mm, yes, most people don't." James bobbed his head and stared at the western horizon, where the sun was sinking and turning the sky purple and orange. "Across the world around, oh, say, two thousand years ago, magic finally became systematized to a point where each generation could build upon the foundation left by the one before. All of those advancements were recorded and maintained and added to the overall tradition, much like with science and technology in more modern times."

Ezeudo nodded. When it was explained that way, it made sense.

"Anyway," James went on, "after the disturbances of what in Europe was referred to as the Dark Ages, things went backward somewhat, but in more recent centuries, they began to recover and even to expand upon what came before. A reasonably talented junior student of today towers over the masters of the ancient days, all because we have organizations in place to preserve knowledge and systematically train people according to the wisdom of the past."

"I see," Ezeudo replied. "I knew this, in a manner of speaking, since all human knowledge follows that pattern as long as the culture is not disrupted."

James turned to look at him. "More or less, yes. And it is when culture is disrupted—or when the organizations grow weak or make serious errors in judgment—that individual rogue actors are able to flourish. The sorts of people who try to teach themselves everything *by* themselves and to brute-force their way through their problems because they don't have teachers who can show them the smarter, gentler, and more efficient methods of achieving the same end goal. Renegades who make problems for everyone else. Vigilantes who think they're doing the right thing, but mostly they are just creating disruptions and making messes someone else will have to clean up."

Ezeudo frowned. "I have reasons of my own to distrust organizations. I thought the United Nations might be the greatest force for good in our world, and sometimes it does good things, but often it is corrupt or incompetent. Most governments, religions, and corporations are far from perfect. But...I understand what you are saying."

"Good," said James.

"Yes," the other man went on, "though I do not agree with all of your methods, it is true that I have advanced with incredible speed under your instruction. And though I have done fairly well for myself by being, how do you say, a lone wolf, I have seen other cases of men and women who caused terrible suffering to themselves or others by their refusal to recognize any authority but themselves. There is, I suppose, a balance to be aimed for between the extremes."

James put a hand on his arm. "See? I *knew* bringing you into the fold would be a good idea."

For the first time in far too long, Ezeudo laughed. "Thank you. I did not know myself that it would be a good idea, but maybe, just maybe, it was."

CHAPTER SIXTEEN

Many martial arts masters over the years and centuries had told their students that anger was not the way to true mastery. Kera had tried to heed their advice, but she found it tough. Anger to her was fuel, and she had a lot of it to burn today.

The post to which her unfortunate punching bag was attached trembled and shook, its chain and fixtures squeaking in fear and anger as Kera pummeled the living shit out of it. The technique was still there, sort of, but mostly she was just subjecting it to a street-fight level beatdown.

Her imagination was restless in assigning an identity to her imaginary opponent. Most of the time, it was El Peluquero. She recalled the cold fear he had inspired in her and the cruelty of his henchmen and reached out to retaliate.

But other times, she found herself beating the shit out of different targets, ones that did not seem so morally clear.

The bag kept changing into Pavla, and striking it then, Kera felt as though she were hurting herself as much as she might hurt the Czech witch should she get the opportunity to pound her face in for real.

Sometimes it became random other people from the past who had wronged her or wronged others.

And in brief flashes between all the others, the bag became her. She attacked herself.

I went into that situation without anywhere near enough fucking information, she acknowledged, palm-striking the beleaguered leather, then kneeing and kicking it as hard as she could.

We technically succeeded, but it was way, WAY too close. And a man died. Sure, he was a professional killer working for a drug lord, and I only shot him because he was trying to kill me and someone else. But I didn't want to. It should not have happened. We ought to have planned it out better. We fucked up.

Finally, striking from the elbow while in a firm stance that generated power, she hit the bag hard enough that it swung perpendicular to the floor and brushed the opposite wall.

Yeah, Kera thought. *Eat that, you prick. Whoever you are. Whoever deserves it most.*

She turned around, intending to finish up, and the bag, swinging back, smashed into the space between her shoulder blades. She stumbled forward in alarm, then tripped over her own feet to roll across the floor. Though technically soft, the bag had enough mass that it felt like it had punched her nearly as hard as she had punched it.

What a great way to end a sloppy, unbalanced training session, she concluded. *Awesome. Good job, Kera.*

Her cheeks burned red as she pushed off the ground and stood. Sadly, there were witnesses.

Chris blinked as he stared at her. "You okay, babe?" He started to get up to come over and help her.

Part of her appreciated the gesture, but she held up an open palm to stop him. "I'm fine, yeah." She didn't make eye contact.

Stephanie sat at the table across from Chris. "Girl, come eat with us. Food's cold by now, you know, but you got the sense to own a microwave, so it's no problem. And you've been going at that damn thing for an *hour.* Take a break."

Kera sighed. Her friends seemed to recognize that she was embarrassed and tired and embarrassed about being tired since it was causing her to make stupid mistakes. They weren't going to judge her or make fun of her.

"Okay. Thanks."

She strolled over to the table and examined the waiting meal. Chris and Stephanie had collaborated on a lovely panful of chicken tetrazzini with lots of extra cheese and veggies, as well as a bevy of hotdogs with chili, onions, and mustard. The two dishes didn't go together well, but none of them cared.

Predictably, Chris had eaten only a cursory amount: one chili dog and a square of the casserole barely big enough to fill the remaining space on his plate. He was, after all, a normal un-magical human.

Stephanie had put away about twice what Chris had. Though a fellow thaumaturge, she had not expended much energy today.

That left the other half of the meal for Kera if she wanted it. She was pretty sure the leftovers would be minimal.

While she heated up a massive plate's worth, her friends started discussing their earlier shooting session, obviously trying to draw her into the conversation to help get her mind off whatever had upset her.

"So," Chris began, "I think my accuracy is improving, especially at longer range. I still can't draw and shoot as fast as Kera can, though."

"Yeah," opined Steph, "handguns seem like a whole different skill set. Like, accuracy matters, but it's more about getting the gun out and putting a couple rounds somewhere on the target as fast as possible. I still feel more comfortable with the rifle. I like being able to take my time a little more and get it perfect, no matter how long the range is. Though we haven't been able to try, what, two hundred or three hundred yards."

The microwave dinged. Kera opened it, stirred the tetrazzini with a fork, and removed the chili dog, which was warm enough, before giving the casserole another minute. She turned toward the table, chewed her first mouthful of chili dog, and swallowed.

"I don't think our range *has* three hundred yards to spare," she pointed out. "To practice at that kind of distance, we'll probably have to head into the mountains or a place on government land. You can usually get away with recreational shooting within the safety parameters and so forth. In fact, that's a great idea. It would allow us to practice drawing and pivoting techniques without range masters breathing down our necks. Of course, it also means we'll have to be that much more, uh, fastidious about safety."

The microwave beeped again and Kera pulled out the steaming tetrazzini, then took it over to the table to sit down.

Chris piped up. "Well, hey, I have an all-terrain vehicle, don't I? Let's organize a field trip."

Stephanie laughed. "We'll have to make sure our papers are in order, though. Sounds like shooting out in the middle of nowhere is kinda in the legal gray area?"

Kera shrugged as she dug a fork into the pasta. "It's legal. But we might have some slight problems if we run into, y'know, other Californians who aren't accustomed to people using firearms for anything other than gang shootings."

Her friends snickered at that, but inside, Kera cringed.

She had killed Vincent Anastidis and Pauline Testrovosky essentially by accident, and she knew their names. She might never learn the name of the man she had shot last night, and it definitely hadn't been an accident. She had done it to save herself and protect the warehouse owner, yes, but on some level, she had intentionally taken his life.

It was ugly. She didn't like it.

As she thought about it, the anger at the world and everyone in it, including herself—*especially* herself—came back. She wolfed down the food in sullen silence while Steph and Chris kept talking about pleasant everyday bullshit.

As soon as she was done eating, Kera went back over to her punching bag and once again began kicking the crap out of it.

Chris, his attempt at a cheery expression fading rapidly, called, "Hey, hun, didn't you say you would only be working out for a bit? You've done enough for one day. Come on, relax."

She ignored him. In the back of her mind, she appreciated that he cared, but now was not the time. She elbowed and punched the leather surface of the sack, embraced it only to knee it, dodged its clumsy rebound, and then knocked its imaginary head off with an axe kick.

Stephanie looked at Chris. "You know, my mama always taught me that it was rude as hell to talk about a person who's in the same room without including them in the conversation, but we need to do something. She's gonna wear herself out badly enough that she can't function at work, and then she'll be too tired to deal with...whatever else we end up having to deal with. I don't know if she'll listen to me."

"I can hear you," Kera pointed out, her voice gruff. "I'm right over here, for fuck's sake."

Chris sighed. "Okay." He stood up and walked over to his girl-friend, at first hesitating at the periphery of her "threat range," then advancing. He stepped between her and the bag as she retreated from it to line up another attack.

She glared at him. "Let me work out!"

"Kera, stop." He stood firm and his voice was authoritative, though his face and eyes were gentle. "You've worked out enough. This is clearly about something else that's bothering you. Talk to me about it."

She looked to the side as a tremor of anger went through her. "Yeah. It bothers me that I had to fucking *kill* a guy, and that even then, we barely pulled that cockamamie plan off, all because of under-preparation. And ignorance. And sloppiness."

Chris' face fell. "Oh, babe. I'm sorry I didn't have more info to give. I should have waited until—"

"No," she interrupted him. "I was the one who leaped into action, and I dragged Steph with me. Because I'm reckless and stupid. I wasn't prepared, I don't even know how to *be* prepared, and every time—"

"Hey," Chris counter-interrupted, "it isn't *your* fault either, really. And as for what's going on this moment—not in the past but in the present—tiring yourself out isn't going to help. Not to sound like your grandma or whoever, but your ability to figure out the next steps we need to take will be much improved if you pause, eat something healthy, and get some rest. Mental unwinding, followed by sleep. You barely slept last night. Or this morning, technically."

Her nostrils flared as she inhaled, but when she let it out, she relaxed. "Okay," she said. "I'll try. If you want me to eat healthy food, though, why did you make chili dogs?"

Chris laughed, and Stephanie echoed it from the table.

"Hey," Steph called, "we got fruit for dessert. That shit has all kinds of antioxidants to counteract that processed meat. Right?"

Chris nodded. "Right." He put a hand on Kera's shoulder, and she allowed him to lead her back to the table, where she had second helpings of everything, followed by fruit.

Chris watched as she dug into her dessert.

"Hmm," he commented. "I don't know. That *is* an awful lot of fruit. No wonder she put on, like, two pounds in the last couple weeks."

She half-laughed, half-squinted in irritation, then nudged him in the side. "Shut up. Apples and grapes aren't fattening. And I've gained more than that, which at least is pushing me out of the 'blatantly underweight' category."

Stephanie added, "But don't they have a lot of sugar? Fruit and all. I mean, it's not the same thing as eating cake and washing it down with soda, but still."

Kera decided she ought to look into that for future reference.

"Anyway," Chris said, leaning closer with a mischievous look on his face, "you're probably going to need another shower. You smell like sweat, girl. It's kind of sexy in a way, buuuut that also means it's distracting. We have other things to worry about right now, and you wouldn't want me all fixated on...you know."

She laughed. "You'll pay for that. Sooner or later."

Stephanie pretended to look away. "Oh, Lord. I'm not getting involved in this. You do smell like, well, like you just been beating the hell out of a bag for the last hour, though. No offense."

Finishing the last of her grapes and deciding a shower *did* sound nice right about now, Kera mumbled, "Yeah, I'll take that under advisement. Thanks."

After a couple more bouts of teasing, she headed toward the bathroom. Her long workout had left her drained, but the big, nourishing meal was already helping.

As she stepped over the threshold, the doorbell rang. Something within her perked up in alarm. Spinning around, she saw that Chris had jumped to his feet and was paces from the door himself.

"Hey," she called. "Check who it is before you let them in!"

He turned his head and nodded, redirecting his path to the window. Kera backtracked and came up behind him, and Steph stood from the table.

Chris peered out the window. "Umm. It's a small Asian girl with long hair and an average-sized Latino guy in sunglasses, shorter hair. They're my age or so, no one I think I've seen before. They both are dressed somewhat formally. They don't look overly cheerful. Sound familiar?"

The description he'd given could apply to many different people, but in point of fact, they *did* sound familiar. Kera hurried over and flung open the door. If they were who she thought they might be, she would rather confront them directly.

The pair standing before her stared in surprise, and she could tell that both were trying not to cringe in fear.

Or turn and flee.

She, meanwhile, was trying not to punch either of them in the face.

Kera demanded, "What the *hell* are you two doing here, and what do you want?"

The woman took a deep breath and was about to speak, but the other—the individual Kera knew as Mustang Man—beat her to the punch.

"Yeah," he muttered, his sunglasses conveniently obscuring if he was looking at her or the pavement, "I was just asking myself the same thing."

CHAPTER SEVENTEEN

The Asian woman flicked her eyes at Mustang Man in a furious glare, then looked at Kera again.

"Pardon me," she began, in a polite, professional tone that matched the quality of her suit-dress, "but we are here because we want to...help you. Please, just hear us out. We remember who you are, and we're sure you remember us as well."

Chris and Stephanie had come up behind Kera and were peering past her at their guests, tense and wary. Neither of them was familiar with the newcomers, but they grasped quickly enough that Kera had a history with them—and not a *friendly* history.

Kera crossed her arms over her chest and glowered at them. "Yes, I recall telling you and your friend, the big guy, to behave yourselves. So far, it seems like you've mostly been heeding that warning, so that's a good sign. What in God's name do you think you can help me with, though?"

Then it struck her and she felt like a fool, though she willed herself not to blush in front of them. If they knew where she lived, they could have easily deposited a cardboard envelope full of info on her doorstep.

"Allow us to explain," Lia asked. "My name is Lia, by the way, and this is Johnny. I'm not sure we were ever properly introduced. Would you be willing to step outside for a moment?"

"Hi," Kera replied and waved at Johnny, who reluctantly returned the gesture. He still seemed to be avoiding her gaze, and his demeanor suggested a child being forced by his parents to pet someone's dog and he was afraid it would bite.

In answer to Lia's question, she said, "No, how about you two come in instead? Two of my friends are here. Between the three of us, I shouldn't have to mention that you would be better off not even thinking of trying anything."

Johnny grumbled, "We wouldn't dream of it."

Kera stood aside, watching her new guests closely as they trudged in, then shut the door. Finally, she introduced herself. "My name is Kera, though if you figured out where I live, you might have been able to get that information somewhere anyway. Have a seat at the table if you like. We were finishing up a meal. Help yourselves to what's left, though we're basically down to fruit at this point."

The pair moved slowly toward the table, scoping out Steph and Chris to ensure that neither was going to freak out and do something hostile. They simply watched the newcomers. Kera's friends sensed that she considered it safe enough to allow them in, though the tension among them was obvious, and held off on doing anything.

As their guests sat down, Kera decided it might be best to reassure her companions. Also, she wanted to surprise the pair with something—a bargaining chip of sorts.

"Stay here," she said to Lia and Johnny, "and eat for a minute. I need to tell these two," she gestured to Chris and Stephanie, "why you're here and who you are. It will only take a second, and then we can talk. Deal?"

Lia's face scrunched with concern and skepticism, then she

spread her hands. "Very well. We won't move or do anything stupid."

Kera believed her. "Good." She motioned for her friends to huddle close and she took them out through the side door.

Once they were outside, Chris asked, "Are you sure about this? I can tell you're not exactly a big fan of those two. Are they the ones who...you know?"

"I don't know," Kera responded, "since that could mean a few different things. Wait, hold on."

She cast a sound-shield around them to protect the privacy of their conversation. "That's better. Anyway, they used to work for Pauline. I let them go with a warning that they needed to get their acts together or face severe consequences. And I'm pretty sure they're the ones who left me the care package."

"Well," Stephanie began, "I'm okay with it if you are. I mean, you invited them into your home, so they can't be too bad. Or at least, if they're dangerous, they're too scared of you to risk what you'd do to them."

Kera smiled. "Exactly. Still, they might start snooping around if we leave them to their own devices for too long. When we go back in there, I want you two to keep an eye on them for a minute while I sneak in the stack of documents. That way, when I pull it out, I can gauge their reaction in case they lie. I can, to a point, sense when people are lying anyway, but watching their faces always helps."

Chris locked his fingers together and flexed his hands. "Okay then, I'm in. If they pull out guns, I'll just use my highly advanced combat skills and psionic abilities to deal with them."

"That won't be necessary," said Kera. "But thanks. If anything happens, get down and get out of the way, and protect Zee. I don't want him getting hurt again. Steph and I are better equipped to take care of shit."

"Damn," Chris pouted.

Stephanie inhaled. "All right, as long as you know what you're doing."

Kera canceled the sound shield and opened the door. They walked back inside.

Lia and Johnny looked up. They had, as instructed, been sitting there idly munching on grapes and otherwise doing nothing. Johnny in particular relaxed, grateful they weren't forcing him to wait for any great length of time.

"Okay," Kera announced, "let me use the bathroom quick, then we'll get started."

Steph and Chris moved in, flanking their guests, as Kera used a mild cloaking charm to disguise the details of her movements while she ducked behind her bed and grabbed the sheaf of papers. Then she went into the bathroom for a minute to keep up the charade.

I was about to take a shower, wasn't I? Hah! Well, those two can just deal with me smelling like a pair of gym socks. I'll consider it the last part of their penance for all the fucked-up shit they did previously.

She emerged with the documents partially hidden under her shirt but mostly with magic and pulled up a chair and sat down. "Tell me what it is you think you can help me with." She folded her hands in front of her and gave them each a keen stare.

Johnny turned his head toward Lia, who cleared her throat.

"Since you have taken to fighting crime and are trying to make this city a better place, I thought that we, me especially, could do nothing better to prove we're turning over a new leaf than assist you. I suspect that at this point in time, your biggest concern is the violent takeover of the underworld being carried out by El Peluquero. Please correct me if I'm wrong."

The second part of what she'd said was almost exactly what Kera had expected to hear. The first part about wanting to redeem themselves by joining her came as a mild surprise, though.

"So," Kera began and hefted the thick stack of files, print-outs, and dossier material onto the table so that they seemed to appear from out of thin air, "is this your handiwork, by chance? I was wondering who the hell left it on my doorstep."

Lia and Johnny froze, blinking. The former nodded. "Yes. I applied for a job at a shipping facility in Playa Del Rey owned by El Peluquero with the intention of gathering information on him and his followers and how their operation runs. My, ah, past experience in a similar industry and my professionalism got me the position easily after the usual hazing and flirtation."

It made sense now that Kera thought about it. "I'm not sure, though," she commented, "why you want to go to all this trouble and put yourselves at risk. Is it because you figured I was going to come after you, and this is your way of proving beyond all doubt that you're on the right side of the law now?"

Johnny chuckled. "I got a bullshit retail job. That's *my* way of proving I'm going legit. Hope it's good enough for you."

Kera turned to look at him. "It is. There's no shame in honest work. I'm a bartender, remember? You tried to strongarm my boss and then shot up my bike. I've *almost* forgiven you for that, though, so keep up the good work, and we'll call it even."

"Sure." He took his sunglasses off for the first time and rubbed his eyes. "And I'm willing to go along with Lia's insane idea here, but don't involve me too much, right? I want to *keep* my job. I do *not* need to end up on the news. Someone might recognize me from the old days and start blabbing. I don't want to end up like Pauline."

Lia waved a hand. "We've been over this, Johnny. You won't have to do anything that will get you in trouble."

Shrugging, Kera agreed there was no need for him to break any further laws or attract unwanted attention. Then she turned back to the main subject at hand.

"Right, so, El Peluquero. You two know what I'm capable of. And honestly, even I am hesitant about this guy. We've had a couple run-ins with him and his men. The first time we couldn't do anything without getting killed. The second time, we thought we had things under control, but we barely escaped with our lives."

Immediately she wondered if it had been a good idea to blab her fears and concerns to them. They might be less inclined to aid her if they thought she was afraid.

As if confirming her doubts, Johnny shot Lia a grimacing glance. She clearly saw it but pretended not to.

"Yes," Lia replied, "that is a fair assessment. The Barber is no one to be trifled with. In addition to the violent methods he has been using against his rivals, he's also dealing in exceptionally dangerous and addictive drugs. And he seems to have connections to the illegal arms trade, which makes him that much more formidable. But he's not invincible."

Chris spoke up. "True. No one is."

Johnny squinted at him. "You the type who lives dangerously, friend? No offense, but you look more like a fuckin' office worker." His tone was mocking.

Resisting the temptation to smack him or magically toss him across the room, Kera decided to let Chris fend for himself.

He shrugged. While she could sense that he was rankled by the comment, it didn't affect him much.

"Yes," he stated, "I *am* an office worker. But since I met Kera, my life has gotten a lot more interesting, and she has taught me quite a few things. I don't claim to be a huge badass, but I'll do what I can to help."

Good man, Kera thought, and a tingling surge of pride in him swelled in her gut. *He didn't back away, stumbling over his words. He owned up firmly and maintained his dignity.*

Johnny put his sunglasses back on, perhaps to disguise that he was rolling his eyes, but he shut up.

Lia waved a hand. "Whatever. If you've been reviewing those documents, you have some idea of the scope of El Peluquero's operation. It also hints at his weaknesses, which are not obvious, but they do exist. We think we can help you exploit those weaknesses to take him down."

Kera felt Stephanie's discomfort. During their battle in Van Nuys, it had seemed like the Barber's men had a contingency plan in place for every possible development and were always two steps ahead. The only thing they couldn't have prepared for was magic. Otherwise, they would have won.

Kera relented. "Okay. Please tell me about them."

Lia, who was no stranger to giving presentations, outlined everything she knew about the drug lord's business. From her past experience working for Pauline and her formal business education, she was able to identify problem areas that could represent soft points in his proverbial armor. Kera nodded as she spoke.

"My conclusion," Lia explained, "is that El Peluquero is at his weakest at times like now, when he is in the process of consolidating his power in a given area. He doesn't seem to show his face much, and rules largely through intermediaries and the strength of his mysterious reputation. His position is tenuous."

Kera was beginning to see the possibilities. She readjusted her shirt, felt the sweat residue, and reminded herself to take a shower after her guests departed. "Go on," she urged the other woman.

Lia did. "The Barber prefers to take over the workforces of his rivals after he has eliminated them. That is smart, insofar as it prevents him from being too widely hated, but it also means his newer and lower-level employees do not feel any personal loyalty toward him. They are motivated by fear and opportunism and would likely abandon him if they could. His calculating and pragmatic approach breeds respect with criminals, but again, they are not loyal to him on a gut-emotional level. This also means that without him holding things together, his operation would dissolve into smaller, weaker factions post-haste."

Kera's eyes went distant. There was much to consider. When

her mind had finished its initial processing of all the new information, she shifted gears. There was more she needed and wanted to learn from the small woman before she agreed to her implied proposal.

"Lia," she began, "thank you for all you've done. You too, Johnny, since I'm guessing you helped as well. Plus, you look extremely unhappy to be here, which is part of what makes me think your story is true. It was brave of you both to infiltrate that place, not to mention come and talk to me. Of course, the warning I gave you that night at Pauline's place? That still stands."

Johnny smiled, though there was no warmth to it. "Yeah, we figured."

Before Lia could attempt to wrap up the conversation, Kera asked, "There's one more thing I need to know. What exactly do you want from me? What do you expect in return for having aided me with this project?"

Lia's mouth opened and shut, and Kera could feel the pulse of her emotions. It was obvious that her motivation, whatever it was, was important to her, yet she couldn't verbalize it clearly.

In the interim, Johnny piped up. "What I want is to be left alone. Like I said, I'm trying to go straight. I don't want any more trouble. All I ask is that you give me the benefit of the doubt. Like, if one or two of my old friends show up and start talking about dumb illegal shit we did in the past, that doesn't mean I'm planning to do anything like that now, okay? If they suggest it, I'll say no, and if that isn't good enough, I'll leave town."

He waited, breathing out, for Kera's response.

She did not like the man. He had personally affronted her in the past in ways beyond what many other people had, though they were worse than he was. Something about his sly, abrasive demeanor annoyed her.

Yet, she found herself respecting him for the first time since he had crudely hit on her at the Mermaid prior to threatening her boss. Like Chris, he was owning up to his personal shortcomings while maintaining his self-respect. Standing his ground and facing the world.

"Johnny," she said, "I think that's more than fair. If you're sincere, and I think you are, there won't be any problems, and I will honestly wish you the best with the rest of your life."

He was as still as a statue for a moment, and he said nothing. Then he sniffed and ran a hand through his slick black hair. "Well, that's a relief."

Lia put a hand on her friend's forearm. "You were never an evil person, Johnny, just kind of an asshole at times." She turned back at Kera, and her eyes were like deep black pools. "I hope the same is true for me. I suppose my reason for doing this is to prove to myself that it *is* true. That despite how disastrously misguided Pauline was at the end, my reasons for following her really *were* as idealistic as I told everyone. That it wasn't all a sham, and I'm not simply an amoral careerist who is willing to go along with things I know to be wrong."

While Kera contemplated what she had said, Stephanie commented, "Sounds right, in all honesty. Most people who have any decency will start to question what they've done at some point in their lives."

Kera glanced at her friend, then back at the two hopefully-reformed criminals. "I'm inclined to agree. If we go through with this, and nothing you've said or done turns out to be a ploy against me or a way to advance yourselves with the new boss or something like that, I will consider you trustworthy."

Lia closed her eyes. She did not move or speak, but the emanation of relief and fulfillment from deep within her was obvious.

"Thank you," she stated. Her eyes flicked back open, and she was back to business. "Now, I had mentioned that there's something coming up that will provide us with an opportunity to move against the Barber. It's info I only became aware of yesterday evening, so it was not with the documents I left for you."

Kera leaned in closer. "Yes?"

"In two nights," Lia elaborated, "El Peluquero will be moving against a major shipyard down in Long Beach. His power is currently greatest in the western part of the city, and since his ploy to take over that place up in the Valley failed, he particularly wants to consolidate his influence in the south before he moves on."

Nodding, Kera said, "Makes sense." Her hands clenched, and she thought back to her and Steph's difficult encounter at the warehouse in Van Nuys. It had provided her with a great many memories she would rather not have, but if what Lia had said was true, they'd succeeded. They had stopped the Barber from expanding northward.

Lia went on. "Since it's a large facility and it's so important to the growth of his empire in Southern California, he will be overseeing the operation personally."

Grim silence fell over the room. All five grasped the implications.

Kera breathed in and held it. "Then we'll be there, too."

CHAPTER EIGHTEEN

Pavla stepped out the church door and gravitated toward the rear corner of the property, which was close to the nearby encircling derelict buildings. Out back, it was like one was standing on the corner of a normal city block, which was oddly comforting to her despite how rundown the neighborhood was. It reminded her vaguely of one of her old loitering spots from when she had been a young woman in Prague.

She needed a cigarette. She seldom smoked these days since it was a foolish and unhealthy habit. Magic healed the damage to her lungs, but it was better to avoid such things altogether. Still, once in a while, it helped her relax.

Night had fallen within the last half an hour, and the city had that lovely tension that seemed to engulf large metropolises when natural light was replaced by the artificial electric kind. There was a sense that the grinding slog of business and work was coming to an end, and now, at last, the possibilities for fun and trouble were opening up.

It was bittersweet. Leaning against the old church's corner bricks, smoking in light puffs and holding the smoke in her mouth before breathing it into the air, Pavla could think of nothing but her own endlessly grinding slog. For her, nighttime meant the beginning of work and a battery of tasks that never seemed complete.

Still, she tried to enjoy the moment. Olina and Belen were gone, mercifully, until the wee hours of the morning. Anezka had dispatched them on a largely pointless errand to shop for groceries and supplies while judging the mood of the city among the average folk.

After three or four peaceful minutes had passed, gentle footsteps and the swishing of long skirts sounded from around the church, and Pavla felt a familiar aura approaching.

It was Anezka. At once, Pavla grasped that her superior had come out here to meet her as an equal for the time being. She liked her better this way. Sadly, it seemed that it happened less and less as time went on.

"Good evening, Pavla," she opened. "I have not seen you smoke in a year or more."

Her tone and demeanor were softer, less haughty and formal.

Pavla gave a wan smile. "It is a vice I like to indulge from time to time. All people have them, do they not?"

"Of course." Anezka laughed, and then it was as though they were schoolgirls together, sharing gossip. "You know about my chocolate drawer. Do not pretend otherwise. We still possess the same silly tendencies as all other people in the end. Belen seems to have a fondness for pornographic romance novels. *That* is something that does not bear thinking about."

Pavla laughed. "Somehow, I am hardly surprised. There is nothing I would put past that little woman. She thinks she will be inducted as a formal member if she kisses our boots enough."

"Oh, I noticed," Anezka confirmed, tittering. "Americans are so ambitious, such self-promoters. Every one of them dreams of becoming a celebrity, which is perhaps why they spend so much time mocking other celebrities. Envy, at bottom."

Shaking her head, Pavla quipped, "Ah, yes, Kera mentioned

something about that."

Abruptly, the pleasantries were over. It was as though all the moisture in the air around them had turned to ice and frost.

"You realize, Pavla," Anezka said, her voice lowering to little more than a hiss, "that you are at the end of your grace period. Your past performance and reputation have protected you thus far from failures that would already have been punished in a lesser witch."

Pavla maintained control over her emotions and did not react in an untoward or excessive way. She didn't try to disguise her cold disgust, either. She was tired of being threatened.

"Of course I realize that," she spat, "since you and the other senior members, to say nothing of Olina, have taken to reminding me of it every single time you have seen me lately."

Anezka's eyes narrowed, and Pavla knew it was foolish of her to have responded with anything other than groveling deference. The woman next to her was no longer her old friend. She was back to being the haughty, unforgiving grandmistress of the coven.

"Take heart," she suggested, and there was sardonic cruelty in her voice, "because I promise you shall *not* be reminded again. You will never hear this admonition another time after tonight. This is your final warning. It is either Kera or you. One of you must die. If you do not destroy her, we will have no choice but to fill the void you've left and destroy both of you."

Pavla gave a single slow nod. She understood far better than most people could, given her long membership in the organization. Part of the reason Anezka had risen to leadership over the coven was her complete willingness to always, *always* put the ruthless needs of the institution first and her personal sentiments a distant second.

"I know," was all Pavla said.

Anezka stood watching her, and a small flicker of her human self—the part of her that was Pavla's friend—returned.

"Why, Pavla, have you given even the slightest thought to disloyalty? Why have you considered failing to back the Orthodoxy against this one stupid young witch? For decades we have watched your back, lifted you up, showered you with honor for your achievements, and given you a place in the world in which to exercise your talents."

Pavla took a long drag on her cigarette. It was little more than a tiny nub of ash by now, so she extinguished it and flicked it into one of the piles of debris surrounding the building. If a fire started, it would amuse her. They could easily put it out.

"It's true that the Orthodoxy has been good to me. Without it, I would be a thoroughly average and anonymous individual at best."

Lately, though, she had been wondering if that would be a bad thing.

"Or," she went on, "worse yet, my powers might have drawn the wrong kind of attention from the authorities or from angry citizens. I have been able to use the gifts the universe gave me, and for that, I am thankful. You know this, Anezka."

Her superior smiled. "Perhaps I do, but I know something else, as well. You *did* consider backing this person, this Kera MacDonagh, against us. Perhaps you only considered it for a moment. Perhaps you have considered it over and over for weeks. Do not insult me by denying that you have done so."

Pavla looked down at her feet. She didn't slump her shoulders since the posture was not one of shame but of contemplation.

"Betraying the Orthodoxy is not something I have seriously thought about," she stated, "but it is true that I would rather Kera avoid destruction. She is a...*valuable* person in more ways than one."

"Oh?" Anezka replied, raising her thin black eyebrows in mock surprise. "Do elaborate. Beyond, of course, that her power would have made her a useful asset to us."

Pavla hugged her arms around her midsection and stared into

the night sky. With all the light generated by the city, she couldn't see the stars.

"Kera was the first person I have gone after," she explained, "who has made me realize how far I have come. How much has gradually changed over the decades."

She couldn't tell if it would be better to shut up and say only what Anezka wanted to hear or to be at least partially honest. She worried that if she did nothing but repeat the official mantra in a sullen tone, Anezka would suspect her of further secret disobedience.

But if she admitted to part of the truth, it might satisfy the grandmistress enough to get her off Pavla's back.

Anezka listened, unspeaking.

"I trained Kera," Pavla continued, "and that is something I have rarely done before recruitment was complete. It happened more...naturally, organically, than what I am used to. It was the little steps, followed by more little steps, building up to further small steps, which gradually amounted to a huge leap."

Anezka ran the fingers of her left hand through her dark hair. "Yes, that is how training is supposed to work. What do you mean?"

"I mean that witnessing her journey in accelerated time made me examine her and how *she* changed over the brief period we worked together. Seeing that, I saw myself and how I have changed, too. The girl I once was..." Pavla sighed. "She would not recognize the woman I am now."

Anezka moved closer by half a step. "Are you implying that you feel you have taken the wrong path in life? I hope not."

Pavla frowned. "I did not mean to cast aspersion on the Orthodoxy. It has more to do with the nature of the threats around us."

"Good," the grandmistress affirmed, "since you, and I and all of us have seen what happens in the world when there is no strong order to hold things together. Misinformation spreads.

What was once rigorous becomes sloppy. Divisions increase. The authorities have no choice but to step in. The world of witchcraft is better off with us presiding over it, and I hope you remember that the next time you doubt the necessity of what you must do to stop a rogue actor from destroying much of the progress we have made."

Pavla shivered. Her earlier impression, that the air had grown colder when Anezka's mood shifted, was not entirely in her head, nor was it a magical effect. It *was* getting chilly out despite it still being summer. The weather in Los Angeles was strangely erratic at times.

"I did not say I will refuse to do what I must," Pavla pointed out. "I understand why our coven exists, and I agree. I simply do not like the world we live in these days. Things have grown so ugly and complicated. I only hope that we can somehow still make a difference."

With that, she considered the conversation over. She placed a hand on Anezka's shoulder and gave her a fast, light kiss on the cheek. It was partly a friendly and familiar gesture and partly a formal display of reverence and obedience.

The grandmistress said nothing; her pale face was impassive. Pavla turned and walked away.

She went back into the church and grabbed her jacket for protection against the brisk night air and her satchel of materials. There was work to do.

As she left the Orthodoxy's temporary headquarters behind, Pavla reflected on what was to come: preparations and further planning on top of all the organization and scheming and calculation she had done previously. Steeling herself. Resolving to do it.

The time had come to set the trap. Her target must fall into it. And, if her predictions were even close to correct, and her courage held, she *would* fall into it.

"And then," the witch mumbled under her breath as she strode into the dark maze of alleys, "this will finally be over."

Kera had to keep biting her tongue to keep control of her amusement. It was *so* tempting to risk screwing everything up by making a smartass comment. She kept trying to think of a way she could joke about the subject without pissing Johnny off too much.

He had changed his mind with startling rapidity. It was as though after having proven to himself that he could convince other people to tell him what he wanted to hear—for example, that he wouldn't have to participate in the coming raid—he had reverted to going along with whatever they wanted.

He was coming with them after all. The team they took into battle against El Peluquero would consist of five people instead of four.

Finally, it occurred to her.

"Be careful, Johnny," she called to him. "If you do too good a job, I might start getting the idea that you want to be here."

Lia snickered.

"Ha, ha," Johnny retorted. "Believe me, I'd rather be...well, not at my regular job, but maybe at home with a fuckin' beer or something. Or a joint. That doesn't count as breaking the law, does it?"

Kera extended her hand flat and wiggled it. "Ehh. I'll allow it."

"Hey, Kera," said Chris, "when this is over, I promise I'll help clean up the place." If anything, he was making the least mess of the five, but she thanked him anyway.

They had transformed half her warehouse into a workshop. There were a lot of preparations that needed to be made before they conducted the raid: gear and equipment to get ready, supplies to be organized, papers to go through, and computers and phones to set up with the necessary programs.

While they worked, Lia explained in more detail what they could expect. In particular, she seemed to have reliable, accurate, and highly detailed information about where the Barber would be and what he would be doing.

"El Peluquero will not arrive right away," Lia pointed out. "He will begin by sending in his most trusted and elite operatives to secure the location and eliminate major resistance, as well as to establish escape routes and contingency plans against any intrusions by law enforcement. Or vigilantes."

Kera smirked. As formidable as their opponent was, she doubted his men had reported *exactly* what had happened in Van Nuys. Upon seeing thaumaturgic spells deployed against them, they had probably fudged the details to avoid appearing crazy or incompetent. Their boss was not expecting to be attacked via magic.

Lia went on. "The operation will take place across two adjacent blocks of the wharves. This time, rather than trying to kill the shipyard's leadership as they typically did before, they are going to seize control of the place while the current owners are away and essentially hold it hostage. They plan to assassinate the owners later, and draft their workforce and commandeer their stock in the meantime."

"Devious," Chris remarked. "Some of the corporate sharks who run the types of places I work for could take lessons from this guy. If they haven't already, that is. Who knows?"

"Eh," Johnny countered, "he hasn't been in LA long enough to advise the white-collar criminals yet. Give him time, and he probably will."

Lia snapped, "*Anyway,* as I was saying, the documents and briefings I read and the phone calls I listened in on were somewhat vague and coded, but by reading between the lines, I was able to guess the nature of their plan.

"There is a long walkway that runs along a wall between the two big wharves. Once his men are confident that everything is secure, El Peluquero will be on the walkway, so he can easily go back and forth to observe both blocks. Most of it is exposed, which means his troops can keep an eye on him the majority of the time. But not *all* the time."

A hush fell over them, and the five paused in their labors to listen intently. Kera felt sizzling excitement grow within her. Perversely, she was kind of looking forward to the struggle to come. Part of her thrived on conflict and danger. She had always been that way.

Catching her breath, Lia continued, "There are two points on the walkway where a person cannot be seen by any of the people on either side. Basically, small support struts. Once the Barber is behind one of those on the opposite side from where we'll strike, we will make our move."

"Oh," said Stephanie. "See, it makes more sense now. Like, I was wondering how the hell we're supposed to get away with disguising me as him. Sure, the illusion might work, but if the real him is right next to me? I don't think so. I'm not much of an actress, truth be told."

Kera laughed. "You'll be fine. Anyway, if I can get the rest of the job done quickly enough, it will only be for like a minute anyway."

Chris, who was tinkering with their phones, piped up. "I believe in you, Steph. You're a waitress, right? You have to pretend to be cheerful, even to customers who are total asshats. Think of it that way."

Stephanie patted him on the shoulder. "You know, I think you're right. Still, we should probably do drills on my performance before showtime."

For another five minutes, they worked in silence. There was a sense among all of them that the task they faced was doable but far from easy. They had no way of being certain about what they were getting themselves into.

Kera, her mind moving on to something else, snapped her

fingers and turned again to Lia. "You said earlier that the Barber's guys are going to clear things out and set up escape plans for him before he arrives. Do we know which direction he'll be coming from? What kind of vehicle he'll be in? Or what his points of egress are, and what their evacuation plans might be? That would be helpful so we can cut him off in advance if he tries to flee the scene."

Lia frowned. "I'm afraid not. They didn't mention anything of the sort. The impression I get is that El Peluquero makes those plans with his top bodyguards and deliberately avoids sharing the information with anyone else, probably so his other minions can't divulge it if they're captured or compromised."

"Operational security," Johnny mused. "I hear the prepper and self-defense guys talking about that sometimes. This dude probably has a military background, or his troops do. Mercs who make better bank off a 'private entrepreneur' like him than they did from their governments."

"Yeah," Kera agreed. "Could well be, which means we need to be super on-the-ball when we go after them. Okay, so to tie it all together... Steph, you're going to imitate the Barber when he's out of sight and distract his followers. While that's going on, I'll sneak around behind you all and destroy the drug shipments in their containers. That way, even if the bastard gets away, his victory will be hollow, and the assholes who own the shipyards won't get to distribute that shit either."

Chris chuckled. "Nice. An army marches on its stomach, they say, and criminals can't feed themselves if they don't have drugs to sell." His face grew serious. "Though they could probably sell some of their guns or hire themselves out as hitmen to other syndicates. Ugh, sorry I said that."

"No," Lia reassured him, "you're correct. Drugs are the easiest way to make a profit in the underworld. El Peluquero might be able to switch to a different industry, but it would disrupt things enough that we would buy more time to deal with him."

Kera interjected, "Yeah, but if all goes well, we'll capture him this time, and then it will be over. That's phase two. That's when you guys—Lia, Johnny, and Chris—move in to help get the Barber into a car so we can deliver him to the police."

Lia raised a hand. "If I may, it might be better to take him to federal law enforcement in case he has paid off or threatened anyone local. People like him rarely get as far as they do without a certain amount of aid from dirty cops."

Kera shrugged. "Okay, we'll look up the nearest FBI field office. I'm not sure I trust them either since they seem to have their own agenda half the time, but the important thing is that El Peluquero can't have his men kidnap their kids or transfer a six-figure sum into their bank account in exchange for letting him go."

Johnny cleared his throat. "You could kill him. That would make things simpler."

The room went quiet.

"Well," Chris observed, "he has a point. But Kera will be doing most of the heavy lifting, so I think that's up to her."

Her nostrils flared as she breathed in, then slowly exhaled through her mouth.

"I'd rather not," she stated. "I don't like killing people. If I *have to*, I will. But if we can take him alive and let the law deal with him, that is by far the preferred way to do it. And please don't argue with me about this. It isn't only about how much I like it or don't like it, it's also about letting LA feel like things are under control again. If the Barber gets bumped off under shady circumstances, people will think it's another gang hit or something. 'Motorcycle Woman' doesn't need to get tagged with the reputation of being a murderer, either, or the authorities might shift gears and decide *I'm* the biggest problem in the city these days."

Stephanie nodded. "Yeah, you're right. We need to do this, but we need to look like the good guys while we're at it. That's how we win the long game."

"All right, fine." Johnny sighed. "I guess it's nice to know you didn't enjoy killing Pauline. That's not, you know, a criticism, I'm just saying. Do us a favor, though, and don't get me, or yourself, or anyone else killed by wanting to do this the kind, gentle way. Okay?"

Kera grumbled, "We'll try our damnedest. Lia, is there anything else we should know?"

Lia brushed her hair away from her eyes. She took to manual labor pretty well, but it seemed unusual to see her under circumstances other than pure corporate professionalism. Then again, the first time she and Kera met had been in a taekwondo fight at Pauline's headquarters.

"Yes. Getting to where we need to be, especially in regards to incapacitating El Peluquero, will be easier thanks to a shortcut I discovered."

Kera practically bounced on her feet with curiosity. "Yeah?"

"There is a tiny stairway that leads up onto the wall, the one spanning both wharves. It's blocked off and disused now, but it should be easy for you, with all of your...abilities...to access it. I don't think the Barber or his men know about it, but I could be wrong. Nonetheless, it would make a good, unobtrusive point of entrance and exit."

They all returned to their various tasks, sensing that most of the talking that needed to be done was complete.

"Lia," said Kera, "thanks again. How did you get all this information, anyway? Or don't I want to know? Sorry, that sounds bad. Don't take it the wrong way."

The woman's face tightened in annoyance, but she got over it. "Much of it is part of my new job. The rest I acquired via a combination of hacking, conjecture, deduction, and talking to people."

Chris laughed. "That'll do it. Especially the 'hacking' part."

CHAPTER NINETEEN

Johnny had more or less promoted himself again. Given that he had hands-on street-level experience and knew enough of the lingo to fit in easily with a bunch of mob-owned dock workers, he had reluctantly agreed to act as one of the "field operatives" for their mission.

"*Don't* thank me yet," he grumbled as he laid out his nice suit and jacket on the counter and hastily changed into casual clothes. "It's not like I'm going to do all the heavy shit myself. I'm your mole, not your goddamn bodyguard. You two have *magic*, after all."

Kera and Stephanie were in the process of suiting up behind a sheet Kera had hung on her chin-up bar to act as a makeshift screen.

She said, "Good point. And no, we don't expect you to take on six guys in hand-to-hand combat while we fiddle with a computer, so don't worry. If things get ugly, we would appreciate it if you remained nearby in case we need you, but we probably won't. You can make yourself scarce if the lead starts flying."

"Fantastic." He grunted as he slipped on cargo pants and a light flannel shirt. "Man, I haven't dressed like a stereotypical cholo in, like, ten years. Well, maybe eight. Something like that. Fuck, I hope I don't bump into anyone I used to know back in the barrio. There were a couple guys who went down to Long Beach. I dunno where they work now, though."

Stephanie zipped up her black catsuit. "It's nice to know I can fit into this thing. Taking up magic might be the best thing I ever done for my figure."

"Ehh," Kera opined. "It's overrated. Half my clothes got way too baggy. I guess that's one nice thing about form-fitting leather."

Chris, waiting nearby and casually listening to all that was said, chimed in, "By all means, keep wearing form-fitting leather. Ideally, it's not only for superhero stealth missions. Is there some way you could wear it into the shower, but, like, accidentally leave your phone camera on and pointed at the stall? I have to ask."

Kera bit her lip. "We'll see about that. Maybe later. How are you two doing on your end?"

It had been determined that everyone should contribute to the mission according to their skills. Thus, if they were, say, a law enforcement task force in a movie, Chris and Lia would be the ones who stayed behind in the van with the headsets looking at screens and shouting dramatic warnings to the men and women out kicking ass.

Lia said, "Everything is fine. At least, all of the, um, mundane programs and tech we'll be using is. I still feel that we ought to do a test run of this bizarre idea of yours to enchant the camera. You don't seem overly confident that it will work, and frankly, I've never worked with anything like that before."

She seemed uncomfortable. Earlier, during a rare moment of letting her guard down, Lia had admitted to having watched the Playa Del Rey shipyard's security cam footage and being severely creeped out by the sight of Kera phasing in and out.

Steph answered the question before Kera could. "We would

love to do a test, but since it's a spell neither of us has tried before, we can't risk wasting all the energy that will go into it. We'll have to see how it goes when we get there, and if it *doesn't* work, a regular camera setup with you guys reporting the details should still be helpful, right?"

"Right," Chris agreed. "In a way, it will be kind of disappointing if all we have to do is keep the machine running and let them beam the info straight into your heads. It would be more fun if I got to do all the reporting of what's on the feed into your earbuds. Black ops shit."

Kera laughed, but her mirth was short-lived. "Understandable, but people get killed during black ops. And if you guys are shouting into a microphone, someone might hear and come investigate the mysterious vehicle sitting around the corner. Someone with a rocket launcher. That would be bad."

Lia pointed out, "I have reason to believe El Peluquero *does* have rocket launchers, by the way. That's not an exaggeration. He has virtually every form of small arms known to man, including a couple of crossbows."

"*Crossbows?*" Johnny blurted. "What the hell century is this?"

Kera scratched her head. "I think it's the twenty-first, but an arrow through the neck is just as lethal as it was in the fifteenth. And crossbows make a lot less noise than guns, even a lot of suppressed guns, so I'm assuming that's what they're for."

Chris squinted. "Unless he believes in vampires. And if he does, he might also believe in witches."

"Doubtful," said Lia. "The Barber is known for being extremely pragmatic. His organization is run like a modern corporation with military overtones. They do not seem like the type of people who would indulge in superstition."

Stephanie stretched in her new outfit. "Okay, great. Except magic *isn't* a superstition, and we can't be sure he doesn't know that."

"True." Kera looked around, her mind wandering. "But we're

going to have to chance it. We don't have time to do an intel roundup on obscure shit like that."

She noticed that Johnny had finished dressing and was standing in place, looking at the wall and doing nothing as though absorbed in gloomy thoughts. Kera came up behind him and gently put a hand on his arm. He tensed but didn't withdraw or say anything.

"Hey. Johnny." She kept her tone gentle. Though he still wasn't her favorite person, he'd improved enough that she was willing to be nice. It was obvious that he was still afraid of her.

He cleared his throat, and without looking at her, he asked, "Yeah? What?"

"Why are you helping me? You act like you don't want to be here, and you said we weren't allowed to 'force' you to do anything. I said you didn't have to if you didn't want to. You pretty much volunteered for this, you realize. Lia said she's here to redeem herself, basically. I'm curious what your rationale is. Enlighten me?"

His mouth squirmed on his face while he tried to think of something to say.

"I'm not sure. I guess it's something lame like 'the enemy of my enemy is my friend.' That's not exactly right, but it's the best I can come up with. I don't want this Hairdresser guy taking over the city, especially since I work close to this fuckin' wharf he's moving on. Next thing you know, his guys are going to be coming up to me and saying, 'Hey, Johnny Torrez, we heard you used to work for blah blah blah' and making me offers I can't refuse. Like I said before, I'm done with that life."

Kera detected a mishmash of emotions within him. He was confused, to some extent, about his own reasons, but he was not willfully being deceitful.

She shrugged. "Fair enough. I believe you. If you were to say that it was partly because you want to make sure we're okay—Lia especially, and maybe even me—you wouldn't have to be embarrassed by it. I wouldn't make fun of you."

"Whatever," he grumbled. "Let's just get this over with and do it right. Actually, I don't want my face showing up on a goddamn camera later. Can you, like, cast a spell to make me look like someone else?"

Kera was annoyed with herself for not having thought of that earlier or suggesting it. "Yes. It will take some of my energy, but not too much. I think between Stephanie and me, we can manage. We'll wait till we're almost there, however. It might wear off too quickly if we do it beforehand."

He responded with a wan smile. "Okay. Thanks."

The next step in their preparations was loading the vehicles. Given that some of the stuff they'd be putting into Chris' Jeep and Johnny's Mustang was either inherently illegal or at least highly suspicious, Kera was more grateful than ever that she lived in a warehouse.

Once the big front door was open, they pulled in both vehicles side by side and closed it behind them before loading the computer setups, cameras, changes of clothes, emergency food and water and caffeine for the two thaumaturges, first aid kits, and of course, the weaponry.

At last, Chris and Steph had legally armed themselves along with Kera with a Magnum revolver and a bolt-action rifle respectively to complement her semi-automatic pistol. The hope was that none of the guns would be necessary, but as the saying went, better to have them and not need them...

Johnny and Lia were packing heat too. Johnny still had his old Beretta from his gangster days. He did not legally own the gun and had been thinking of getting rid of it for that reason alone, but he didn't like the thought of being unarmed.

"If I have to use it again," he pointed out, "I can probably get away with saying I pulled it off one of the guys at the wharf. Not that suspicious to find a secondhand gun at a place owned by a bunch of criminals."

Lia, meanwhile, who technically did not have a criminal record, had acquired a subcompact .380 pistol and slipped it into her dress. She too hoped it would be unnecessary.

With everything done, Kera addressed the troops.

"Okay, everyone," she announced. "We've been working toward this all day. We're about as well prepared as we're likely to get, and we have good insider information thanks to our new friends. El Peluquero is no one to mess around with, but he's also used to winning. He doesn't have any way of knowing what we're plotting, and he isn't prepared to deal with a well-organized strike like this, combined with magic. We're going to win."

Chris clapped. "I have a positive feeling about this. Really, I do."

Grinning, Kera snapped, "Shut up, Chris. But thanks. Seriously though, after everything I did to try to clean up this city, this son of a bitch has come in and is sending things back into the shitter. We're going to dismantle his empire and see that he ends up in jail where he belongs. Steph and I were able to foil one of his operations already. Barely, yeah, but still. With all five of us, *we can do this*. Don't panic or doubt yourself. Crazier things have happened."

With that, they went to their assigned vehicles. Kera and Stephanie would be riding her motorcycle, as usual; Johnny would be alone in his car (but might have to getaway-drive for someone else, if necessary); and Lia and Chris would be in his Jeep along with their remote viewing tech. It would be a more cramped setup than the standard "party van" in the movies, but it would suffice.

Before he climbed behind the wheel, Kera gave him a hug. "Be careful."

"You should talk," he observed, "but thanks. I will. Love you."

She smiled, and for a second, she was afraid she might get misty-eyed. "Love you too. See you later."

Since the plan required Johnny, Lia, and Chris to arrive near the Long Beach docks beforehand, Kera and Stephanie were the last ones to leave. The last thing they did before they mounted Zee and took off was look at a map of the area in which they would be operating.

The wharves of the shipyard El Peluquero was moving against were located off Terminal Road on a narrow peninsula that extended into the harbor. Though the roads were busy during the day and not far from residences and even police and fire stations, at night it was a quiet, obscure area. There were no houses or businesses immediately nearby.

"Okay," Kera murmured, fixing the location in her mind. "Got it. You ready?"

Steph climbed onto the bike behind her and wrapped her arms around her friend's waist. "Let's go."

Pavla had determined with relative ease that El Peluquero's next activity would be at a shipyard located off Terminal Road on a narrow peninsula in Long Beach.

While scoping out the location beforehand, she had cast a couple of spells designed to obscure it from attention. The cops would not show up or notice any untoward activity unless it was something as blatant as an exploding fireball or an extended gunfight with unsuppressed automatic weapons.

"Good," she said to herself, and a calm feeling of satisfaction came over her. After all the uncertainty and strife she had been through lately, it seemed things were going to work out exactly as planned.

The trap would be sprung. Her target would fall.

She had several ruses and snares set up, though they were all of a similar nature. There were three main endpoint traps surrounding the wharves, with six peripheral trigger spells farther out, designed to funnel a magic-sensitive individual toward one of the inner three.

It was an ingenious setup, she felt. She had read about such things being used, but not very often, and the details were of her own invention.

Each of the six outer traps was like a beacon, a kind of psychic will-o-the-wisp calling out for help in the language of pure emotion. It would tug at the heartstrings of a compassionate person. Alternately, it would provide an irresistible form of bait to a ruthless person, the type who moved in to kick people who were down. Either way, it would work. It was all a matter of interpretation.

Once the outer traps had been sprung, they would direct the target toward one of the three inner ones. That was where the hammer would fall. The primary snares were a combination of pure spell-weaving and material components.

First, the unfortunate individual would stumble onto an echo of the phantasmal cry for help, thinking they were nearly upon the aura of a person hiding nearby. Then the ruse would come to an end and the curse would be sprung, physically immobilizing the victim.

At the same instant, a net of translucent mesh, woven throughout with bits of iron and silver, would drop from on high. Pavla had located several overhead objects where the nets could be easily concealed with the help of a bit of cloaking. Once within the net, not only would her target be unable to move, but they would be unable to perform the slightest magic, finding it blocked on all sides.

She looked at the sky. It was beautiful out over the sea; she had spent much of her life in landlocked countries or regions and had forgotten how wistful the ocean made her. The clouds were dark since the sun had faded.

Pavla climbed onto a pile of rocks beside the pier from which she could observe all that happened. Though he was not her target, she was also curious to see what the Barber was up to and if any of his men would prove sensitive to the magical lures she had placed. If so, she would need to counter-enchant them to keep them from springing one of the traps prematurely and giving away the game.

With the inspection of everything else complete, Pavla double-checked her final last-resort measure.

In her purse was a Smith & Wesson M&P Shield in 9mm. It only had a seven-round magazine, but for such a small gun, one she only intended to use if all else failed, that ought to be more than sufficient.

She smirked. It was amusing that California had such strict firearms laws, yet it had only taken her about ninety minutes to find a reputable black market dealer who could supply her with a "no questions asked" pistol for a relatively reasonable asking price. Of course, she had used her abilities to convince him to sell it to her for almost nothing.

It had been years since the last time she had fired a gun. The Orthodoxy occasionally made use of them, usually Russian military surplus, but the general attitude was that they were crude weapons reserved for emergencies and that magic should always be the first, second, and third resorts.

But she had been decent at it. The noise and recoil did not intimidate her, and a simple low-energy-cost spell to focus and stabilize her perceptions would help with aim.

She wondered what Olina would think of her packing heat American-style. Most likely, the insufferable little woman would scoff and sneer and tell everyone back at the church about it as evidence of Pavla's incompetence.

"Oh, Olina," she said under her breath. "You will soon see how competent I am when I put my mind to things. When I know exactly what I must do." Fortunately, she had thrown off the other witch long enough to get the traps set, thus ensuring there would be no mistakes and no sabotage.

She checked the time. Olina ought to be arriving shortly, around the time Kera would probably be showing up. She was looking forward to it.

CHAPTER TWENTY

Since Ezeudo was continuing to string himself along, barely possessing the strength to complete his lessons as it was, James was all too happy to give him a nice, long two-hour break. He needed one himself.

And today was a special occasion. Sort of.

James stood about twenty yards from the front of his estate's front doors, his hands folded behind his back, patiently watching as a black limousine pulled up and came to a stop fifteen feet away from him. The chauffeur emerged and opened the rear passenger door, and out stepped Mother LeBlanc.

"Hiiii," James greeted her, unfastening one of his hands from his back to wave. "Welcome back. How was your trip? And all the other usual pleasantries, et cetera."

Her smile was partially amused, though to some extent, she looked annoyed that he would start joking around the instant she arrived after another long, tiresome journey.

"Thank you, James, and the trip was fine. New Orleans has changed a great deal in some ways. In others, it is the same as it always has been and likely will be for another millennium. Would you be so kind as to help me with my bags?"

He stepped forward and took one of her two suitcases. It was a polite gesture more than because she truly needed the help, of course. The chauffeur had been about to do it, but James waved him off.

"Someday," he mused, "I would like to visit that place. Sure, they say it's not the same since that wretched hurricane in, uh, 2005 I believe it was, but it's often regarded as one of America's most cultured cities. I think it was Truman Capote who ranked it alongside New York and San Francisco as among the most interesting and distinctive in the United States."

LeBlanc scoffed. "Alongside New York? N'awlins easily outclasses it, despite being smaller and having New York's awful summer weather last for three-quarters of the year there. Particularly these days, when New York has been commercialized to the point of self-parody."

James chuckled. "You may be on to something there. Most of the time, I'm quite content up here in the hills. New York has its charms, but I'd rather not drive through it. That reminds me, did you arrive at Albany? I believe you said you'd be doing that to save on the drive."

"Yes," she told him. "The layover was only forty-five minutes, which was hardly enough time to refresh myself in the ladies' room and cross the terminal before going through the ticketing rigmarole. Still far easier than having our poor driver take us through the Big Apple on our way up here, as you insisted on doing last time."

"Hah!" James riposted. "That was some sort of criticism, wasn't it? Well, it's nice to have you back, regardless."

"Perhaps it was," said LeBlanc in response to the first part. "The world may never know. Anyway, I would rather get settled in before you give me the full report, but if I may ask for the capsule version, how is our guest doing?"

There were a thousand things James could have said, and he

had been wracking his brain all day in search of the right way to explain everything to her.

For the moment, his only comment was, "He's coming along. It's been stressful, but he's managing."

"How vague," LeBlanc observed. "Nevertheless, that means it has not been a disaster unless you are doing an excellent job of lying to me. Let me unpack and have a cup of tea, then we'll meet in your study for a brief conference. I should also like to speak to Ezeudo afterward. Is he present?"

They reached the front doors, which one of the servants had opened. Stepping through and heading at once toward the stairs, James replied, "Yes, but he's taking a two-hour respite. Normally his breaks are shorter than that, but frankly, I needed one as well. Besides, you deserve a proper reception."

"That's sweet of you," she said in a flat tone, though he knew she meant it. "In any event, I would like privacy during the first round of our discussion. He can be brought in later."

They began ascending the steps to the second floor. "Right, right." James glanced toward Ezeudo's room; the door was closed. "There are a couple other things I'd like to talk about, too. Ripples in the pond from our recent adventures."

LeBlanc sighed. "Oh, dear. Yes, I heard about some of those while I was back home. I'm amazed that Lady Mitchell hasn't harangued us about it yet."

James felt his gorge rising. "I'm sure it's only a matter of time."

He dropped the suitcase off, then left LeBlanc to her own devices and retired to his study. He was confident she would rejoin him when she was ready. About half an hour later she did, knocking twice and letting herself in a second later.

James had prepared drinks for both of them, bourbon on the rocks. He handed her a tumbler, and once she had closed the door, he cast a sound shield around the room. LeBlanc could have done it, but she was probably more drained than he was after her flight.

LeBlanc sat in her favorite leather chair across from him. "Thank you for the drink. Now, then. Ezeudo. Tell me all about it."

Reclining in his seat and taking a slow, deep drink that was halfway between a sip and a full swig, James reorganized his thoughts and elaborated upon them.

"Lauren Jones has been in and out pretty regularly, and between her efforts and my own, we have kept Ezeudo on schedule. But only barely. He is smart and talented and is clearly trying his hardest, but he's also in early middle age, older than I am. He has half a lifetime's worth of habits to unlearn so he can relearn everything according to our methods, and we are running out of time. I'm pushing him hard, I know. So far we're doing okay, but he's fast approaching burnout. I don't think we can keep this up for a full year."

Mother LeBlanc frowned into her glass as she took a draught. "That is not surprising. You set up a highly optimistic regimen, from what I recall. But James, there is something I don't understand. Why are you so keen on finishing within a year? You seem virtually obsessed with the idea. Is this some ridiculous male honor or competitiveness thing? You promised it would only take him twelve months, so you feel you have to live up to that in order to preserve your trustworthiness?"

"Ehh," he answered her, swirling his ice cubes in the tumbler and watching the eddies of their meltwater mixing with the liquor. "That's part of it, I'll confess, but only the smaller part. A third, roughly, or maybe more like a quarter. The rest is...more complex."

LeBlanc leaned forward in her chair, her bright eyes fixed on him. Her expression and demeanor were neutral, curious, and accommodating. "Tell me."

Again, Lovecraft reviewed all the things he had planned to say to her, but they suddenly seemed stupid and poorly thought-out.

To stall for time while gradually approaching the main subject, he took a detour.

"As long as I have been a member of the Council of Thaumaturgy," he began, "our mission statement, our *raison d'etre* or whatever you want to call it, has been remarkably consistent. And yes, I realize I'm one of the younger, newer members, but still, I get the impression that things didn't change much before I joined, either."

"Correct," affirmed LeBlanc. "Your pronunciation of *raison d'etre* needs some work, though. One of these days, I'll get around to teaching you proper French."

He raised his glass. "Right, thanks. Umm. Anyway, our 'thing' has always been to preserve the knowledge and the craft and the discipline of our art. Each of us has his or her particular fixations and areas of expertise, but there's a sense that there is stability from generation to generation, going back *centuries*."

LeBlanc nodded. James went on.

"But it seemed to me that stability was turning into stagnation. None of us is getting any younger—notwithstanding those like yourself who don't age in the conventional sense—and we have not made any efforts to engage with the modern world. As I said when we first published the book, our traditions were in danger of dying out within the next hundred years. Unless we replenished our ranks."

Sighing, his friend said, "Yes, James, we have been over this before. If you are concerned with attrition over the next *hundred* years, then why the hurry to train Ezeudo in only *one?*"

"Because," he shot back, and his tone was snappier than he had meant it to sound, "the cat's out of the bag, and we were the ones who let it out. Mainly me. Don't you see? There isn't any going back to the old world where thaumaturges would trickle in over the decades, and everything remained a nice cozy secret. Our little cross-country trip convinced me of that."

LeBlanc's brow grew creased with concern and contemplation. "What you mean is that you believe releasing the book has spread our secrets too far and wide for us to maintain control over it all? We dealt with the various failed candidates, James. Or have you observed the rising of others?"

He gulped down another larger mouthful of his beverage. "Yes and no. I haven't specifically scried any manifestations of power, in part because I've been too busy training our newcomer to deal with that and in part because I wouldn't want him to see that. He might start asking questions. He has a slightly suspicious nature and a rather inquisitive mind, and we don't need him distracted by other things with all the work we've thrown at him."

At that, both of them heard footsteps approaching the study, the footsteps of a tall, lanky individual, undoubtedly Ezeudo. At the mouth of the hallway, they stopped. There was a moment's hesitation, then their student turned and walked away, probably after realizing they were having a private conversation which he ought not disturb.

"So," James continued, "instead, I've been sneaking peeks at the Internet, keeping abreast of what all has been going on in Los Angeles and in other parts of the country and the world. Things have become...interesting. Perhaps you heard about some of it."

He proceeded to fill her in on the apparent copycat vigilantism in LA, likely the work of other independent actors trying to fill Motorcycle Man's shoes, and on the buzz that the Eastern European coven known as the Orthodoxy was trying to expand into the United States.

LeBlanc listened to all of it without interrupting, and she frowned as she took it in. The picture James painted grew more worrisome the longer he spoke.

"We thought," he concluded, "that we had everything under control. That we had shut down the powers of all those troublesome individuals who would not have made good students and put it all to bed. Yet I suspect that we, er, 'activated' far more people than we realized."

His partner looked at the wall. "That was what I too feared," she said in a low voice.

"Yeahhh." James finished his drink and set the tumbler roughly on his desk. "I am starting to believe there are many, many more human beings out there with the capacity for magic than we had ever suspected, and I am no longer sure we *can* get it back under control. Like I said, the cat's out of the bag. It's a brave new world."

LeBlanc stood and began pacing the room, one hand still gripping her bourbon. "Unrestricted, untrained magic-users cannot be allowed to proliferate. The chaos would be unacceptable. Blaming you for the present situation, while technically accurate, is pointless, as we must now focus on how to deal with it. We must activate the entire council and request that everyone pitch in. Perhaps we can even speak to the Orthodoxy and determine how they might feel about a temporary alliance."

James winced. "I don't think that would be a good idea. The second part, I mean. We are essentially an academic fellowship. The Orthodoxy is more like a crime syndicate. As I understand it, they started as some sort of underground resistance against the Orthodox Church's efforts to stamp out witchcraft, hence the ironic name. But since then, they've essentially turned into the fucking magical mafia. Inviting them to have dealings with us would be a great way to let them observe our weaknesses so they can take over our turf."

LeBlanc stopped. "Yes, the rumors I have heard about them are not encouraging. But if we don't do something, thaumaturgy will soon be everywhere, and by that point, there would be no way to put the proverbial cat back into the bag without being highly obvious about it. Then everyone would know about magic one way or another."

"Exactly," said James. "Maybe, LeBlanc—and I'm being serious about this—maybe *there is no way to keep it all a secret anymore*. It could be that we're entering a new era, in which case the old ways might no longer be workable and we will have to either adapt somehow or wither into irrelevance."

To his shock, LeBlanc reacted by turning away from him and hurling her tumbler. It shattered against his wall, spilling the small amount of liquor and melted ice left within, and fragments of crystal rained down.

Muttering under her breath, she cast a couple of quick spells to gather the debris into a ball and remove the moisture and potential staining material as well. She commanded both to float into the nearby trash can.

"Pardon me," she commented. "I owe you a new glass."

James blinked. "I have twenty or so more. Seeing you this upset is a rare occurrence, though. For what it's worth, I *am* sorry I ever thought of putting together that goddamn book."

She trudged back to her chair and sat down. "Yes, of course, you're sorry. We all are. What will this brave new world look like, James? Will it all be sunshine and rainbows? Will everything descend into chaos? Will there be special government restrictions placed upon magically inclined persons with robots to hunt down the ones who don't comply like in that comic book with the mutants or whatever it was? Will there be a magocracy that rules humankind from on high with powers beyond their understanding, passing judgment on all their activities and punishing their behaviors as they see fit?"

James shrugged. "Well, that last one isn't too different from the way Big Tech operates right now, but I digress. Any of the others might happen too, but I think we can achieve a workable equilibrium. It didn't take long to forge an alliance with those FBI agents, right? Granted, we mind-wiped them at the end, but still. Once people get over the initial shock, there must be a way to come to an understanding. And if not and we have to go to war to defend ourselves, having someone as talented as Ezeudo in our corner sooner rather than later would be beneficial, don't you think?"

"Yes," replied LeBlanc, "and having him as our eyes and ears in Europe will also prove helpful. But you risk alienating him if you push him too hard. In older times, there were stories of students who were disciplined so cruelly that they rebelled and became dangerous rogue casters. We cannot allow *that* to happen. We have to consider all the angles..."

The two thaumaturges talked for another half-hour, largely repeating themselves and coming to no clear resolutions. They were both tired.

Neither realized that their sound shield had been compromised.

Ezeudo, back in his room, sat on his bed and listened. James had recently taught him how to cast a barrier the human ear could not penetrate, and on his own, he had managed to deconstruct the charm, and he'd found several small weaknesses within it. Thus, casting it backward while focusing on the flaws, he was able to create a pipeline to within the shielded study.

His face grew angrier, more lined and solemn, as he followed his teachers' conversation. Though their intentions were not overtly malevolent, many of his worst suspicions had been confirmed.

"So," he murmured to himself, rubbing his knees and measuring his breaths, "that was why they brought me here. To be their soldier or spy because they are afraid of the consequences of their own mistakes. Their whole purpose in coming to Europe was to cover their tracks. How foolish of me to assume that they wanted only to help me when they are not even charging me rent."

As the thaumaturges argued over whether to keep him on the current hectic schedule or to amend it and grant him fourteen months instead of twelve, Ezeudo's mind wandered. He wondered how Guillaume and his expat friends in Geneva were doing.

And he wondered how the rest of the world would be doing

soon.

————————

Olina gritted her teeth. To her annoyance, though not to her surprise, Pavla had held out on giving her the information about where tonight's operation would be taking place, then she had gone, cloaked and incognito, somewhere into the city, leaving her partner in the dust.

Thus Olina had had no choice but to send Pavla a text message asking where the hell she was supposed to meet her.

Oh, sorry, Pavla had texted back. **I thought I already told you or you would be able to find me if not.**

She was doing it to make Olina look incompetent. Of that, she was certain. Still, the indignity of being forced to beg for information was a small price to pay for the ultimate victory they would finally achieve tonight.

At last, the girl Kera would die. And since Pavla had admitted she couldn't do it without Olina's help, Anezka would be unable to deny her value in bringing the mission to its close. *Promotion.* Promotion awaited her. It had been close to a year since her last one, and she'd found it nearly unbearable.

Pavla had revealed that the trap was set at some dockside place along the Pacific down in Long Beach. She wondered why criminals were so obsessed with docks and warehouses. Didn't they also host fancy dinner parties? She would much prefer to conduct a hit operation at one of *those.*

Olina hailed a taxi, took it to a random pub half a mile from her destination, and charmed the driver to get out of having to pay him. Just for fun, though, she had made sure he left the meter running so he would have to explain to his superiors why he had given someone a ride without collecting his fare. They would probably assume he had traded drugs or sexual favors for it and fire him. The thought amused her greatly.

Once she set out on foot, Olina checked her phone again. It seemed Pavla needed her to check the security of some traps she had set. They were basic but cleverly disguised net-snares, the Czech witch explained, which were controlled by triggers designed to mimic Kera's friends crying out for help that would then trap her within nets of silver and iron.

Olina found this method rather crude, particularly for a caster of Pavla's exalted standing, but she didn't much care. The only thing that mattered was capturing or killing Kera.

First, though, Olina sought out her reluctant partner. She wanted to confirm with her own eyes that she was there.

It wasn't difficult. Pavla had taken up position behind a pile of rocks acting as a breakwater right next to the sea, one with a good view of the wharves.

"Hello," Pavla said as the small blonde woman approached. "Thank you for showing up. I know that we have had our differences, but tonight, all of that will be resolved. The problem that has plagued us for so long will be removed."

Olina flashed a bright but insincere grin. "Good. It should have been removed weeks ago, but at least there will be no more delay. Now, where are these traps? I can sense the sympathy beacons but not the snares, so it would appear you cloaked them properly. You are good at something after all."

Pavla's jaw tightened, but she made an effort to smile back. "Yes. Try to ignore the beacons. Those should work with minimal difficulty. I will point out the locations of the main traps." Her smile widened. "Both of them."

Nodding, Olina paid close attention as Pavla explained that one was set up close to them, near the rear corner of the dockside loading area, and another was on the other side of the wall connecting the wharves. In both cases, the net would fall from a tall lamppost.

"Yes, very well," Olina muttered and strode off toward the first one.

She possessed a variety of foresight that allowed her to extrapolate how a machine or mechanical process would work in advance of it operating, even if its internals were hidden or its operations were obscure or highly complex. It was an uncommon ability, one Olina had used many times in her efforts to advance herself.

She found the first trap easily once she knew where to look, Pavla's cloaking spell ceased to hide it, then a brief precognitive flash told her that it ought to function without a hitch. The American girl would blunder toward the fake aura, get herself paralyzed, and look up in horror as the net fell on her head, leaving her helpless.

It was a comforting thought. After all the trouble that Kera had caused, it would be preferable to take her back to Anezka alive so the Orthodoxy could devote some time to finishing her off. Humiliating her, making her suffer. Killing her on the spot would be too quick and easy.

Olina snapped out of her reverie and started down the wall toward the second and final trap. To her left, the shipping facility was coming alive with activity as a small group of men arrived. They were probably the regular workers, though it was possible they were some of El Peluquero's advance scouts. Olina was well-cloaked, so she paid them little heed.

Halfway down the path, though, she heard something. It was a man's thoughts, pushing outward into the world despite his voice being impaired.

Help me, please. I'm hurt. If they catch me, they'll kill me. If some-one, anyone, can save me, I'll give them whatever they want. Anything I have is theirs. Please, God! Let someone come by! If they find me first, I'm dead.

Olina stopped. Though similar to the distress beacons Pavla had set up elsewhere, the message was different. It didn't seem to be a psychic distress call made to sound like one of Kera's friends.

It seemed to be someone associated with the shipping facility. A snitch who had fallen and broken a leg, perhaps?

She had to see who he was. If he was in a predicament like that, Olina could demand things from him in exchange for help. Or for *not* helping if she were to suddenly decide to change her mind.

She peered under the dock, then climbed down onto the wet sand of the shallows and looked up toward the nearest light post, seeking to orient herself.

Something like an electric field struck her, springing out of nowhere, and before her mind could stabilize enough to cast a counterspell, her body froze. Seized up, as though everything but her eyes had turned to stone.

There were still ways to summon the aid of the divine powers. She tried not to panic, scanning her mind for a powerful nonverbal spell that required mental energy only. A flicker of motion disturbed the light above her. Moving her eyes upward, she saw a net weighted by small pieces of metal falling toward her head.

Pavla, you idiot! You told me the wrong location for the trap! And why the hell did the beacon sound like some worker or informant? She's so stupid. How could she have made a mistake like this?

The net landed, its weight knocking her over so she lay half-submerged in the sandy mud below the dock, her mind going half-dead at the touch of iron and silver. She could think of the spells, but they would never reach the higher forces. Her only option now was to wait for Pavla to realize her error and come rescue her.

About five minutes later, the slim silhouette of the Czech approached. For the first time ever, Olina was glad to see her.

Pavla stepped into the light and looked the smaller woman over. A flickering smile played about the corners of her mouth, and Olina felt cold dread pooling in her stomach.

"Ah, good. The trap worked *perfectly*."

CHAPTER TWENTY-ONE

El Peluquero turned to Neron and held aloft a small object dangling on a silver chain. "Do you know what this is?"

Neron looked at his boss, then at the item, which reflected the lights of passing street lamps as the car sped down the asphalt through the darkened city.

"Um," he coughed, "it's, uh, a medallion. A keepsake from someone important to you?"

The idea of the Barber having loved ones back home seemed strange to him, and he instantly regretted having suggested as much. He felt like a fool, as though this were a quiz and he had given the wrong answer. He ran a hand over his smooth head.

El Peluquero looked at him with his usual blank yet oddly intense expression, though his nondescript face did not appear angry or disappointed. If anything, it was the first time Neron could recall him looking almost...kind? Warm? Pleasant?

"It is a good luck charm," the boss stated. "I believe that is the common term here. In my home country, it is worn to protect against sorcery. Do you believe in sorcery?"

Uh-oh, Neron thought. *Finally, he's addressing those stupid rumors about that Pauline chick being cursed or whatever. Is he trying to figure out if I'm as gullible as the kids who move the product?*

He gave a tentative and conservative reply. "I'm not sure what I believe, *Jefe*. I don't claim to understand everything in the universe, so you might say I'm open to, uh, evidence. If I see something to convince me it's real, then I guess it's real."

The Barber nodded, and not a single hair on his head fell out of place.

"My feelings are the same. A great many have been talking about sorcery lately. That young lady you hired? Her former employer met a mysterious end. And there are rumors that the supernatural may have been involved in the..." he paused, and any minimal trace of warmth he had shown vanished utterly, "*ill-fated* incident at the Van Nuys warehouse. Of course, the men did not say as much to me, but I hear things."

Neron nodded, waiting for his superior to finish before he commented.

"Yes," El Peluquero went on, "and I believe in being prepared for every possible contingency. That is why I have come so far." He put the chain over his head, draped it around his neck, and hid the medallion beneath his black suit.

Marveling that such a calculating man could give the time of day to horseshit gossip from the lowly grunts, Neron said, "Well, hey, it can't hurt. Besides, I'm pretty sure we prepared for everything *except* sorcery, ha, ha. This is gonna go off without a hitch. It'll make up for the Van Nuys thing. Long Beach is way more important anyway."

"Yes," his boss replied. "We will not fail again."

———

Zee's roar softened to a growl as the bike slowed, and Kera pulled off the road into the mouth of a dark alley. They waited until a couple of cars behind them had passed before doing anything.

"All right," Kera told Stephanie, "this is where we split up. From what Lia was saying, the hidden stair is right in the middle of that dividing wall. So you get in there and stay hidden but where you can see and hear them, then wait for our friend the Hairdresser to pass. Get a glimpse of him, imitate him, and head back the way he came but to the left."

Steph nodded. "Got it. It don't even sound that hard, though lots of things seem easy 'til you have to do them for real."

Kera hugged her. "Don't be nervous. I mean, it's okay to be afraid, but don't second-guess yourself. Have a shield spell ready. Unless they somehow hired a thaumaturge who's better than *me*, we have plenty of ways to get out of this alive even if things go south."

Her friend laughed. "Yeah, true."

"Meanwhile," Kera went on, "I'll be circling around the long way to the eastern wharf. It will probably take me longer to get there than it takes you to get into position, so be patient. I'll try to send you a mental signal if something goes wrong. Once I'm in place and El Peluquero passes, we spring into action. I'll notice when you stand up and start impersonating him. That's when I'll take out the drug supply."

And then, she thought, *we have to rely on Johnny, Lia, and Chris to get everything else right if we're also going to pull off Phase Two and take the Barber out of the picture once and for all.*

For the first time in many days, Kera found herself missing Pavla. If she'd had more training, she might be more certain of herself. Despite her encouraging words to Stephanie, she kept thinking back to all the screw-ups at the warehouse in the Valley, and this was a bigger job than that had been.

"Ready?" she asked.

Steph nodded. "As I'll ever be. I think we can do this."

"Yeah," Kera agreed, hiding Zee in the alley and moving eastward. "Good luck. It'll go off without a hitch. We won't come close to failing again."

Pavla knelt beside her unwanted partner, who stared at her with a mixture of undisguised fear and seething hatred.

"Olina," she began, "as I said before, you really are quite stupid. There are many normal humans who possess less than a tenth of the special abilities you have who could have anticipated what I had in store for you."

The eyes darted around in a desperate bid for someone to come rescue her, then stared at Pavla as though trying to kill her through the raw force of anger alone. It was the only thing she could do at the moment.

Pavla went on. She didn't want to waste much time, but she was only human, after all. She *had* to savor the moment a bit, given how much unpleasantness Olina had put her through.

"I am smarter than you after all, but you are in luck because I am also far more merciful. If our positions were exchanged, I have no doubt that you would spend two or three days torturing me before dumping me into the sea, would you not? I will do no such thing. Instead, I will do something that is...in a way, worse."

Again, the eyes within the frozen, helpless face moved in crazy circles before staring back into her own.

Pavla extended her hands toward Olina's temples. "You don't need to know about me, do you? Or about Kera. Or about the Orthodoxy, except perhaps in the most general way. I think you would be happier if you remembered none of that."

The truth registered in Olina's tiny brain and her eyes almost pulsated with the emotional tornado behind them.

The only problem, Pavla recalled, was that it was difficult to wipe someone's memory while holding them in stasis at the same time. Furthermore, since iron and silver did not discriminate between targets, she would have to remove the net, if only for a moment, to grab the smaller woman's head and perform the spell.

She doubted Olina was canny enough to break free in that brief instant of opportunity, but people were full of surprises.

Pavla snatched the net with her left hand and pulled it up and over her captive's head. The metals woven into it made it deceptively heavy, and one of the open portions got snagged on a piece of wood protruding from the dock. She tried to free it and toss it away while with her right hand, she focused on the spell keeping Olina paralyzed. It was an "automatic" spell, tied to the location rather than the caster, but it still could weaken if she wasn't careful.

Then Olina's rolling, blazing eyes came to a stop, fixed directly on her. She pounced up, free, her mouth falling open and letting out a guttural, animalistic rasp as her hands closed around Pavla's throat.

"You! How dare you!" she roared, and foam ran from the corners of her mouth. Pavla fell back, seizing the smaller woman's wrists and trying to pry them off before both witches tumbled into the mud and shallow water.

Pavla struck Olina with a blunt-force concussive blast at the same instant her foe cast a crude spell that caused seizure of the muscles. Olina flew back, crashed into one of the dock's wooden pillars, and screamed in pain. At the same moment, Pavla rolled deeper into the lapping waves of the Pacific, her body paralyzed with momentary agony.

I should have killed her. Pavla cursed herself. *Trying to show her mercy was utterly stupid. Now I may be the one who dies.*

As she gradually regained control of her body, Pavla struggled to her feet. Olina was ranting and raving in her native Norwegian and throwing out claw-like hands in another magical evocation.

The water before her began to freeze, threatening to trap Pavla in place, not to mention put her at serious risk of hypothermia. She tamed the muscular-convulsion spell and surrounded herself with a thin shield of heat, which met the freezing water in a cloud of steam. The visual obscurity it created allowed Pavla to roll to the side as Olina stomped toward her. The blonde witch was only half-coherent; total rage was impairing her ability to cast or strategize but making her faster, stronger, and more vicious.

It was only then Pavla realized that a few seconds ago, noise and commotion could be heard from the shipyard above and behind them. Men shouted and feet stomped. Two staccato gunshots rang out, followed by an odd rushing that largely blended with the sounds of the sea.

Either Kera and her friends had arrived, or El Peluquero's men had begun their armed takeover of the facility. Perhaps both.

Pavla cast an inverted shield over Olina, protecting herself from any offensive spells but also trapping the other witch within a dome. Olina crashed stupidly against it, but it took her only a second or two to begin cutting through it, unmaking the spell to renew her assault.

While plotting how to deal with her, Pavla looked at the wharves and blinked. El Peluquero was down at one end of the dividing wall, curtly barking orders to a half-dozen of his para-military goons...and yet, he was also at the other end of the same wall, shouting at some of the workers on the wharf proper and waving his arms.

Does he have a body double? No, wait. I sense magic. Someone is imitating him. It must be part of Kera's plan.

Olina broke through the shield, and Pavla had no more time to speculate on anything other than the woman who was trying to kill her.

The air tingled. Pavla grasped what was happening and launched herself fifteen feet into the air, away from the water, just in time to avoid being electrocuted as Olina struck the waves and moist ground with a spider's web of crackling lightning.

As she soared away, there was more gunfire from the shipping area. This time, it was a controlled burst of automatic fire from a carbine or submachine gun. She saw the muzzle flash and watched as men rushed around, yelling and repositioning themselves to deal with the disturbance. None of them had noticed the battle between the two witches along the shoreline, though.

Floating earthward, Pavla hurled waves of confusion and fear spells, but Olina avoided or blocked them, rushing toward her and flinging fire and lightning. Pavla blocked it with a rudimentary shield of physical force, then was able to generate enough wind across a short space to knock Olina partway off-balance.

It produced all the hesitation she needed. Pavla drew her gun and aimed it as Olina was preparing to cast another attack spell.

The smaller witch froze, her eyes again glowing with antipathy as they had while she was paralyzed.

"Don't try it, Olina," Pavla urged. "I won't hesitate to kill you in self-defense. Then you would lose all hope of advancement, would you not?"

Olina bared her teeth. "You wouldn't dare. Someone would find out, and then you—"

Footsteps pounded toward them, and both women glanced aside as a figure in a black catsuit sprinted toward them, trailed by two men in combat fatigues. Pavla's eyes bulged as she recognized the first individual. It was Kera's friend Stephanie. She had been grazed by a bullet or a knife and probably struck in the face by someone's fist or the butt of a gun.

The two European witches sprang into action. Pavla moved first, redirecting her pistol toward the two men and firing a single shot. She couldn't tell if she hit them, and if she did, their armor likely stopped it, but it was enough to distract them for a second. Then she encased them within another inverted dome-shaped shield barrier. They crashed against its walls and stumbled into one another, but they would be trapped for several minutes or longer.

Olina ducked past Pavla and went straight for Stephanie, who didn't see her at first.

Pavla spun and lunged, her left hand grasping the trailing tatter of Olina's jacket. She pulled her back and wrapped her left arm around Olina's neck.

Stephanie stopped and stared at them in surprise. Since Olina was too discombobulated to cast a spell, Pavla hurriedly dug into her pocket, left her pistol there, produced a certain item, and tossed it to Stephanie.

"Take this and get to safety!" Pavla shouted. She brought her other arm around Olina's head and manhandled her to the ground.

Olina spat and cursed in Norwegian again, followed by, "You are dead, Pavla! Dead! Anezka will skin you alive for this. I am on my way up. I am important! You are old, out of touch, obsolete, and—"

"Forget about it," Pavla said and cast the spell she had been meaning to use all along.

The air tingled again, but in a way different from when Olina had summoned lightning. The small blonde woman's eyes went vacant, and her jaw went slack. Her struggling and snarling came to an abrupt end. Within her mind, certain things vanished and a void opened up, only to be filled by the gray haze of uncertainty and misremembrance.

Olina forgot everything she had ever known about Kera and Pavla. It was as though she had never met or heard of either of them. Related to that, her career with the Orthodoxy, especially recently, were vague and confused as well. The past weeks became a fog that began to dissipate as soon as she focused on it like the details of a dream that vanished when one woke up.

Pavla threw her down into the mud, where she lay twitching and drooling. In another five minutes, she would collect herself and be fine, more or less, aside from the knowledge that had been erased from her brain. Pavla wondered if Olina might become a slightly less insufferable person with no memory of her chief rival or the girl she had been assigned to murder.

Looking up, Pavla saw Stephanie gazing at her, then circling around to rejoin the fight on the wharves. It was heating up; the Barber's men were converging on the eastern containment area, where someone was giving them a great deal of trouble.

Pavla had little doubt about who it was.

She walked away, her gait easy and casual, and climbed back over the breakwater to leave the shipyard behind. Her mind had grown strangely calm.

I am done, she decided. *I am no longer a member of the Orthodoxy, which means I am now a dangerous rogue witch in their view. I can never go back to any place they control. But things have changed too much. I have grown to hate the person they were forcing me to be. I will not be that person anymore.*

As she worked her way inland, renewing the cloaking spell that protected her from the sight and hearing of normal people, there came a slight rise in the land along the road. From there, she could see the wharves again.

She stopped. There was too much chaos to determine who was winning. Pavla did not want to intervene since it wasn't her fight, but for Kera's sake, she watched and rooted for her.

CHAPTER TWENTY-TWO

Kera reached up and fiddled with her earbud, waiting for the word from Chris and Lia. She had finally arrived in position near the extreme eastern rear corner of the wharf. She had a good view of the mass of boxes and crates and machinery the place's owners had unloaded and the dividing wall where the wannabe new owner would soon be marching.

Now it was simply a matter of trusting that Stephanie and Johnny were in their places, too.

And that nothing had gone wrong.

Nothing *else*, that was. Already things were proving more complicated than they had hoped, and they were running out of time.

Isn't it always like that? I think the military has some saying about stuff like this. You have to plan for every worst-case scenario, and even then, there ends up being shit to deal with that you could not have foreseen.

First, she and Steph had encountered a patrolling guard far earlier and farther away from the facility than they'd expected. Neither had seen or heard the man until he was nearly on top of them. They were cloaked, or he might have put two bullets in each of their heads before they could have reacted.

As it was, Kera had been able to hit him with a sufficiently powerful relaxation spell to knock him out, then the two thaumaturges had dragged him into an alley and tied him up.

They had escaped detection, but someone would wonder where the man was soon. Not to mention, Kera had had to expend a good chunk of her magical energy sooner than she wanted to. Every little bit left her with less strength for the main event.

Furthermore, as Kera circled to the east, she had seen Stephanie narrowly evade detection by a sniper with night-vision goggles perched on a nearby roof. The man had binoculars, too. He might be able to see far enough to glimpse Chris' Jeep, though it was a good half-mile away and hidden behind a building. Kera wasn't sure if the angle was right for the sniper to see over it.

El Peluquero was taking no chances. He'd had a firm grasp on the entire peninsula before he made his main play.

Now, as she watched the workers mill about and the paramilitary thugs assume their positions, corralling them, her earbud came to life.

"Okay," said Chris' voice. "All quiet so far. I can see what you're seeing, so the camera enchantment thingy is working, I guess. Can you see what we've got on the Jeep cam?"

She couldn't risk speaking, but they had set up a code whereby any silent pause from her could be assumed to be a "yes." If there was trouble, she would either cry out or send a psychic emotional distress signal to them.

"All right," Chris went on. "I'm assuming that's a yes. Not that we're in the thick of the action back here, but—oh, hey, caravan of two vans and one car between them heading your way."

Lia's voice added, "It's almost certainly him. All three vehicles are filled with men armed to the teeth, and the central car has blacked-out windows. Wait, you can see that, can't you?"

In point of fact, the spell was only half-working. Kera got flashes of vague, hazy images in her mind like daydreams that quickly faded, but they were enough to get an idea about what was happening farther down the road. Three dark vehicles were moving down the street, blocking the light.

Johnny reported next. He was on the western wharf, out of sight from where Kera currently crouched. "Nice quiet night," he muttered as though he were talking to himself while he loafed around with the other semi-captive laborers. "I thought this was gonna be more dramatic. Is the almighty Hairdresser actually showing up in person?"

Someone snapped at him to shut up. Based on what he'd said, Kera was pretty sure no one knew what was going on with Stephanie.

Sending out her mind, she could feel, if only faintly, her friend's emotional aura, but it was a steady throb of tension and nerves. Steph was keyed up, worried, but nothing seemed to have happened to have changed her state of mind.

Off to Kera's right, in the direction of the hidden staircase, a man shouted, "Hey! What are you doing here? Identify yourself!" Radios crackled and other voices relayed messages, mostly in Spanish, though with some English and semi-comprehensible military lingo mixed in.

Stephanie's psychic signature screamed in terror.

Shit! It took all of Kera's self-discipline not to jump up and bolt toward the middle of the dividing wall. If she did, the plan would be ruined. Steph had ways of protecting herself. Kera had to have faith.

But their time was up. Unless her friend pulled off a miracle, they were going to have to spring the trap prematurely and deal with the drugs and the drug lord via brute force, haste, spit, and elbow grease.

Kera felt Stephanie's emotional core moving, and there was a general commotion somewhere between the two main wharves, along with pounding footsteps. Steph had been discovered, but she had broken free and was running away.

Then two gunshots rang out, and Kera's heart jumped into her throat. No! No, no, no.

But the aura kept moving. It was heading toward the water.

In Kera's ear, Chris' voice said, "The caravan stopped, but now it's advancing again. And we got gunshots and chatter on their radios. I think they found Steph. Oh, crap."

She couldn't wait any longer. Kera sent Chris a signal—not distress, but the equivalent of a battle cry.

"Whoa!" he responded. "Um, I think Kera is leaping into action here. Everyone hold onto their butts."

As she leaped up from her hiding place and charged onto the wharf, her mind cycled through its options and selected one that was better than simply trying to beat the hell out of everyone who looked like a bad guy and potentially getting them all killed.

If Steph couldn't pull off the illusion, maybe she could. The image of El Peluquero and his chilling voice were firmly lodged in her memory. She muttered the charm under her breath and flailed her hands through the motions, jumping into the imitation of her target at the same time she canceled the cloaking spell.

She burst onto the wharf amidst the crates of drugs at a fast trot, and the men there started in surprise at the sight of her.

"You men," she ordered in a crisp, mechanical, somewhat accented male voice, "begin opening up all these crates and removing the product. We have a slight problem, but it is under control."

The workers scrambled to do as they were told. If the drugs were loose, destroying them later would be easier.

The armed guards moved toward her, seemingly as shocked as the laborers. "Sir," one of them began.

"And you men," she commanded, "head that way." She pointed to the east. "We found some suspicious activity over there. Make sure it is secure before you return." There was nothing out that way, of course.

The guards ran beyond the eastern wharf, fanned out in scouting formation, and began combing through the adjacent docks and lots.

Kera wanted to break into a full run, but she suspected that El Peluquero wasn't the running type. His minions might suspect something was up. Looking ahead, she saw a dark figure running away from the dividing wall onto the beach that stretched beyond the docks, where the transition from sea to land was more gradual. Two armed men were in hot pursuit.

Do something, Steph! Don't just run. They'll shoot! I hope she's shielded at least.

Then there was more commotion: a flurry of shadows and the sense of spells being cast. Lots of them—more than she had realized at first, all of them centered on the area by the far docks. Too much chaotic information flooded Kera's mind to be sure of what was going on, and she couldn't see very well, either.

But the psychic vibe she got from Stephanie suggested her friend was all right for the moment.

I have to let her deal with the problem on her own, Kera told herself. *Where the hell is the Barber? We can deal with the drug shipments later if we take care of him now.*

She heard cars pulling up not too far away. Bingo.

Johnny's voice said, "Okay, I was able to slip away in all the racket. Didn't someone say I'm supposed to start dumping the drugs in the ocean if Kera and Steph can't handle it? For fuck's sake. You did say that, right? I'll see what I can do."

"Affirmative," Lia snapped. "The rear van from the caravan is coming back this way. Oh, shit. Target has arrived at the wharf, but what are these guys—"

Chris blurted, "Fuck it." Then brakes squealed and Kera heard the roar of an engine, followed by crunching metal.

Now what are they doing? This entire plan has gone straight down the toilet drain, Kera raged, jogging onto the dividing wall to get a centralized view of the whole mess, regardless of whether it looked suspicious. *We might as well have not even made a plan, and all showed up drunk. And now El Peluquero is coming out in person, and I get to deal with him alone.*

She'd rather have to fight harder by herself than have any of her friends die, though. She had no idea what was happening to them.

As she mounted the wall and waved her hands vaguely at some men looking up at her, Chris' voice came again. "We're okay. Rammed 'em. Wait. Crap!"

There was some static, followed by a burst of automatic gunfire, followed by three pistol shots.

Chris! Kera's mind screamed. She shouted it through the radio, trying to reach him and make him understand she needed to know if he was alive.

Then she felt his emotional aura like she had felt Stephanie's a moment ago. He was scared but alive. Beyond that, she didn't know what had gone down. Lia had been in the Jeep with him, but she couldn't pick up anything from her.

Someone was coming onto the dividing wall from the western wharf's end, Kera saw. Quite possibly the Barber and his bodyguards. And the half-dozen guards she had sent east on the brief wild goose chase were returning far more quickly than she would have liked.

"Sir," one of them yelled toward her, "we didn't find anything. Requesting permission to—"

"No," Kera barked, struggling to maintain the illusion. "Go around that way and check the shallows. Someone escaped to the beach over there." That would send them toward Stephanie, but by now, she ought to have had time to escape. The main goal was to get them as far away from their true boss as possible so Kera would not have to deal with all of them at once.

The trooper in the lead squinted at her. "With all due respect, are you all right, sir? Wait. Wait a minute! What the *hell?*" He pointed at her, and the other men took off their goggles to examine her more closely. The illusion was failing.

Okay, time to make up a Plan B so I can shift to it. Or is this Plan C by this point? Plan X?

Kera took a deep breath, then spread her hands and flooded the eastern wharf below her with a minor tidal wave of relaxation and confusion, with a short-term memory wipe thrown in for good measure.

The guards slumped and staggered before toppling over, unconscious. Behind and around them, the workers did the same. The entire wharf was littered with passed-out men.

Kera felt her strength ebb by nearly a quarter. It should not have taken that much out of her, she thought; but casting spells efficiently required focus and emotional discipline. Since she was on the verge of panicking, it was the best she could do.

Somewhere out in the shallows or on the adjacent beach, she heard a woman's voice cry out. It was impossible to say if it was Stephanie, but oddly, it sounded like someone else. As Kera spun, she saw El Peluquero, surrounded by four geared-up troopers, striding down the walkway toward her.

Goddammit. Kera steeled herself. Well, no shame in pulling the same trick twice. She prepared another knockout wave and allowed herself to hope the battle would be won with no more casualties than a few bruised asses as men fell over.

The Barber, up close, was not as tall or imposing as he had seemed from afar, but there was something about his icy, unemotional demeanor that unnerved her. "Who are you?" he asked. "For a minute, you looked like me. How was that so?"

Beside him, the three men with rifles aimed them at her. There was another man, a bald guy, who pulled out a pistol and waited in the rear.

"Watch," Kera quipped. "I'll show you."

She cast the spell. Another huge chunk of her stamina

vanished as the squall of magical calm rushed down the walkway. The three armored riflemen dropped like sacks of potatoes, hitting the ground hard and rolling off the wall to crash onto the wharves below.

But nothing happened to the Barber. He stood calmly regarding her, though his eyebrows lifted in mild surprise when his men dropped. His hair was not even mussed.

Behind him, the bald guy moaned and stumbled, leaning against the railing and staring vacantly into the sky. Somehow, the spell had only partially affected him. It was because he was standing behind his boss, Kera realized. That had afforded him partial immunity.

But why the *hell* was El Peluquero immune?

Her blood went cold as the man let out a low, dry laugh, shaking his head. "Ah," he mused. "You truly *are* a sorcerer, then. It is strange that this does not surprise me. I should have asked all my men to be as prepared as me, but they might have thought me a madman."

Kera stared at him. He stripped off his suit jacket, and beneath it, his body was more muscular than she had expected.

"But," he went on, "can you fight when you do not have your magic to help you?"

You have got to be fucking kidding me. Kera's jaw dropped. Then a crazy exhilaration swelled up within her, and she fell into a Shotokan horse stance.

"I'll show you that, too," she said. As she twisted her hands into fists, she cast two quick enchantments on herself, a luck charm and a speed and strength augmentation, though neither was powerful as she'd like. She might need to reserve her energy. She was in uncharted territory since nothing had gone according to plan.

El Peluquero lunged, faking a strike at her head, and as she drew up a knee to protect herself and pivoted to kick him in the torso, he smoothly stepped around her and drove his knuckles into her kidney.

She cried out, lashed with her fist, and grazed his cheek as he ducked away. They separated, now on opposite sides of the walkway, facing each other again.

The exertion of what he'd done and the light blow he'd taken had slightly disheveled the Barber's hair, but otherwise, he was as unflappable as ever. "You have some skill," he observed. "But I can tell when an opponent is tiring. You must have had a long night before you met me."

"Yeah," she retorted, "and yours is over."

They plunged toward each other again. The path atop the wall was narrow enough that there was only a limited space in which to dodge to either side, so deft, precise movements counted. The next clash might well go to the one who could employ superior direct force.

Kera simply drove her fist toward the man's face as fast and hard as she could, trusting her luck spell to protect her from massive retaliation. El Peluquero blocked and redirected the punch with his forearm, and while she could tell she'd bruised the hell out of it, he barely flinched.

His other hand struck her hard in the groin. She yelped and fell back, in shocking pain.

Was that the good luck outcome? Is the spell even working? Would he have torn my guts out if I hadn't cast it?

She risked the stamina expenditure of a minor healing spell to numb the anguish and hopped back to her feet as the Barber advanced again. His eyes were dark and flat.

The man was the most terrifying kind of opponent— collected, efficient in all his movements, and totally vicious. Were it not for her considerable martial arts experience combined with her magic, he would probably have killed her during their first exchange. His style was one of the brutal, military ones, perhaps

Krav Maga or Systema, combined with dirty tricks he might have learned in his youth.

They clashed again, and this time Kera had a good enough idea of how he fought that she avoided his clawing strike toward her neck and managed to knee him hard in the solar plexus. He fell back, doubling over but maintaining enough control over himself that she could not risk an immediate follow-up.

Especially since behind her, the bald guy was coming to. He pulled himself to his feet, blinked, and raised his pistol. Kera spun and kicked the gun from his hand.

"Shit!" He dove and rolled toward it rather than trying to fight her hand-to-hand as his boss was.

Kera barely repelled another disabling strike from the Barber and found herself trapped between the two men. She went after the smooth-domed henchman again, grappled with him, and successfully tossed his gun over the walkway, where it clattered behind a crate.

Then both he and El Peluquero assailed her with fast punches and kicks, and for a moment, she could do nothing but block and dodge.

"Boss!" the bald man exclaimed. "She's a woman! What do you say we do with her after?"

Rather than answer the question, the Barber replied to the first part. "Yes, Neron, I had noticed."

I still have my gun, Kera remembered. *They're going to kill me, and maybe worse. I'm going to have to use it again, aren't I? Fuck!*

Her brain was overwhelmingly focused on her two enemies. In the chaos of the three-way battle, they became hard to tell apart in the dark, with both wearing black shirts and pants, and they were of a similar size, too. She was dimly aware that there was a commotion somewhere nearby. Gunshots, yelling, fighting.

Kera seized the opportunity. Both El Peluquero and Neron had withdrawn after knocking her back, but within the next second, they would dogpile her again.

She leaped eight or nine feet into the air and drifted past the walkway on the wall and down to the wharf.

"The fuck?" Neron marveled.

Kera landed behind the crate where she had knocked the bald guy's sidearm. She grabbed it—a Sig, she was pretty sure—in her left hand and drew her Glock with her right, aiming the pistols at the two men.

For a brief instant, she saw something like fear in the Barber's flat eyes.

Then Stephanie's voice screamed, "Kera! No!"

A shot rang out. Kera fell back, dropping both guns as pain exploded in her left forearm. She swung her head and saw Stephanie halfway across the wharf, launching a blast of water upward. It struck the sniper on the building across the street, and he bellowed as he tumbled from the window to the street below.

Steph caught up and pulled Kera back. The bullet had only grazed her arm; the luck spell must have kicked in when she needed it most. Still, it would be hard to fight with that hand. She was in no shape to take on two men at once.

They needed to either win now or flee. If they fled, El Peluquero would consolidate his strength on the value of the current shipment and then hunt them down like dogs.

"Steph," Kera gasped, "we need to take those two guys out right fucking now." The Barber and his right-hand man had leaped down from the walkway and were in the process of retrieving the fallen pistols.

"How?" Stephanie asked. "I saw what happened. Magic don't work on the Barber, and I don't have my rifle."

Kera took in the scene before her. Neron had scrambled for his own gun, found it, and was weaving between the crates to rejoin his boss and finish her off. At the moment, she was half-protected by a piece of shelving, and he probably didn't want to risk a ricochet that might harm his employer.

El Peluquero, meanwhile, was slowly advancing toward them.

He had picked up her Glock and tucked it into the back waistband of his pants. He had a different idea about how to kill them now, it seemed.

Mere feet behind him was a big tank of propane.

No, Kera thought. *I can't kill another human being like* that. *Shooting someone in the head is bad enough. But there's so goddamn much at stake...*

"Fire spell," she groaned, cringing within as she said it. "Magic doesn't affect him, but it can affect the things around him. I need your help to cast it since I'm drained and beat to hell. Remember what I said? Fire is like water. Remember that."

Stephanie nodded. "I remember. And these motherfuckers are *not* going to kill us no matter what."

Kera began. She focused on the propane tank, channeling energy toward it, beseeching the powers of the universe to heat up that distinct location as much as they could. She felt her strength ebbing as the air shimmered.

Stephanie took her hand and whispered the rest of the incantation under her breath.

El Peluquero hesitated, sensing something was wrong.

Neron ran up beside him. "Boss! Get out of the way! They're trying to—"

As he dove toward his employer, Kera poured what little she had left into channeling pure heat around the Barber toward the tank. Stephanie, letting the heat and flames flow like the waves of the ocean behind them, ignited the air. And the gas.

"Shield!" Kera gulped.

Stephanie conjured one just as the propane tank exploded, the roaring fireball engulfing El Peluquero, whose face finally showed alarm and pain as the wave of heat blasted him aside and reduced him to a blackened husk. Neron fell back, wreathed in fire, and crashed into the base of the dividing wall before stilling.

The force of the explosion and the burning wave were stopped by the shield, but the two women were driven back and fell to the ground as the barrier wavered. The fire was spreading across the wharves.

"Let's get out of here," Steph suggested.

Kera, barely conscious, nodded.

As they struggled across the dock with fleeing workers running past them, a Mustang pulled up. "Hey!" Johnny shouted, flinging open the door. "You guys okay?"

"Somewhat," said Kera.

Stephanie helped her into the back seat, then asked Johnny, "Where were you?"

He ushered her into the passenger side, then slid back into the driver's seat. "I decided to see if I could get one of the cranes going. It worked!"

"It worked?" Stephanie repeated, her tone quizzical. "Just like that?"

"Yep." He pointed, and the two witches could see one of the huge cranes, apparently unmanned, going through the repetitive motions of picking up full cargo containers of drugs before dropping them far out in the bay. "I guess I got it running on a preset sequence. I knew you guys wouldn't want to leave before doing something about all their precious product, right?"

Kera waved a hand. "Yeah, that helps. Thanks, Johnny. Now take me immediately to my bed." She passed out.

Stephanie pulled out the enchanted bandage roll Pavla had tossed her. She had already used some of it to bind her wounds and was amazed by how fast it helped. She tore loose another length and wrapped it around Kera's bloody arm as Johnny drove them away from the wharves, rejoining Chris' Jeep on the road back home.

Across the wharf and across the surf, from a high point in the road farther inland, a woman watched and listened.

"Yes, Johnny," she remarked. "It 'just worked.'" She laughed. "Oh, well. It will not hurt for him to believe he did that himself.

And Kera deserves to know they accomplished what they set out to do."

She frowned, and her spirits sank. In all likelihood, Pavla would never see her again.

Turning slowly, she walked back into the city, ignoring the approaching sirens. Soon she would have to disappear for a time. Perhaps a long time.

But there was one more thing she needed to do first.

CHAPTER TWENTY-THREE

Kera woke up, knowing damn well that it was going to be one of those mornings where the act of getting up would make her regret doing so. She would feel like crap for at least an hour thereafter. Maybe more like three or four hours.

Still, she swung her legs out of bed, rubbing her head and sighing. Her clock said 12:06, so technically, it was one of those afternoons. Close enough.

She massaged the various places on her body where she had been attacked, battered, or wounded. All were far better than they would have been without the infusion of healing magic, but then again, having to cast healing spells on herself was part of why she was so exhausted. It was worse than a hangover.

Her arm was the worst since she had been shot, albeit not very badly. Somehow, Stephanie had healed the worst of it. She would have to ask her about that later.

There was good news, though. Chris was up, had brewed a pot of coffee, and was making eggs and toast.

"Good morning-ish," he began. "Brunch will be ready in another five minutes or so, but there's fruit if you can't wait that long."

Kera poured a large, strong cup of coffee. "I think I'll live. Thanks so much, though. I'm gonna need it."

She sat down and caffeinated herself, gradually returning to something that resembled normalcy by the time Chris set a heaping plate of food in front of her. She smiled at him. The yolks of the eggs had broken when he flipped them and the toast was a tad darker than she would prefer, but she wasn't about to complain.

After they were done eating, Kera felt up to a little conversation. She was still hungry, but the worst was over.

"Hey," she told her boyfriend, "you did great. We couldn't have pulled it off without you. And Lia, in all fairness."

After they had rammed the rear van of El Peluquero's entourage, they had been forced to shoot the one minion within who hadn't been knocked out by the crash. Neither Chris nor Lia had been hurt. The Jeep was noticeably dented and scuffed and scratched, though.

He raised his coffee mug. "You should talk. That whole thing was an ugly business, yeah, but we probably saved a lot of lives. Not only gang hits and the risk of innocents getting killed in the crossfire, but also all the people who would have overdosed on the crap they were going to peddle or ended up in jail or clinics or homeless on the streets as a result of getting addicted. Sure, crime never goes away completely, but I think we bought the city some relative peace for a while. 'We' meaning you, mainly."

"Well, thanks," she replied, "but it was a group effort. The people providing support are as important as the ones with boots on the ground. Plus, it helps to have someone to feed me."

He chuckled. "Don't mention it. I'm not a great cook, but I'm learning."

Kera wondered if now was the time for the surprise she had planned for him. After mere seconds of consideration, she decided it was.

"I have a gift for you, Chris. It's something I made recently. I was keeping it a secret, and I thought about giving it to you sooner, but, well, other things got in the way." She blushed for some reason.

He raised his eyebrows. "Oh, really? Well, I think I'm technically supposed to say 'you didn't have to do that,' but since you *did*, I'm curious to see what it is. And I'm sure I'll love it."

That was the plan.

Kera got up, fished one of her extra school bags from beneath her bed, and pulled out a small object wrapped in black cloth. She had purchased most of the components, but assembling them and putting on the finishing touches had been her doing.

"Here." She handed him the little pouch.

Chris set down his coffee and unwrapped it with both hands. He blinked and spent a moment examining what lay within—a tiny pendant made of nickel on a thin leather cord. The central ornament was hollow and inscribed with an old Celtic luck symbol. Within it was a tiny ball of metal suspended within a piece of amber.

He smiled. "It's beautiful. Does it have, um, magical significance?"

"Of course," Kera explained. "The symbol means good luck, so that's a start. Amber just looks pretty. But that little pellet thingy inside the amber is a mixture of iron and silver I injected myself. Then I enchanted the amber, which was difficult, but it could be done. I got the idea from Pavla before everything went to hell with her, and she showed me the basics of making charms."

He looked at her, squinting in curiosity.

"Normally," she continued, "iron and silver block all magic, but that's such a small amount that if you're wearing the thing, I can still heal you or protect you if I need to. However, the spell I put on the amber essentially means the anti-magical properties of the metals will be activated only in the case of one specific type of spell: memory-wiping charms. As long as you have that thing on you, your mind cannot be wiped clean of anything. Especially not by me."

She sat rubbing her feet over one another in the awkward silence that followed.

Chris' eyes opened wider, and his expression grew warm and soft. "It's a gesture of trust?"

"Yes." She blushed again. "I know it's tough for you, after...after what I did, before. So accept this token of my faith in you, I guess. I'm giving you the power not to be affected by my powers because it isn't necessary in your case. If that makes sense."

He reached over and hugged her. "It does. This means a lot to me, Kera. Thank you so much."

They started to separate, but their faces paused at the moment the tips of their noses brushed. Then, in unison and with neither of them making the decision for the other, they kissed.

It was a light kiss, and it did not last more than five or six seconds. But it was more than good enough for Kera. And long overdue.

She giggled and ignored the little voice scolding her for acting like a dumb schoolgirl. "That was nice," she stated.

"It was," agreed Chris, "even though both of us just ate a bunch of eggs." He squeezed her hand. "How are you doing, anyway? I can tell you're still in some pain after last night."

She shrugged. "I'm getting better. Still hungry, though. Always hungry, anytime there's something important that needs to be done. No offense about the eggs, but today I think I need two or three extra meals. It's like being a novice witch again. Ugh."

Chris laughed. "Well, after we get freshened up, we can go out for a nice lunch, which is technically the follow-up meal for brunch anyway. I might not be able to eat much myself, but I'll try."

In any event, Kera could take care of any leftovers.

Chris added, "In fact, I think I'm fine with most of our date nights revolving around the consumption of a shit-ton of food. It's the one thing no one can argue with, especially since neither of us is a picky eater."

Kera stood up and stretched. "I know, right?"

Chris reflected on something as he admired her body. "Hmm. If we make a habit of it, though, I'm going to need to start working out. Which I should be doing anyway since I sit at a computer desk for a living."

He stood up, and they took their dishes to the sink.

"If you do," Kera pointed out, "I can give you some tips on how to get started."

"Well, duh," said Chris.

Mr. Kim checked the expiration dates for the milk on the refrigerated shelves in the back for the third time. It had been a slow night. Generally, he did not close up shop early unless there was a specific and important reason, but he contemplated doing so today.

As he wandered back to the counter, he made himself refrain from texting Sam again. He and Ye-Jin had sent their son on his own "vacation" with some friends up in Sacramento, staying behind to watch the store and to continue her cancer treatments.

So far, all was well. Sam had been texting them twice a day to confirm that he was okay. Then again, they had not seen Kera in that period.

It pained Mr. Kim to think Kera might suffer or come to a bad end while he avoided her instead of helping. Before long, he would have to text her as well. He could not stand it much longer, but protecting his own flesh and blood had to come first.

The door opened, and in walked a slender woman: white, brunette, thirty or so. She was dressed in a casual yet subtly classy way, though her clothes were damp and had wet sand residue on them.

She looked harmless, but for some obscure reason, Mr. Kim's gut clenched in fear at the sight of her.

"Hello," he greeted her. "May I help you?"

She was coming toward the register rather than browsing the shelves. "Yes. In truth, I may help you."

The voice, tinged with a European accent the man could not identify, sounded disturbingly familiar. And the woman was reaching into her pocket.

Mr. Kim froze. His first instinct was to cast a spell to protect himself and force her away, but his magic was gone. Instead, he fumbled for the hidden drawer where he kept a loaded .38 revolver.

Before he could retrieve the gun, the woman's hand emerged and opened, then emptied three small medallions onto the counter. "Here you are," she declared. "You may keep them. One each for you, your wife, and your son."

Their eyes met. Despite the enchantments she had used to disguise her voice and her appearance, he knew who she was— the person in the alley who had recommended they get out of town for a while.

Oddly enough, she gave him a soft, almost sad smile. "When I came the other night to warn you, it was to make sure that no one could use you against Kera. Do you understand? But I have taken care of that. The threat is past. And now, these will protect you."

Mr. Kim relaxed slightly but remained on guard. Her words made *some* sense, but clearly, she knew far more than he did about whatever the hell was going on.

"Protect us from what?" he inquired.

"The Orthodoxy." Pavla looked aside and brushed a lock of brown hair back over her ear. "They are dangerous, but they do not know about you. And with those charms, you will remain hidden from their sight. There were...internal conflicts, but they have been resolved. I did not want innocents to become involved."

Mr. Kim grasped the gist despite lacking the full information. Behind him, he heard Ye-Jin coming downstairs, and he was glad Sam was gone. Just in case.

"Well," he told his guest, "thank you for coming clean, young lady. You do not need to convince me that the charms are real. I know such things. I only hope that whatever troubles you were dealing with, they will no longer bother you. Or anyone else."

Pavla nodded, and a lump appeared in her throat. "Yes. Thank you. Be well. You, your family...and your friends."

She turned and walked away, disappearing out the door at the same time a woman with two kids stepped in and made for the ice cream display.

Mrs. Kim put a hand on her husband's shoulder. "Who was that? And what are those?" She gestured at the pendants.

"Gifts," said Mr. Kim, "from one of Kera's friends. I think. We will ask her about it later. I think Sam can come home now." He put his hand atop hers. "Things will be all right, my love."

The wordless bond between them suggested she felt it too. For the time being, they were safe again.

Neron awoke, wondering if he was in Hell. It was dark and he was in pain, so that might be the case. He didn't know if he was alive or dead. And while he had never been the superstitious type, after what he had seen at the wharf—the last thing he could remember—the existence of Hell seemed as possible as any other myth to him. If there *was* an afterlife, he highly doubted he would end up in Heaven.

He tried his voice to see if it worked. "Hey," he gasped. His throat was sore, and his voice sounded dry and scratchy. "Where am I? Is anyone there?"

Footsteps approached, and Neron's sense began to return to him. His eyes had been opened, and they began to see again. Bright white lights and tiles. A mattress beneath him. Bandages all over his body. Pain.

He dismissed the idea that he had died and been condemned to the abyss. Everyone hated hospitals, true, but it seemed ridiculous that Satan would have patched him up and put him in a bed before getting started with the eternal damnation.

He had survived.

"Oh, sir," a man's voice said, "you're awake. Please, do not move. You need to heal yet. You are past the most critical stage, but for your own sake, we respectfully request that you remain in bed for now."

What a polite doctor, he thought and turned his head to glance at the man, who looked nervous. He also was wearing casual clothes rather than a typical white coat. And the infirmary around him looked like a converted basement room, albeit clean.

Well, then, things are looking up. Not only am I alive, but the boys got me to one of "our" hospitals instead of an official one, so I won't have the fuckin' cops showing up to ask me a bunch of friendly, innocent questions about what happened that night.

The subject of "what happened" raised other questions for which he wasn't sure he wanted to know the answers.

"Doctor," he asked, "what happened to me? How bad is it?"

The man breathed deep and turned his eyes to the floor. "You had a concussion but are recovering from it well. However, you were very badly burned, sir. You are lucky to be alive, and we have done everything we can. You should recover most of your, ah, faculties, including sight and speech. Your face was damaged, however. It may be impossible to completely restore your appearance."

Neron said nothing for a moment. When it looked like the

man was about to leave, Neron queried, "How long ago was it? And did both of us survive?"

The doctor swallowed and put his hands behind his back. "Four nights have passed, sir. And I am afraid not. The other man died on the scene. We are, ah, still in the process of identification. We might need to access dental records."

"Oh," Neron replied. "Let me see a mirror."

Though the man hesitated, he agreed after a couple of seconds and held a small mirror over the bed. Bracing himself for the worst, Neron looked into it.

Half of his head was still covered by bandages, but from what he could see of the other half, his features were oddly warped, and his skin was an unpleasant deep pinkish-red. There was probably no way to know what he would end up looking like until the healing process was complete, but he was scarred for life. He would never look normal again.

He waved a bandaged hand, and the doctor took the mirror away. "Could be worse," he rasped. "Where are we?"

"We are in a facility," the doctor stated, "hidden under a processing business your organization previously made a deal with. In Santa Monica. The other men who survived and escaped are handling all the arrangements. They will be in to report on things tomorrow if that is acceptable. If you would prefer, sir, I can call them in sooner."

Neron's brain turned over the facts before him. The man waited for him to speak.

Ever since the doctor started speaking, something had seemed wrong, but now it was coming together. The man was excessively respectful and polite, and he seemed frightened. Neron's first suspicion was that he was a legitimate normal-person doctor, and the boys were forcing him into service by threatening his family or something like that. But no, it was something else.

The other man, he'd said. Dental records for identification. Your organization, he had specified.

They didn't know who had died and who had lived—Neron or El Peluquero. The two men were close to the same size, and the Barber's hair had undoubtedly burned off in the fireball. They were acting on the assumption that Neron *was* El Peluquero, just to be safe.

He smiled.

When he opened his mouth, he imitated his late boss' strange accent to the best of his ability. Of course, his throat was messed up, so it might be hard for them to tell anyway.

"Yes," he proclaimed. "Call them in. It is unfortunate that Neron died, but the bitch who killed him and did this to me will not escape retribution. We need to make plans to deal with her and soon."

The man *bowed*, and Neron had to clamp his jaw shut to keep from laughing, though the muscular tension of it caused the pain in his face to flare up.

"At once, sir," said the doctor.

Neron called after him, "Thank you. Tell them that we are not finished yet. Not by a long shot. No one takes out my right-hand man *and* destroys a huge shipment like that and gets away with it."

CREATOR NOTES
FEBRUARY 25, 2021

Thank you for not only reading to the end of this story but these author notes as well!

Sometimes you win, sometimes people reject a conversation with an author completely based on the title of their series.

Like this one!

The (very) short and sweet is I was informed not that long ago that I was up for an interview, but that the focus would not be on the Badass series but more on what I've done to build my publishing company.

The impression I received was that the name of the series was not really daytime news-friendly.

Oh, well.

Do many of you read comic books?

A couple of years ago, one of the artists who works with me and I set about to see if we could do a comic book. The test showed me that it would be EXPENSIVE at the time to build a page at the quality level I wanted.

So, I dropped the effort.

Now, with the new leadership running LMBPN Publishing, I

have the time to go back and dust off the different projects we have tested over the years.

I am going to see if we can figure out how to profitably do a comic book series. If we can, I'll probably do a Kickstarter to fund the project.

Comics are anything but cheap to publish. Lots of money to make a comic book. Either money or time, actually, for those who have the talent.

I don't have the talent, and I'm very impatient.

So, Jude and I are working once again to see if we can disrupt the creation of comic books to where LMBPN might start building stories around our own IP.

Anyone ready for a Badass Witch Comic? How about a ZOO? Kurtherian Gambit? How about Skharr DeathEater?

It might take us a while, but I thought I might pull back the curtain just a little and let you know some of what we are checking into.

Once more.

I hope your month is fantastic!

Ad Aeternitatem,

Michael Anderle

BOOKS BY MICHAEL ANDERLE

Sign up for the LMBPN email list to be notified of new releases and special deals!

https://lmbpn.com/email/

For a complete list of books by Michael Anderle, please visit:

www.lmbpn.com/ma-books/

CONNECT WITH MICHAEL

Connect with Michael Anderle

Website: http://lmbpn.com

Email List: http://lmbpn.com/email/

Social Media:

https://www.facebook.com/LMBPNPublishing

https://twitter.com/MichaelAnderle

https://www.instagram.com/lmbpn_publishing/

https://www.bookbub.com/authors/michael-anderle

www.ingramcontent.com/pod-product-compliance
Lightning Source LLC
Chambersburg PA
CBHW060310260626
47160CB00007B/2554